MW01148239

The Boarding House

by

Sharon Sala

Bell Bridge Books

This is a work of fiction. Names, characters, places and incidents are either the products of the author's imagination or are used fictitiously. Any resemblance to actual persons (living or dead), events or locations is entirely coincidental.

Bell Bridge Books
PO BOX 300921
Memphis, TN 38130
Print ISBN: 978-1-61194-133-3

Bell Bridge Books is an Imprint of BelleBooks, Inc.

Printed and bound in the United States of America.

We at BelleBooks enjoy hearing from readers.
Visit our websites – www.BelleBooks.com and www.BellBridgeBooks.com.

10 9 8 7 6 5 4 3 2 1

Cover design: Debra Dixon
Interior design: Hank Smith
Photo credits:
House © Gary Blakeley | Dreamstime.com
Child's Face (manipulated) © Lane Erickson | Dreamstime.com

:Lhb:01:

Dedication

We come into this world as pure and innocent as a soul can be, and from the moment of our first breath, we are at risk.

As a parent, our greatest fear is that something or someone will harm our child, and the vigilance and ferocity with which we protect them is at a life and death level.

It is the perfect pairing – a helpless child and a loving and protective parent - except when the parent is the wolf and the child, the lamb, with nowhere to run.

I dedicate this book to all the children who grew up without a hero.

I applaud your instinct for survival, and I pray you have found peace.

Chapter One

Memphis, Tennessee—1993

Despite the long blonde curls and crybaby blue eyes, Ellie Wayne wasn't like most five-year-old girls. Momma said she was fragile. Not fragile like the stuff Momma ordered from the QVC—fragile like sugar flowers on the bakery cakes at the Piggly Wiggly.

Daddy said she was ephemeral. Ellie didn't know what that meant, but she thought it was good. It sounded better than being fragile. *Fragile* was something that didn't last. She didn't really remember it, but they all said she'd been a sickly baby and even now was still prone to every kind of ailment that came along, unlike her twin, Wyatt, who was her shadow.

Fern Wayne, Ellie's mother, came from sturdy stock, but her large breasts and wide hips had been misleading. One would have assumed she would be perfect for childbearing—perfect for the family Garrett Wayne wanted, and to be fair, Garrett hadn't been looking for beauty when he'd gone after Fern. He'd wanted a daughter. He didn't care how many boys she birthed to make it happen, he wouldn't be satisfied until he got his girl.

It had been easy for him to overlook her odd, androgynous features by focusing on the blonde hair and blue eyes she'd inherited from her Swedish ancestors, and there was the money she would one day inherit as the only child of Johan Strobel, as well. Strobel Investments was well-known in Memphis. Garrett always said you would be surprised at the number of people who traded on the New York Stock Exchange.

He and Fern had married within six months of their first date and were pregnant before the honeymoon was over. Everyone assumed Fern would birth fine, healthy babies, and yet her first attempt had been dismal. Garrett had been disappointed in Fern, but had taken one look at the four pounds and seven ounces of Ellie's frail, naked body and fallen deeply, madly in love.

His silent condemnation of Fern hung over her spirit like a

swinging scythe, taking swipe after swipe at her failure to breed hale and hearty children, until she imagined she could feel the sharp slice of the blade only a breath away from her throat. To counteract a future failure, Fern began hanging all sorts of religious icons upon the walls in the nursery. There were small crosses and large crosses—plain ones and ornate ones—crosses that had been blessed by holy water and some that had been blessed by her tears. She hung framed pictures of the Virgin Mary, of Jesus Christ, and of angels—all kinds of angels in every size and color—as physical proof of her piety in the hope that God would let Ellie live.

The fact that Ellie was now five years old had proved to Fern that all of her praying had worked. But the guilt of birthing a sickly child, along with the burden of raising her, had done a number on Fern. She'd grown old before her time, complaining constantly of womanly ailments usually left to middle-aged women and had taken up a life that revolved around bottles of pills and numerous glasses of wine—enough to get her through each day.

As for Garrett, he knew his worth down to the penny and ignored his flaws. He was a lanky man with a long, narrow jaw and a wild shock of red hair. His beak of a nose over-powered his face, centered between a pair of wide-set eyes in a shade of watered-down green so pale they seemed to have no color. His lips were thin, but curved often in a smile upon seeing his daughter.

Despite Ellie's fragile hold on life, Garrett was determined she would not die—tending to her when Fern took to her bed to pray. He bathed the little runt of a babe, changing her diapers, delicately cleaning her lily—which was what Fern called her girl parts—doing everything for Ellie but the nursing. And if his teats could have produced milk, he would have done that, as well. But no matter what he did for his infant daughter, from the time she could voice an opinion, her allegiance had always been to her twin, who was the boil on Garrett's life. From morning to night, it was always about what she and Wyatt played and where she and Wyatt went. Garrett found himself angry, even jealous, over her single-minded devotion.

And, the older Ellie got, the more withdrawn her mother became. She was no longer available as a wife for Garrett or a mother for Ellie. Garrett believed it was because Fern feared a second pregnancy would be a repeat of the first—something she knew he would not abide—but the truth was Fern Wayne had run clean out of prayers.

So this was Ellie's life—a father who dominated her every move—a mother who was little more than a ghost—and the center of her world, her twin, Wyatt.

It was Sunday, and Ellie was in her bedroom in her silk panties and socks, waiting for Daddy to come dress her. She knew how to dress herself, but Daddy always made her wait. She kept digging her toe into the thick pile of the carpet, wishing she could dig a hole big enough to hide in.

"You could dress yourself, you know," Wyatt muttered.

Ellie frowned. Wyatt had the adjoining bedroom and got to dress himself, but Ellie didn't have that freedom, even though they ran back and forth between rooms. "Daddy says no."

"You don't have to do everything he says."

"Yes I do. So do you." Panic edged her voice. "Right?"

"I'm sorry, Ellie." He reached out to calm her. "I didn't mean to upset you. You're right."

Ellie nodded, but she was getting cold without any clothes. Chill bumps were breaking out on her skin and being undressed was making her nervous.

When she finally heard the sound of footsteps hurrying toward her room, she slapped her hands on her chest, covering the tiny raisin-like nipples just as Daddy came rushing into her room.

"There you are, my darling," he said, eyeing her thin, reedy limbs. "Oh no, you're cold, aren't you? Here now. Let's get dressed lickety-split and you'll be all warm again, okay?"

Ellie felt Wyatt's disapproval, but he made himself scarce. He didn't like Daddy, and Daddy tolerated Wyatt, interacting with him only when Ellie insisted. She didn't understand how a parent could love one child more than another, but she was only five. She figured things would become clearer when she got older. Grown-ups were always telling her, "You'll understand when you get older," so she assumed it was a fact.

She stood like a mini-mannequin waiting for window dressing and bore Daddy's ministrations like a soldier; then one foot at a time, she slipped her tiny feet into the stretchy white stockings he was holding. Her breath caught in a moment of panic as Daddy pulled them up her legs, taking care to smooth out the wrinkles with his long slender fingers.

"Don't want to leave any droopy spots, do we?" he asked as he finally pulled them up over her panties.

Ellie exhaled. "No Daddy. No droopy spots."

Then he went to her closet and stood for a few moments, searching through the hangers.

"Ah . . . here it is. This dress is my favorite." He turned around, holding a blue wool with small white sheep appliquéd around the yoke. "How about this one?"

She nodded, holding up her arms as he slipped it over her head then buttoned it down the back. It was soft. And it was warm. Ellie began to relax.

"I want to wear my shiny black shoes, Daddy."

Garrett frowned. "It's cold out so I thought we'd do the furry boots."

Ellie began to panic. "It's okay. I'll wear the boots."

He shook his head and smiled as he cupped Ellie's chin with the palm of his hand, then ran his long thin fingers down the side of her cheek. "No. No. If my little angel wants to wear the shiny black shoes, then she shall. That's what families do for each other. I do a favor for you. You do a favor for me."

Ellie didn't want to do Daddy any favors, but it was already too late to take it back.

He got the black shoes from a shelf in her closet and then sat her on the side of the bed.

"One foot in," he said, buckling the shoe on her small, skinny foot. "Second foot in." Ellie aimed her foot at the shoe as he slipped it on. "Just like Cinderella, right?"

Ellie's heart began to pound.

"So if you're Cinderella, then what does that make me?"

Ellie shivered. Daddy was staring at her with those funny green eyes. The words got stuck in the back of her throat. She looked around for Wyatt, but he was nowhere to be seen.

Garrett prompted her again as he buckled up the last shoe. "Who does Cinderella love? Come on. Tell Daddy. Who does Cinderella love?"

"Her prince. She loves her prince."

"That's right. So that makes me your prince, doesn't it, Ellie?"

"Yes."

Ellie gritted her teeth. Her words sounded squished, like they'd been forced through lips too tight to open, only Daddy didn't care. He just laughed. She watched his eyes crinkle so tight she could barely see the color. Wyatt called them frog green and reminded her how lucky they were that their eyes were blue. She shivered as Garrett slid his hands beneath her arms and lifted her down from the bed.

He held out his hand. "Now off we go or we're going to be late for church."

"Is Momma coming?" Ellie asked.

He took her coat from the closet. "No. Momma isn't feeling well. She's still in bed."

"Can Wyatt come? I want Wyatt to come, too."

Garrett paused. This was one of the few times that she reminded him of Fern, and he didn't like it.

"No, Ellie. Wyatt doesn't go with us. This is our time. You're Daddy's girl, remember?"

The First United Methodist Church sat on the corner two blocks down from Ellie's school. Ellie loved the old church with all of its multiple steeples and gables. She thought it looked more like a castle than a church. All it needed was a moat and a dragon. Ellie would sit quietly during services without really listening to Preacher Ray, pretending she was the princess locked up in the tower, just like in the story *Rapunzel* that Momma sometimes read to her when she was sick. Ellie also liked the lemony smell of the polished wood and the way the sunlight came through the stained-glass windows, spilling all kinds of colors into her lap as the choir sang songs about Jesus.

Every other Sunday, the choir sang *Washed in the Blood of Jesus.* Ellie didn't much like that song. She couldn't imagine taking a bath in blood, even if it would wash away her sins. She wasn't too sure what sins were either, but according to Wyatt, sins were things people did that were bad and got them sent to hell. If that was so, then that's where Daddy was going. She just hoped when he went, he didn't insist on taking her with him.

After church was over, Daddy paraded Ellie down the aisle, soaking up the compliments as if they were about him instead of her. It wasn't anything she hadn't heard before, and she stayed mute, which she knew was exactly what Daddy wanted, until she overheard someone say what a beauty she was.

"Yes, she has a baby-doll face, for sure," Daddy said.

Ellie frowned. She wasn't sure what that meant because her baby-doll Rita had a big, flat face, a little bitty nose, and a mouth that didn't open. As soon as she got home, she yanked free of his grasp and ran ahead of him to her room, grabbed her dolly from the bed, then carried her to the dresser mirror.

She looked at both their reflections, trying to figure out what Daddy meant. Rita's eyes didn't blink and her mouth didn't open so you could see her teeth. Even more confusing, Rita's hair was straight and brown, not blonde and curly like Ellie's. She laid Rita back on the bed as she heard Garrett calling her to come eat, but she was going to remember this. Next time Daddy wanted to play, she was going to send Rita. Maybe then he'd leave her and Wyatt alone.

Even though Daddy didn't like Wyatt, he was the other half of Ellie's world. Wyatt wasn't afraid of snakes or spiders—not even the big, black, fuzzy ones that could hop farther than Ellie could jump. Wyatt called them *trantlers.* Wyatt was brave and smart and knew stuff—important stuff. Wyatt wasn't even afraid of storms, or monsters under the bed.

But Ellie was afraid. She was afraid of almost everything and had known, for as long as she could remember, that when the monster came, there was nowhere to hide. Not under the bed. Not in the back of her closet. The only thing between her and the monster was Wyatt—the other half of her soul.

That night, about an hour after Daddy tucked Ellie into bed, it began to rain. She heard drops hitting the window like tiny rocks, *pop, pop, pop,* then faster until the sound was lost within the wind and the oncoming storm.

Lightning flashed. Thunder rumbled, rattling the glass in the window close to her bed. Ellie gasped and pulled the covers up over her head as Wyatt slipped in.

"Don't be scared, Ellie," Wyatt said. "I'm here. I'll keep you safe."

"Is it gonna come a twister?"

"Naw . . . it's the wrong time of year for a twister," Wyatt said. "This is just wind and rain."

Ellie snuggled a little deeper beneath the covers as the sound of their own breath amplified within the small dark space.

Breathe in. Breathe out.

In through the nose. Out through the mouth.

She opened her eyes and realized she could still see tiny flashes of the lightning through the covers, but it wasn't scary anymore. She began to pretend she was seeing fireflies, soaring from tree to tree, then up into the sky, and the rain and thunder became giant water balloons being popped by the fireflies' lights. It was a good place to be, deep beneath the covers, in the dark, with Wyatt at her side.

The fantasy ended with a *scratch, scratch, scratch* at her bedroom door. It was the monster. He was here. She reached out in the darkness, her voice hardly more than a whisper.

"Wyatt. Did you hear that? The monster is here. He's coming to get me."

"I heard," Wyatt said.

"I'm scared," Ellie whispered, then crossed her legs and squeezed them tight against her lily, but it was too late. She could already smell the sour odor of pee-pee. Ellie Wayne had wet the bed.

The *scratch, scratch, scratch* of the monster's footsteps was in the room now and coming closer.

Ellie closed her eyes and rolled up in a ball. Maybe if she got small enough, the monster couldn't find her. She said a silent prayer to Baby Jesus, just in case He was listening, and promised she'd take a bath in that blood every Sunday if He'd make the monster go away.

Then just like that, the darkness was gone and the covers were at the foot of the bed. Ellie could smell the monster's breath. It was always the same. Wyatt said it smelled like roadkill. Ellie thought it smelled a little like Momma's Christmas pudding just before she lit it on fire.

"No, no, no," she sobbed and started to shake as she felt the monster's claws sliding across the sheets, coming closer and closer for her body.

"Don't cry, Ellie, don't cry," Wyatt said. "I'll go with the monster. You stay here and sleep."

Chapter Two

The rain had stopped by morning. Ellie was in her bed alone when she woke. It made it easier to pretend that what happened last night had been nothing but a really bad dream. She got up slowly, thankful it was a teacher's meeting day, which meant no school today. She and Wyatt could go down to the creek that ran along the back side of their property. Daddy didn't like for her to get dirty, and Momma was always scared she was going to get sick, but sometimes Ellie just had to break rules or go crazy.

"Wanna go hunt crawdads?" Wyatt asked as he walked into the room.

Ellie nodded as she pulled a clean pair of panties out of her dresser and put them on.

"Can we go barefoot?" Ellie asked.

"Naw . . . you know Momma won't let us, but we can take our shoes off after we get to the creek."

Ellie grinned and quickly finished dressing, then she and Wyatt headed for the kitchen, following the smell of frying bacon. She liked having secrets with Wyatt.

Fern was at the stove when Wyatt and Ellie walked in.

"Good morning," Fern said. "Are you hungry?"

"Yes, Momma," Ellie said. "I want bacon and toast and Wyatt wants eggs."

Fern paused, then turned around, eyeing what Ellie was wearing. "It rained last night. It's all wet and muddy outside, so I think you should play inside today."

Ellie moaned. Wyatt muttered under his breath.

"Momma. We want to go outside. We won't get muddy, we swear, right, Wyatt?"

"Right."

Fern's lips pursed. "You and Wyatt always manage to get into trouble."

Ellie refused to answer. She knew from past experience that she couldn't outtalk Momma. It was better just to let her talk to herself.

Fern carried the bacon and toast to the table and slid it under Ellie's nose.

"Smells good, Momma, but don't forget Wyatt's eggs."

Fern rolled her eyes. "Have I ever forgotten?" She laid a plate of fluffy scrambled eggs onto the table, then poured two glasses of juice.

As soon as they'd downed their food, Wyatt and Ellie were out the door. Fern followed them onto the porch, still calling out warnings as they disappeared over the hill and headed down to the creek. Even before they got to the trees, they could hear the swift rush of running water.

"Ooh, I bet there's lots of water in the creek today," Ellie said as she ran headlong toward the sound.

Wyatt was more hesitant. It was his job to keep her safe and he knew what would happen if he didn't.

"It will be too deep to wade in," he reminded her as they reached the trees on the ridge above the creek.

Now it was time to slow down. From here on, the ground sloped downward rather sharply, and even though it was grassy, the recent rain would have made it slippery.

Wyatt was thinking that very thought when Ellie suddenly slipped, and down she went with a squeal, taking him with her.

They hit a bush, then a tree, then lost their grip and slid farther, moving ever closer to the water below.

"I can't stop!" Ellie cried.

Wyatt clenched his jaw, his focus centered on the half-grown sapling they were about to hit.

Ellie reached toward it, but it was Wyatt who grabbed hold of the trunk and stopped their descent.

"Oh my gosh," Ellie gasped, as she rolled onto her back to catch her breath.

From where she was lying, she could see pieces of the sky through the trees. Parts of it were dotted with white puffy clouds, and parts of it were a pure, clear blue, and all of it was framed in rich spring green—like God's version of a patchwork quilt. Ellie thought it was beautiful. If not for the fact they were covered in mud, it would have been worth the fall.

"Wyatt?"

"What?"

"You saved my life."

"I know."

"We're awful muddy now. Momma's gonna pitch a fit."

"We'll wash the mud off in the creek, and our clothes will be dry by the time we get home."

Ellie nodded then started to laugh.

"What's so funny?" Wyatt muttered.

"We aren't supposed to get in the water, but now we have to take a bath in the creek or Momma will know what we did."

Wyatt grinned. "So let's get going."

Ellie carefully pulled herself upright, and then crawled on her hands and knees to a more level spot before heading for the water.

A small turtle had taken up residence on an outcropping of rocks, positioning itself in such a way to catch the few rays of sun coming down through the canopy.

"See, even the turtle is drying out," Wyatt said as they reached the creek. "Take your shoes and socks off. I'll wash off the mud."

"We'll have to take our clothes off, too," Ellie said. "I know how to scrub. I watched Momma do it in the sink."

Wyatt shrugged. Getting naked was no big deal to him, but Ellie didn't like it.

"What if someone sees us?" Wyatt asked.

Normally, it would have been Ellie asking that question, but today felt safe. The monster only lived in the house. It didn't come to the creek.

"We can hurry," Ellie said and quickly stripped. Wyatt cleaned up their shoes, then Ellie took the clothes down to the creek and knelt by the water.

Her naked limbs were snow-white and thin, like the trunks of new cottonwood saplings. Her hair brushed against her shoulders as she bent over the water, scrubbing the pieces of the clothing back and forth, just like she'd watched Momma do.

The water was cold, but the sun was warm against her back. She could feel the tickle of new grass against her legs and feet where she knelt. She liked the damp, earthy smells of moss and mud, and the rush of blood coursing through her body, keeping pace with the runoff from the rain. It made her feel alive and clean.

She thought about asking Preacher Ray on Sunday if she could get washed in the creek instead of being washed in the blood. It seemed like a less messy option.

"Are you done?" Wyatt asked.

"Soon as I wring out my shirt."

She was reaching for her panties when she heard her Daddy's first shout.

"Ellie! Where are you?"

She froze.

Wyatt shook her. "Get dressed."

Every piece of clothing she tried to put on was too wet. It either stuck to her skin or she couldn't find an opening. And all the while, Daddy kept coming closer.

"Ellie! Answer me. I know you're here."

Ellie moaned. "Oh no, oh no, I can't get them on."

Wyatt was in a panic. He kept trying to pull at the tiny bits of clothing. Finally, he found the neck of her T-shirt and yanked it over her head. "Your arm. Put your arm in here."

At that moment, Garrett stopped at the top of the creek bank and looked down. The fact that his daughter was naked and standing at the verge of the rushing water nearly stopped his heart. She'd fallen in.

"Ellie," he yelled and started down through the trees, crashing through brush as he ran.

Ellie's legs gave way. "It's too late. It's too late."

"Stand up, Ellie," Wyatt begged, then saw the thin stream of urine running out from between her knees and realized she was already gone.

He turned to face his father, his fists doubled.

"Ellie. What happened? Did you fall in?"

When Garrett reached for Ellie, Wyatt swung, his fist connecting with the side of Garrett's jaw. Granted, it wasn't much of a blow, but it was unexpected enough that Garrett stopped.

"Don't touch her," Wyatt yelled.

Garrett's eyes narrowed angrily. "Don't touch her?"

"You heard me," Wyatt shouted.

"Ellie, get up. You're going to get sick out here without any clothes," Garrett said.

"She'll put them on. I'm gonna help her," Wyatt said. "You just stay back and let me do it."

"Wyatt, you need to shut up. I'm the father, not you. Back off. I need to tend to Ellie."

Garrett began unbuttoning his shirt to put around Ellie.

Wyatt started to panic. Daddy was too big and he wasn't listening.

"I'll do it," Wyatt said. "Just leave Ellie alone."

Garrett's eyes narrowed. "Do what?"

"Whatever you want," Wyatt said, and tried not to shudder when

Garrett smiled.

"You know what I want," Garrett whispered.

Wyatt could hear Ellie panting, like a dog that had run too far and too fast. Bowing to the inevitable, he quietly gave up.

"It's okay, Ellie. Hide your face," he said.

Ellie was praying. She was always praying, but Wyatt already knew it didn't do any good. God was always busy when Daddy wanted to play.

Chapter Three

Memphis—May 31, 2000

The school bell rang. It was the last day of fifth grade. When school began again in August after summer was over, Ellie Wayne would be in sixth grade.

She'd just turned twelve a couple of weeks earlier and was walking with a slight sway to her hips like the older girls, even though she didn't have much of a caboose to swing.

But there were big plans on the horizon for Ellie. Tomorrow was Saturday, and Momma was taking Ellie to Dillard's Department Store to buy her a training bra.

She wasn't sure why they called them training bras. It wasn't like her boobies were gonna run laps or anything. But she was excited about the rite of passage and even happier that it was Momma who was gonna take her and not Daddy.

The older she'd become, the more she'd resented his interference in her life. Sometimes she had to lock the bathroom door to keep him from barging in. It might have been okay when she was little, but not anymore. He didn't know Momma was going to take Ellie to Dillard's, and she wasn't going to tell him. Sure as shootin', if he found out, he'd want to come. Then Momma wouldn't go, and Ellie would die before she'd let anyone see Daddy buying her a bra.

She grabbed her backpack and headed out the door, anxious to catch up with Wyatt. They never got to be in the same class, which was Daddy's fault. She'd seen him whispering to her teacher when she'd started first grade. She'd watched the teacher turn and give her a funny look, then touch her Daddy's arm in a pitying kind of way. Ellie didn't know why Daddy needed pitying. Everything in their house went his way.

Wyatt had assured her it didn't matter, because they were together all of the other times, and if Wyatt was cool with it, then so was Ellie.

"School's out! School's out! Teacher let the mules out!"

Ellie winced as a third grader ran screaming past her, shouting the chant at the top of his lungs. Stupid third grader. Stupid boy. All boys were stupid—except for Wyatt.

She hurried through the crowded hallway while keeping an eye out for Wyatt and was all the way out the door before she heard his voice.

"Hey Ellie, wait up," Wyatt said.

Ellie stopped. "I was looking for you."

"Now you found me. Race you home," Wyatt said and tore out running.

Ellie squealed.

It was heaven, running as fast as she could go with the sun in her eyes and the wind in her hair—running away from tedium toward an endless summer of lazy days. She could hear the *slap slap* sound of her tennis shoes on the sidewalk—felt the thump of her heartbeat in her ears—and then something wet running down the inside of her leg.

That wasn't right.

Ellie stopped, and then ran up onto a neighbor's yard and hid behind part of their hedge. "Wyatt!"

Immediately, he was at her side. "What's wrong?"

"I think I peed my pants."

"We're almost home. You can change. It's no big deal. You know what Momma says. Your bladder is weak."

Ellie's voice was shaking as she took a tissue out of her backpack. "Momma thinks everything about me is weak."

She lifted her skirt just far enough that she could wipe off the trickle running down her leg, but when she pulled the tissue out from underneath her hem, she gasped.

It was blood red.

"Oh no! Wyatt, I think I'm dying."

Wyatt sighed. "Naw . . . you're only twelve. Remember what they said about girls in health class? I bet you're getting your period."

Ellie was shaking as she stuffed the telltale tissue deep into her backpack. "Are you sure?"

Wyatt shrugged. "I'm not a girl. Just ask Momma when you get home."

Ellie nodded, checked herself one more time, and then slipped out from behind the hedge and started home at a more stately pace. If this was true—if she was truly getting her period, then this might be the best thing that would ever happen to her.

"I hope it is," Ellie said. "And you know why."

"No. Why?"

Ellie glanced over her shoulder to make sure no other kids were close behind them. Then she lowered her voice. "Think about. If this is my period, then that means doing it can make me have a baby."

"Yeah. So?"

"So Daddy will have to stop the games. Right? They have to be a secret, but if he made a baby it wouldn't be a secret anymore."

Wyatt grinned. "I never thought of that. Maybe you're right. Come on. Let's walk faster. I think I heard Doris say she was making cookies this afternoon. Maybe they'll still be warm when we get home."

Ellie giggled. This might become the best summer ever, a training bra, cookies in the afternoons, and no more secret games.

Doris Bailey had been hired two years earlier after Fern appeared in the kitchen one morning and announced that God had come to her in the night and told her she was not to cook anymore. She'd stayed firm, despite Garrett's shock and displeasure, claiming she knew it was her duty to obey her husband, but that God trumped Garrett, and if he wanted to eat, he'd better hire them a cook. And while he was at it, make sure she was also willing to clean house, because Fern had a premonition that God was going to take her off that duty as well.

Garrett had fussed and fumed, but an empty refrigerator and no clean work clothes had ended the standoff in a timely fashion. Doris had been here long enough now that she was almost a part of the family, except that she didn't sleep in the house.

By the time Ellie and Wyatt ran through the back door into the kitchen, they were breathless. Just as Wyatt had predicted, Doris had made cookies—soft, chewy oatmeal cookies with raisins. Wyatt's favorite.

"Yum," Wyatt shouted and grabbed two from the counter where they were cooling.

Doris smiled. She liked kids, and while this family was a little strange, she was the kind of woman who didn't poke into other people's business.

"Where's Momma?" Ellie asked.

"In her room, I think," Doris said. "But she might be napping."

"Well, she's gonna have to wake herself up then, 'cause I have an announcement she needs to hear."

Ellie stuffed a whole cookie into her mouth and strode out of the kitchen, dragging her backpack behind her like she intended to wipe out her tracks.

Doris paid her no mind. Wyatt was the calm one, but Ellie was always verging on hysterics. Lord only knew what the problem was this time.

Ellie dropped her backpack inside the door to her bedroom as Wyatt made himself scarce, then dashed across the hallway into Fern's room without knocking.

"Momma. We need to talk," Ellie cried, startling Fern to the point that she promptly spilled the handful of pills she'd been about to take. They hit the floor with a faint *click-clack* sound and rolled out of sight.

Fern turned, her pale, fleshy face shaking with anger.

"I swear to goodness, Ellie, you scared the life out of me. You know better than to come into my room without knocking. Now get down on the floor and find Momma's pills. Do you hear?"

Ellie sighed. "Yes, ma'am. I hear." She dropped to her knees and began sweeping them up, digging them out from beneath the dresser, from underneath a rocker, and from beneath the bed.

"'Zackly how many pills did you have?" Ellie asked as she dropped what she had into her mother's outstretched palm.

Fern frowned. "I'm not sure," she said, and downed them without counting. "Now what on earth is so important?"

Ellie put her hands on her hips and cocked them to one side. There was a can-you-believe-it tone in her voice when she loudly announced, "I got my period. Today. On the way home from school. What do you think about that?"

The expression on Fern Wayne's face hovered between shock and disbelief. "Are you sure?"

"I'm bleeding, Momma. So I either got my period, or I'm dying."

"Lord, Lord," Fern muttered and stumbled toward her rocker. "I'm going to have to think about this."

Ellie frowned. "While you're thinking, I'm bleeding. What do I do? I already ruined my panties for sure."

Fern pressed a shaky hand to her lips. "They'll wash," she muttered. "Let me think. My pads are going to be too big for you. Maybe a panty liner will work for now. I'm going to have to call your Daddy. He can pick up some small pads for you on the way home."

Ellie frowned. "I don't want Daddy picking up my pads. This is girl stuff."

Fern smiled. It was a rare thing to see, and Ellie found herself staring.

Fern patted her on the head. "I know, but Daddy does a lot of our shopping. He buys Momma's pads. He'll know what to pick out for you, too."

Ellie's chin jutted. "Whatever. At least this will be the end of the games," she muttered, and then froze. She'd never said that out loud before except to Wyatt. She wasn't supposed to tell. Maybe Momma didn't hear.

But Fern heard. "What do you mean, the end of the games? What games?"

Ellie shrugged. "Nothing. I didn't mean it."

Fern grabbed her by the arm. "Don't lie to me, Ellie. I won't have it."

Ellie began to panic and backed out of her mother's grasp. "Nothing, Momma, nothing." She began to shake. What had she done?

A bubble of horror rose at the back of Fern's throat as she got up from the rocker and followed Ellie all the way to the door, grabbing her before she could escape. She closed the door, and for one of the few times since Ellie started school, picked her up and carried her back to the chair. When she sat down, Ellie was locked in a grip from which she wouldn't escape.

Fern's heart pounded so hard she thought it would burst. Even as the words were forming in her mouth, she knew once they'd been spoken, she could never take them back.

"Elizabeth Ann, what games does Daddy play with you?"

Tears welled and rolled down the curve of Ellie's cheeks. "I want Wyatt."

Fern groaned. Not again. "No. I don't want to talk to Wyatt. I want to talk to you."

"Wyatt knows," Ellie whispered.

"But I need to hear it from you," Fern said, then suddenly yanked her child up to her breasts and started to rock. "Tell Momma, Honey. Tell Momma what kind of games Daddy plays with you. I won't be mad."

"Secret games," Ellie whispered.

Fern moaned. "What kind of secrets?"

"The kind of secrets that make babies, like the game you and Daddy played that made me."

Fern needed to throw up, but it would have to wait. "How long have you and Daddy played those games?"

"Always. I'm Daddy's girl. He says that's what Daddy's girls do."

Shock went through Fern's body in waves, ripping away her soul and leaving her with nothing but naked guilt. It was her fault. It was all her fault. She'd taken to her bed without thinking of the ramifications—without watching over her own child. Now she was shaking as hard as Ellie.

"Always?" she asked.

"Yes, but now he'll have to stop. Right? I got my period, so he'll have to stop. He says it has to be a secret, but if he makes a baby, it won't be a secret anymore. That means it's over, doesn't it?"

Fern looked up. Years ago, after they'd realized Ellie was going to live, Garrett had insisted Fern remove all the religious icons from his daughter's bedroom, claiming Ellie needed bright colors and toys instead. And like always, Fern had obliged him. She'd taken everything out, all the crosses and the angels and the paintings of Jesus Christ and the Virgin Mary, and moved everything into her room, and here they hung. Everything that had happened to Ellie afterward was all Fern's fault. When she'd taken God from her baby, she'd let the Devil come in.

"I'm sorry, Ellie, I'm so sorry," Fern said and kept on rocking.

Chapter Four

Everything felt weird to Ellie. She couldn't remember the last time Momma had hugged her, or rocked her, or even read her a book. And she was rocking her so fast—too fast. Ellie wondered if Momma was thinking speed would make up for lost time.

But time was passing and Ellie'd had enough rocking. She was more concerned about her ruined panties and what Daddy was going to do when he found out she'd told. She pushed herself out of Fern's grasp and got out of her lap.

"Momma . . . about my period . . ."

Fern moaned, then fell out of the chair onto her knees. Prostrating herself upon the floor, she began to pray, mumbling words in between shrieks and moans so loud they hurt Ellie's ears.

Ellie clapped her hands over her ears as she backed toward the door. Then she turned and ran, screaming Wyatt's name.

As always, he came running. "What's wrong?"

Ellie kept her ears covered, trying to block out the sounds from the room behind her. "She knows," Ellie whispered.

"Knows what?" Wyatt said.

"The secret."

Wyatt gasped. "You told?"

Blood was still running down the inside of Ellie's legs. She could feel it inching toward her knees. She wondered if she stood here long enough if she might just bleed to death. It would solve pretty much all of her problems—except the one about going to hell. She didn't want to go to hell when she died. She'd planned all along to go to heaven, but now it wasn't looking so good.

"Someone's coming," Wyatt hissed. "You better run."

But as luck would have it, it was only Doris. She'd heard the screaming and wailing all the way into the kitchen. Certain someone had been injured, she'd come running. When she saw Ellie standing in the middle of the hallway, she breathed a sigh of relief. Whatever was happening, the girl was okay.

Ellie swiped snot off her upper lip with the back of her hand just as Doris grabbed her by the shoulders.

"What's wrong? What's all that crying about? Is someone hurt? Where's your mother? Where's Fern?"

Ellie felt like she was standing outside of herself. She could see her reflection in Doris's eyes, and she'd never noticed Doris's roots were gray. It was a revelation that Doris actually colored her hair. It explained why it was darker some days than others.

"Ellie. Answer me. What's wrong?" Doris shook Ellie by the shoulders to make her point.

Ellie shuddered. "I got my period."

Doris's expression shifted from panic to sympathy. "Oh sugar, that's alright. It comes to all of us sooner or later. What's the matter with Fern?"

Ellie couldn't tell her about the secret. "I think she's praying."

Doris's eyebrows knitted over the bridge of her nose, and her mouth pursed right up into a knot of disapproval.

"Well now," Doris muttered. "There's a time for praying, and there's a time for being sensible. Do you have any pads?"

Ellie shook her head.

Doris hugged her again. "You go right into your bedroom and jump in the shower. Clean yourself up all nice and tidy while I go down to the pharmacy and get you some. I should be back by the time you're done."

Ellie was so relieved her Daddy wasn't going to be the one doing the shopping that she threw her arms around Doris's neck and gave her a quick hug. "Thank you, Doris," Ellie said, and then dashed off into her bedroom.

"Well now," Doris said.

At that moment, Fern let out a particularly loud and mournful wail. Unaware of the unfolding tragedy, Doris rolled her eyes, then gathered herself up and headed back to the kitchen to get her purse.

By the time she got back, all was quiet in Fern's bedroom and Ellie was waiting in hers. She gave Ellie another hug and a brief lesson in feminine hygiene and then made a beeline for the kitchen. She was already late starting supper.

Ellie didn't know what she thought about the pad between her legs. It felt a little strange, but in a way, she felt proud. She began walking back and forth across the bedroom floor, trying not to waddle like a duck.

That was when Wyatt returned. "So, how do you feel?"

Ellie shrugged. "Different."

He frowned. They always did everything together, but this was a place he couldn't go.

"Whatever." He sat down on the side of the bed. "Momma quit crying."

"I know," Ellie said.

"Wonder what it means?'

Ellie shrugged. She was afraid to guess.

"Are you going to tell Daddy?" Wyatt asked.

Ellie turned on him, her hands on her hips, her voice shaking with emotion she couldn't control. "About what . . . that I told the secret, or that I got my period, or that Momma was taking me to Dillard's tomorrow to buy me a training bra?"

Wyatt frowned. Put like that, he decided Ellie was entitled to be pissed.

Ellie sighed. "I'm sorry, Wyatt. I didn't mean to sound mad at you. Don't be angry. You're not just my brother, you're my best friend."

"I'm never going to be mad at you," Wyatt said. "We're together forever, remember?"

Suddenly, Wyatt flew off the bed and ran to the window. "Daddy's home."

Ellie gasped and began looking frantically for a place to hide.

"Stop that," Wyatt said. "Don't let him know you're scared. He likes it when we're scared."

Ellie swallowed anxiously, then pulled herself up with a dignity beyond her years. "You're right. I don't have to be scared of him anymore. I got my period, so he can't play the game."

Wyatt didn't feel like now was the time to mention that since he didn't get periods, he might not be all that safe. The main concern was what Momma was going to do with her newfound information.

They didn't have long to wait.

When they heard Daddy's footsteps coming down the hallway toward his bedroom, Ellie started to pray.

"Be quiet," Wyatt hissed.

Ellie sucked up in the middle of "Baby Jesus." When his footsteps stopped outside their door, breath caught in the back of Ellie's throat. Wyatt tightened his grip as they stared at the doorknob, willing it not to turn.

Garrett had had a long, miserable day at work. The stock market was down and clients had been calling all day, demanding to sell certain stocks while others were trying to buy the same stocks at an all-time low.

Doris eyed him curiously when he'd walked into the kitchen, then quickly looked away.

Garrett frowned. That was weird. She usually spoke. He bypassed the cookie he'd been about to sample and headed straight for his room to change. But as he started down the hall, he realized the house was too quiet. *Ah.* This might explain Doris's odd behavior. He stopped, cocking his head to listen.

Usually Fern's television was blaring, and he should be hearing Ellie chattering away to Wyatt. Even though she was his special girl, her bond to her twin was one thing he had never been able to break. He paused outside her door and knocked.

"Ellie? Are you there?"

Wyatt put his hand over Ellie's mouth.

Garrett was reaching for the doorknob when he heard a sound behind him. He turned just as Fern lurched through the doorway. Her face was splotched, her eyes nearly swollen shut, but she was standing with her feet apart in a fighting stance and her shoulders thrust back as if bracing herself for a blow.

"Get away from that door," she shouted.

Garrett frowned. "How dare you—"

Fern launched herself at him like a guided missile and hit him with a fist to the jaw before he could end the sentence. He went down like a felled ox.

Inside the bedroom, Ellie flinched. "What was that?"

Wyatt headed for the door. "I'm gonna see."

"Wait, what if—"

Wyatt had already opened the door. Ellie had no choice but to follow. The last thing they expected to see was Daddy on the floor with blood pouring from his nose and Momma standing over him, her hands curled into fists.

"What the fuck is wrong with you? I think you broke my nose," Garrett yelled, and grabbed his handkerchief to stop the blood.

Fern drew back her foot and kicked him in the balls. She would have preferred to cut them off, but she'd made a deal with God.

"With me? What the fuck is wrong with you?" she screamed. "Pervert! Child molester! Devil's spawn!"

Garrett moaned and retched as he grabbed his crotch and rolled, desperate to get away from Fern's wrath. *What the hell just happened?* As he did he caught sight of Ellie and knew from the look on her face that he'd been betrayed. He caught a glimpse of Ellie's expression and suddenly, he knew.

"You told," he said accusingly, then grunted as another of Fern's kicks caught him in the balls.

"Hell yes, she told," Fern screamed. "Ellie. Get back in your room."

But Ellie couldn't move. "I had to tell, Daddy," she announced. "I got my period today. That means I can make babies. And that means you can't play the game with me again."

"Jesus Christ," Garrett muttered, staring at her anew. That she would have drawn all of these conclusions on her own had never entered his head.

"Do not even mention the name of our Lord and Savior," Fern shrieked and grabbed him by the back of his suit coat and spun him around. "You need to hear my words, Garrett Wayne, and hear them good. God told me not to kill you. If He had not, you'd already be dead. You're still breathing because I'm following God's command. But if you ever go near that child again, it will be the last thing you do. I'll gladly go to prison for life, just to know you're already in hell." She let him go and pointed at her daughter. "Ellie. Get in your room and don't come out until I tell you to."

Ellie ducked back, slamming the door behind her, then ran for the farthest corner of the room and hid between the wall and her bed.

"I'm here," Wyatt said, and slid down beside her.

Ellie wrapped her arms around her knees and stared over the mattress toward the door, praying it wouldn't open.

Out in the hall, Garrett had managed to crawl to his feet, but he was a sorry lot, standing with one hand on his crotch and the other trying to stop the flow of blood coming out his nose. "Fern, I didn't mean—"

Fern slapped him across the face, splattering blood across the wall. "Shut your mouth. You're evil. Nothing comes out of you but lies. The only thing you didn't mean to do was to get caught. Go clean yourself up and come down to dinner."

"I can't eat. You need to take me to the emergency room. My nose is broken."

"Take yourself," Fern snapped. "When you go back to work on Monday, you tell them whatever you want, as long as it's not the truth. The only reason I haven't already called the police is because if the news got out about what you've done, Ellie would be subjected to ridicule and pity for the rest of her life."

Then she shoved him away from Ellie's doorway and stood guard in front of it until Garrett staggered back toward the kitchen.

Doris had just walked back in the house from carrying trash out to the curb and heard only enough commotion to suspect trouble was brewing. When she saw her employer come stumbling back through the kitchen holding a bloody handkerchief to his nose, she knew she'd been right.

She stepped back in shock. "Oh my, Mr. Wayne, do you need me to—"

Garrett held up his hand then put a finger to his lips.

Doris clasped her hands over her mouth.

He walked out the door.

She heard the car start up then drive away. Moments later Fern came striding through the kitchen with her purse over her arm. "I've got to run an errand. I won't be long. Feed Ellie when dinner's ready. I'll eat when I get back."

"Yes, ma'am," Doris said.

Fern drove away, leaving Doris in the kitchen shaking her head. The money was good, and she felt sorry for little Ellie, all alone in this house except for Wyatt. This had to be the strangest family she'd ever worked for.

By the time the food was ready to eat, Doris was worried. Fern was gone. Garrett was gone, and Ellie and Wyatt were nowhere to be found. Remembering how shook up Ellie had been earlier by starting her monthlies, Doris wondered if she was ashamed to face her. She knocked on Ellie's door then peeked in.

At first Doris didn't see her, then Ellie moved, and it was the motion that caught her attention.

"My goodness, child, what are you doing over there in the corner? Are you ill?"

"No, ma'am," Ellie said as she got to her feet.

"Then it's time for you and Wyatt to come eat."

Ellie shook her head. "Wyatt's in his room, and Momma told me not to come out until she came to get me."

Doris frowned. "Well she told me not to wait dinner on her, and for you two to eat. She said she'd eat when she got back."

Although it wasn't cold, Ellie wrapped her arms around herself to keep from shivering. "I'm not disobeying Momma," Ellie whispered. "I can't."

Doris frowned. "Would you eat if I brought your dinner to your room?"

Ellie nodded.

Doris resisted the urge to roll her eyes. "I'll be back."

Ellie was finishing up her food when she heard footsteps and guessed it was Doris coming to get the tray. But it wasn't Doris who came in, it was Momma. She had a sack in one hand and a screwdriver and hammer in the other.

"Why are you eating in your room?" Fern demanded.

Ellie jumped up. Momma still sounded mad.

"You told me not to come out of my room until you came to get me."

Fern sighed. At least the child had the good sense to mind her. "It's just as well," she said, and then began digging stuff out of the sack.

"What's that?" Ellie asked as Fern shoved a small metal plate onto one side of her door.

"I'm putting a lock called a slide bolt on the door. When you come into this room, you lock this door behind you every time. Do you understand?"

Ellie's eyes widened. Her heart thumped once out of rhythm then curiosity got the better of her as she watched Momma working. "I didn't know you knew how to use tools."

"There are a lot of things I can do," Fern said.

"Are you mad at me, Momma?"

Fern stopped. The quaver in Ellie's voice was a shaft to her heart. "Lord, no, child. Why would you think that?"

"You yelled at me and now that." She pointed at the lock. "Are you putting me in jail, too?"

Fern gasped. "No! Oh my goodness, no. You don't understand. This lock isn't to keep you in your room. It's to keep your . . . to keep people out."

Ellie's eyes widened as the ramifications of this new piece of information soaked in. Of course Wyatt showed up when he'd heard all the commotion, then moved closer, watching to see how the lock was going to work, and how the screw ate into the wood bit by bit until it was flat against the plate.

Fern glanced down just as Wyatt looked up. Their gazes met. Fern blinked.

Wyatt glared. "You should have taken better care of Ellie."

Fern shuddered and reached for her daughter.

Wyatt pulled her back. "I've been taking care of her longer than you have. You can put all the locks in the world on all the doors, but it's not gonna stop Daddy if he wants in."

Fern covered her mouth to keep from screaming. The look in Wyatt's eyes was frightening.

"I'm sorry, I'm so sorry," Fern mumbled. "Look, look, the lock works. Come try it."

Ellie slid the bolt back and forth a few times as Fern showed her.

"I can do it," Ellie said. "But if I get scared, Wyatt will do it for me."

Knowing she'd failed her child, Fern shook her head in a gesture of sadness, grabbed her things, and left the room as if the Devil himself was at her heels.

Wyatt glanced at Ellie. "Well, what are you waiting for?"

"Oh. Right," Ellie said. She carried their food trays out into the hall then ran back inside and locked the door behind her.

"Now what?" Wyatt asked.

Ellie tugged at the back of her panties. The unfamiliar feel of the pad between her thighs kept making her think she was walking with a wedgie.

"There's no school tomorrow," she offered.

Wyatt grinned. "There's no school all summer."

"And no more playing games with Daddy," Ellie added.

"Damn straight," Wyatt muttered.

Ellie gasped. "You cussed."

"Yeah, well, you're not the only one who's growing up," Wyatt stated, and swaggered toward the television to get the remote.

It was after dark before Garrett got back to the house. He had a splint on his nose, and his balls were throbbing. But he'd had plenty of time to think.

It had been a shock finding out that his little Ellie was turning into a woman. He'd noticed the way her breasts were budding, but she was still so small that he'd never assumed the rest of her body was about to follow suit.

The bigger shock had come upon learning she'd actually told about their games. He would have bet his life she'd never tell. His anger at Fern grew as he walked into the house and locked the door behind him.

That's exactly what he had done—bet his life, and if it hadn't been for his wife's fucking piety, it would have already been over.

He'd been blindsided. They'd both blindsided him, and he was mad. But he had a plan. All he needed to make it work was time. Plus, he needed to talk to Ellie. She had to understand there were ways to protect herself now. But when he turned the doorknob of her room and the door didn't give, he couldn't believe it. It only took seconds to realize Fern had put a lock on his daughter's door. Son of a bitch! She'd locked him out of his daughter's life.

This only added to Garrett's fury. Fern's holier-than-thou attitude was one thing, but separating him from his daughter was crossing a line. They didn't understand. None of them understood. He'd never violated her. She was still a virgin. Yes, they'd played games, but he had not violated his child. Still, he knew the scope of his transgressions covered a very gray area and he was treading on thin ice.

He crept past Ellie's door and into his own bedroom while giving Fern's a wide berth. Her reaction had shocked him to the core. He hadn't known she'd had that much passion in her. There had been a moment when, despite her vow to the opposite, he'd thought he was dead. He downed some pain pills, shed his bloody clothes, letting them lie where they fell, and crawled into bed.

Chapter Five

It had been years since Fern had bothered to go to church on a regular basis, but now she and Ellie sat in their pew every Sunday whether Garrett went or not. He didn't like the new Fern, and he missed his relationship with Ellie, although he had only himself to blame.

He bided his time, watching Ellie scurry through the house like a meek little mouse with Fern striding along beside her like an Amazon warrior, her hands doubled into fists if he happened to cross their paths. He felt like he was living in the fucking Twilight Zone.

The splint came off his nose after about three weeks, and the last hue of greenish-purple faded from beneath his eye about a week after that. Doris didn't work on weekends, and when Saturday came around, Garrett was ready. There would be no witnesses for what he intended. This was, by God, his house and his daughter, too, and he was taking them back.

That morning, he woke up to an empty house. It was the first chance he'd had to see exactly what kind of a lock Fern had put on Ellie's door. When he saw it, he smiled. A couple of loose screws would put an end to that.

As much as he would have liked to stay in her room, there was more to be done. He crossed the hall into what had once been the master suite. Now it was Fern's bedroom, and it had been years since he'd been inside. The array of religious icons was daunting. He was a believer, but this bordered on fanaticism.

After a quick glance outside to make sure he was still alone, he began going through Fern's things, looking for her journal. Before he could implement his plan, he needed to remove any evidence that could mess up his plans.

He found the book in a drawer next to her bed and quickly flipped through the pages to see if she'd written about Ellie's revelation, which of course she had. But it was the last page in the book that set the wheels in motion. Taking care not to leave fingerprints on the paper, he began to read.

Dear Ellie . . . my little Ellie . . . I will never be able to tell you how sorry I am. You didn't deserve this, but it's too late for words. I can't ever make this right.

I'm so sorry. Momma

"On a silver freakin' platter," Garrett muttered as he tucked the journal under his arm, then headed into the bathroom to raid Fern's pharmacy.

Across town, Fern and Ellie came out of the supermarket with the shopping cart full of bags. Ellie pushed the cart as Fern dug for the car keys. They paused at the curb for a car to pass when, to Fern's surprise, the driver honked. She looked up just in time to see a couple of teenagers drive past.

"Who was that?"

Ellie eyed the taillights of the car and shrugged. "I don't know, Momma. Did you find your keys?"

Fern stared after the car, then turned and looked at Ellie. Her pretty baby-doll face was already changing—showing promises of the beauty she was turning out to be. Her body was taking shape from the thin, sickly child that she'd been, and when the breeze suddenly lifted Ellie's hair away from her neck in an odd, almost sexy kind of way, Fern flinched. All of a sudden, she didn't see her child, but the woman Ellie would become. The sight hit Fern like a bullet to the heart.

But this was her little Ellie—who was wearing a bra. This was her little Ellie—who'd begun to bleed. This was her little Ellie—who'd been fucking Fern's husband.

It wasn't a fair reaction, but Fern had never been known for rational thinking. She slapped Ellie across the face.

Quick tears sprang in Ellie's eyes and she grabbed her cheek. "Why did you do that?"

"You'd think with the mess you're in you would know better," Fern hissed.

Ellie reeled from the shock. One minute they'd been happy and now this? What had just happened?

"You're only twelve and you let your Daddy bust your cherry, which is a mortal sin. Now I catch you flirting with boys way too old for you."

Ellie shuddered. Momma sounded crazy. "I didn't let Daddy do anything to me, Momma. He just did it."

Fern grabbed the shopping cart with one hand and Ellie with the other and began pushing both of them toward the car.

"Get in," Fern said, as she unlocked the door.

Ellie paused, still trying to regain the prior joy. "Don't you want me to help put the sacks in the car?"

Fern slapped her again. "Don't talk back."

By the time Ellie got into the back seat, she was shaking so hard she couldn't fasten the seat belt. Instead, she curled up on the seat with her arms over her head. She should have known this wouldn't last. Momma was off her rocker all over again.

Fern slung the grocery bags into the trunk of the car, then shoved the cart aside. When she went to get in, she saw Ellie in the back seat, curled up like a snake.

"Oh, for the love of God," Fern said, as she slid behind the wheel. "Get up here right now."

Something inside Ellie snapped. There was no such thing as the love of God. God didn't love her or He would not have given her such crazy parents. She uncoiled herself with a jerk, sat up straight and buckled herself in.

"Hurry up," Fern yelled. "I haven't got all day. Ice cream is melting."

"Then you better drive, Momma, because I'm not moving."

A dark flush spread up Fern's cheeks as she started the engine. "I should have seen this coming. You think what's happened to you makes you all grown-up, don't you?"

Ellie was so mad she was spitting her words. "No, Momma. I think God hates me, that's what I think. I've been scared of Daddy all my life, but I'm done. No matter what you do to me, I refuse to be scared of you, too. You wanna know why I'm not sitting up front with you? You already hit me twice." Then she started to scream. "I'm not stupid. I don't want you to hit me again."

Fern looked up into the rearview mirror, staring at her daughter in disbelief. Ellie's cheek was a bright, ugly red. She looked back at herself. There were tears in her eyes and a rage in her body she didn't know how to assuage. She'd done this. She just didn't know how to take it back.

"I'm sorry," she whispered, and then put the car in gear and drove away.

The silence between them was fraught with an angry energy. Two females who'd been betrayed by the same man had gotten lost from each other and the way back was too far. When Fern pulled up to the house, Ellie was out of the car and running inside before she got her seat belt unlocked.

"Oh Lord, Lord, what have I done?" Fern whispered. Either God wasn't listening, or He was mad at Fern, too, because she didn't get any answers.

With a heavy heart, she gathered up grocery bags and started toward the house.

Garrett was standing in the doorway with a smile on his face. "What happened?"

Fern wasn't about to discuss Ellie with him. "If you intend to help, there are more sacks in the car. Otherwise get the hell out of my sight."

Garrett turned around and left her standing. The sound of his laughter was an ugly reminder of the perilous hold she had on her world.

That night, the mood around the supper table was tense. Daddy had offered to help prepare the meal, even going so far as to fill all their glasses before they sat down to eat. Then they'd passed dishes and scooted food around on their plates in a sick kind of politeness that was making Ellie nuts.

Momma hated Daddy.

Daddy hated Momma.

And Daddy was definitely mad at Ellie.

She kept glancing at Wyatt, but he wasn't talking. Momma kept picking up the saltshaker then putting it back down without using it, and Daddy persisted in crossing her line of vision by reaching for the gravy boat without asking her to pass it. Every time he used it, he would put it all the way back on the far side of the table, knowing he was intruding upon her personal space.

Ellie felt his anger. He wanted her to argue. He wanted to start a fight. She wanted to run away, but there was nowhere to run. Even worse, the slice of roast beef Momma had put on Ellie's plate was too raw. Momma knew Ellie liked her meat well-done, but she was too angry with Momma to ask for another slice. A thin trickle of blood had run out onto her mashed potatoes when she'd cut her first bite. It looked too much like the blood that had run down her legs—the blood that had started all this mess.

Everyone was quiet and far too polite to mention the smell of rot festering between them. The only person who was actually eating was

Daddy. He wolfed down food as if he'd been starving.

Ellie caught her mother glaring at Daddy and then at her, over and over, watching the both of them. But for what? Daddy was too calm and the smirk on his face made Ellie nervous.

Finally, Momma carried her plate to the sink and began doing dishes.

Ellie took it as a sign. "May I be excused?" she muttered, then got up and stomped out of the room without waiting for an answer.

Fern started to call her back, then shrugged and reached for the faucet. As she did, everything started to spin. She grabbed hold of the sink and lowered her head.

"What's wrong?" Garrett asked.

Fern wouldn't show weakness. "Nothing."

"Fine then," Garrett said. "I'll clear the table."

She didn't bother to comment. If he wanted a conversation, she wasn't interested in participating.

Even though she kept getting dizzier, she managed to get the dishes loaded in the dishwasher. But as soon as she turned it on, she headed for her room, staggering with every step.

"Lean on me," Garrett said.

Fern was so weak she didn't argue. By the time he got her to her bedroom, she could barely move one foot in front of the other.

"Want me to stay with you?" he asked.

"Get away from me," she mumbled, as she crawled up on the bed, collapsing face down.

Garrett walked toward the door, then stopped and gave the room one last glance. The telephone was unplugged. The suicide note in Fern's own hand was propped up on her writing table across the room, and Fern was flat on her face, doped to the gills with every sleeping pill in the place. She'd just seen her last sunrise and it was none too soon.

"Sleep tight. Don't let the bedbugs bite," Garrett said and then laughed all the way out the door.

Ellie was about to turn on her television to watch one of her shows when she heard her Daddy laugh. What just happened? Were he and Momma laughing together? Everyone had been mad and hateful and now they were laughing?

"Wyatt, did you hear Momma and Daddy laughing?"

Wyatt was pissed. "I heard it."

It was Ellie's last straw. "That does it. We're going to run away."

Wyatt frowned. "No, you're not, and neither am I."

"Why not? Momma doesn't want us. Daddy doesn't like you, and I don't like Daddy."

"We can't drive a car. We don't have any money or anywhere to go."

Ellie covered her face and fell backward onto her bed. "I hate my life. I hate everyone."

"Even me?"

Ellie gasped. "Not you. I don't hate you, Wyatt. I love you more than anyone else. You're part of me, remember?"

"I know. That's what makes us twins."

They sat together, listening to the sound of Daddy's footsteps moving away from their door. Distance between them was all that mattered.

But by morning, it became apparent that the hell they'd been living had been elevated to a whole new level.

Chapter Six

It was just after sunrise when Daddy began beating on Ellie's door and shouting her name. The loud, frantic pounding yanked her rudely from a dream. She pulled the covers up to her chin, certain he was about to break in.

"Go away, Daddy. Go away."

"No, it's not that, Ellie, it's not that. Get dressed. Something's wrong with your Momma. She won't wake up. I've already called 911."

Ellie's heart nearly stopped. She threw back the covers. "Wyatt! Did you hear?"

"I heard," Wyatt said as he came into the room.

"Do you think it's a trick?"

"I think we need to get dressed. I can already hear the sirens."

Ellie tore her nightgown over her head and scrambled through her drawers for a clean pair of shorts. It took what seemed like forever to put on her bra and pull a T-shirt over her head before unlocking her door and peeking out into the hall.

She could hear Daddy in the front of the house.

"The ambulance is here," Wyatt said.

"I wanna see Momma," Ellie cried and dashed across the hall into her mother's room.

Momma lay face down on the bedspread, still wearing the clothes she'd had on last night. Ellie wrinkled her nose at the sour, fetid smell. "Momma?" she whispered and reached for Fern's arm. The moment her fingers felt the cold, lifeless skin, she gasped and backed away.

"What's wrong?" Wyatt whispered.

"She's cold. Somebody needs to get her a blanket."

"Daddy's coming," Wyatt said and made himself scarce, but Ellie stood her ground.

The moment Daddy entered the room, she spoke up. "Daddy, Momma's cold. You need to get her a blanket."

Daddy moaned and scooped her up into his arms as the paramedics encircled the bed. "You shouldn't be in here," he said and carried her back out into the hall.

But Ellie could see over his shoulder. "What are they doing to Momma?"

Garrett knew the next few hours were going to be crucial to their relationship. He set her down, then got down on his knees and reached for her hands.

Ellie was starting to get scared. She'd never seen Daddy act like this. "Why won't Momma wake up?"

Garrett's chin quivered as his eyes filled with tears. It was easy to cry. There were all kinds of tears. Who would know the difference between tears of sadness and joy?

"Ellie, darling, Momma can't wake up anymore. She went to sleep last night and didn't wake up because she died. Momma's gone to heaven, Ellie, and we can't get her back."

"You lie," Ellie whispered and covered her ears, but it didn't help. Photo-like images of Momma started popping through her head. The way Momma wrinkled up her mouth when she was mad. The way her nostrils wiggled when she laughed. The scent of her perfume. The pillowy softness of her breasts. The drop of spit at the corner of her mouth when she'd slapped Ellie's face.

Momma was dead. She'd been mad at Ellie when she went to bed and now she'd be mad at her forever.

Ellie's eyes rolled back in her head.

When Ellie woke up, Doris was sitting in a chair by Ellie's bed and patting her hand like she was trying to put out a fire. Doris was crying. Ellie had never seen Doris cry.

"Are you sick?" Ellie asked.

Doris shook her head. "No, baby, I'm not sick."

"Then why are you crying?"

Doris choked and pressed a hand to her lips.

Ellie frowned. She hated it when she asked questions and adults didn't answer. It wasn't fair. They sure expected an answer when they asked her one.

Fine, Ellie thought. She sat up, then looked down at her clothes. They didn't match. She never wore stuff that didn't match.

"I need to change my clothes."

"It doesn't matter about your clothes," Doris said and grabbed a fresh tissue.

At that point, Ellie zeroed in on the voices out in the hall. "Where's Wyatt? Who are those people out in the hall?"

Doris shrugged. She couldn't account for the missing Wyatt and wasn't going to be the one to tell this child that her mother had committed suicide and the house was crawling with cops.

Ellie's bedroom door opened. It was like someone turned up the volume. All the voices and noises became louder, but it wasn't until she saw her Daddy's face that she remembered—Daddy on his knees out in the hall—telling her Momma went to sleep and never woke up. He said Momma was dead, but she was pretty sure that he lied. Daddy did whatever he needed to make things work in his world.

"Where's my Momma?" Ellie asked.

Garrett looked like he'd shrunk a foot as he crossed the room to her bed. His eyes were red-rimmed and his hands shook as he touched Doris on the shoulder. "Thank you so much for coming in on your day off. If you don't mind, I need a few minutes alone with Ellie."

"Is she . . . is the body . . . ?"

Garrett shook his head. "The people from the crime lab are still in there."

Ellie stood up on the bed. Her voice rose with her. "Where's my Momma?"

Garrett's mouth crumpled. "I already told you, remember?"

Doris stood up and left the room, closing the door behind her.

The moment the door shut it dawned on Ellie that she and her father were alone. A shaft of panic shot through her so fast she had to sit down. This time, the challenge was gone from her voice.

"Momma said you can't be in here with me anymore."

Garrett sat down in the chair Doris had vacated, making sure to keep some distance between them. The last thing he needed was for her to start talking about their games with a house full of cops.

"I know, Ellie, and I wouldn't be, I promise, except I needed to check on you."

"Momma can check on me," Ellie whispered, but reality was beginning to set in.

Wyatt came in, glanced at his Daddy then positioned himself between them. "Leave her alone."

Garrett flinched. "Ever the protector, aren't you?"

"Someone had to be," Wyatt said.

Garrett leaned back in the rocker, eyeing his progeny and wondering if he was going to be able to pull this off. He was older and smarter, but he'd yet to find anyone more pigheaded than his own seed.

"Ellie, talk to me," he said.

Her head came up and the look in her eyes caught him off guard. "You're lying to me, aren't you, Daddy?"

"I'm not lying about anything."

"Where's Momma?"

Garrett exhaled slowly. The only way this was going to end was for her to see the ugly truth for herself. "The police are here. They haven't moved her body yet, so she's still in her room."

Ellie started to shake. Police were a big deal. It would be hard for Daddy to lie about that, especially if she was to see them for herself.

"Ellie needs to see," Wyatt said.

Garrett eyed him curiously. "Did you look?"

Wyatt nodded. There were tears in his eyes, but his jaw was set. Garrett knew he wouldn't cry.

Ellie gasped. "Did you really see her, Wyatt?"

"Yes."

"I need to see, too," Ellie said. "I think you just need to wake her up. Sometimes Momma takes too many pills, remember?"

Garrett's heart leaped. This was exactly what the cops needed to hear. "Come with me, baby," he said softly.

"Wyatt too."

He sighed. "Wyatt too, but no talking, do you hear me?"

Wyatt nodded.

Ellie crawled off the bed, and when Garrett might have picked her up, she pulled away and walked out of the room on her own. Within seconds, she was backed into a wall by a group of policemen who hadn't seen her.

"'Scuse me. I need to get by," she said loudly.

They jumped at the sound of a kid's voice, then stared at Garrett in disbelief. "Man, she doesn't have any business here."

Ellie frowned. "This is my house. I know the law. You can't make me leave my own house."

Ellie didn't really know the law, but it sounded good, and she was going to see her Momma. She needed to tell Momma she was sorry that she didn't help carry in the groceries, and she was sorry that she didn't tell Momma good night.

"She refuses to believe me," Garrett told the police. "I think she needs to see this for herself."

"Momma's just asleep. All you have to do is shake her hard to wake her up, 'cause sometimes she takes too many sleeping pills."

Bingo. It was all Garrett could do not to smile. Ellie couldn't have done any better if he'd fed her the line.

The officers looked startled, then eyed Garrett with a different air as he took Ellie by the hand and led her into the room.

At first Ellie couldn't see past the men standing around the bed, but someone was taking pictures. When he stepped back to take a photo from a different angle, she realized they'd turned Momma onto her back.

"Look, Daddy. I told you she'd wake up. She turned over."

Garrett put his hand on Ellie's shoulder. When she walked out from under his touch, he didn't push it.

"They turned her over," he said softly. "She's dead, Ellie. She took too many pills and it killed her."

Ellie pushed past the photographer, then past another policeman until she was standing at the foot of Momma's bed. Only this didn't look like Momma.

"What's wrong with her face? Why is it so purple?" Ellie asked.

"Because she died face down, Ellie, and that's where all the blood in her body went when her heart stopped beating."

Ellie reeled as if she'd been slapped. She looked up. Everyone was staring at her. She looked back at her Momma, then poked the toe of her shoe. It flopped lifelessly.

She heard someone whisper the word suicide. She frowned, uncertain of what that meant.

"Momma?" Ellie said it again, and louder. "Momma."

The room was so quiet Ellie could hear the blood rushing through her body. Her shoulders slumped. For once, Daddy hadn't lied. There was no way to describe what she felt, but the bottom line was that she'd just been abandoned.

"I'm sorry I made you mad, Momma," Ellie said softly, then turned around and walked out of the room.

Garrett followed, taking care that they all see his concern for his child. As he'd hoped, Ellie had played right into his plan. She'd confirmed what he'd told the police about Fern's drinking and prescription drug addiction, and the apology in Fern's suicide note fit perfectly with what Ellie had just said. For all intents and purposes, Fern Wayne and her daughter had a fight last night. Despondent, Fern had taken her own life, leaving behind a note to explain the act. No one would suspect the nonspecific note referred to her dereliction as a parent that had led to her daughter's molestation.

Ellie walked through the house, then outside onto the back porch. She was pretty sure she was supposed to be crying, but she felt numb. Wyatt was sitting on the far side of the porch as Garrett came out of the house. She glanced at Wyatt, then at her father, her eyes narrowing.

For a moment, Garrett thought she'd found him out. The look on her face was so accusatory, he was certain somehow she knew what he'd done.

"Why did they say suicide?" Ellie asked.

Garrett sat down on the porch swing, taking care to keep a distance between them, then leaned forward, his elbows on his knees. "It means someone died, but not because they were sick or had an accident, or were murdered. It means someone took their own life. Like Momma."

Ellie's frown deepened. "Momma took her own life?"

Garrett nodded.

"She swallowed a whole bunch of pills when she knew they would hurt her?" Ellie asked.

He nodded again.

"She did it knowing she wouldn't wake up."

"I guess so," Garrett said.

Rage made knots in Ellie's stomach. "She went away so she'd never have to be with us again?"

"I'm sorry, baby," Garrett whispered. "Don't be afraid. I won't go away. I won't leave you alone."

Ellie stood up, and for that moment, was eye to eye with Garrett. "I already knew that," Ellie muttered. She'd been trying to hide from him her whole life and nothing that had happened led her to believe anything was going to be different. "And just so you know, I'm not afraid. You can't ever make me afraid of you again."

Garrett's eyes widened. When Ellie got up and walked off the porch toward the creek, talking to Wyatt as she went, he didn't have the nerve to call her back.

The church where Momma was buried was the same one where they'd gone every Sunday. The one that looked like a castle, and where Ellie pretended she was a princess. But they held the services in the afternoon, so there was no sunshine in Ellie's lap. Like Momma, the sun had already moved on.

Ellie heard the whispers at the cemetery and afterward at their house where everyone brought casseroles and platters of all kinds of foods. She couldn't figure out why they had to feed people at their house when they were the ones who were supposed to be sad. It seemed more sensible that someone would be feeding them. But she was just a kid, and it was becoming more and more evident that until she grew up, her voice would not be heard.

Doris served platters of fried chicken to the people from the choir and to Preacher Ray, who preached the sermon. The creamy mashed potatoes and thick brown gravy were just like Momma liked it, and vegetables and biscuits were abundant. The sideboard was covered with so many pies she didn't think they'd ever get eaten, and the number of casseroles, where the food was all mixed up together, was overwhelming. Ellie didn't mind it all that much, but Wyatt didn't like his food to touch, so casseroles were out.

In between bites and chewing and the clinking of glasses and Momma's good silver scraping against the bone china plates with big pink roses, Ellie heard them talking in low, hushed tones . . .

". . . what a shame . . ."

". . . going to hell . . ."

". . . suicide a sin . . ."

". . . poor Ellie . . ."

". . . poor troubled Fern . . ."

The whispers circled the rooms like vultures circling the skies.

In the midst of it all, Doris sought her out, then handed her and Wyatt a plate of food to share. They carried it to a corner of the room and sat down behind the black leather wingback chair where Daddy watched football. They were out of sight, speaking in whispers or not at all. It was enough that they were together. She wasn't hungry, and Wyatt was just picking at the food on the plate. It was easier for them to take what was offered and go along, than to argue.

Throughout the whole ordeal, Ellie watched Daddy cry and pray and shake hands with people she'd never seen before. She didn't know what to think. It seemed like he was truly sad. But there were other times when she caught him looking at her, and her throat closed up.

How was this going to work?

When everyone went home—even Doris—she and Wyatt would be alone with Daddy. In her worst nightmare, she'd never imagined it would come to this.

"Ellie," Wyatt whispered.

"What?" she whispered back.

"It will be all right."

She shuddered. Wyatt always knew what she was thinking. "I don't think so, Wyatt. We need a plan."

"What kind of plan?"

"I don't know," Ellie whispered. "I'm thinking on it."

Wyatt didn't respond. He knew when Ellie got like this, it was useless to argue.

Finally, the people began to leave. Ellie and Wyatt stood at the door beside Daddy as he shook hands and thanked everyone for their condolences. Ellie didn't know what condolences were, but she was pretty sure Doris hadn't put any on her plate.

It wasn't until Mrs. Markham, the lady who played the organ at church, went to leave, that Ellie's world was yanked into perspective in a way she had not expected.

"Poor Garrett, y'all know I'll be prayin' for you, don't you?" Mrs. Markham said.

"Yes, ma'am, and we appreciate your kindness for the fine pie."

Mrs. Markham beamed. "I suppose it was a success. There wasn't a bite left in the dish when I went to claim it."

Ellie frowned. Vanity. She knew that sin. Mrs. Markham was standing in their doorway being vain about her own cooking when she was supposed to be sad about Momma.

Mrs. Markham looked down at Ellie. She glared back. Wyatt looked away. He didn't want to draw any attention to himself.

Mrs. Markham frowned then. Unruly child.

She patted Garrett's arm. "You take care of yourself. Don't want to orphan anyone, if you know what I mean?"

Garrett muttered something acceptable, but Ellie wasn't listening. She was trying to wrap her head around the fact that if anything happened to Daddy, she would become an orphan. She knew about orphans and looked up at her Daddy in a moment of clarity. Better the Devil she knew, than the one she did not. She didn't want to be an orphan any more than she wanted her Momma to be in that box out in the cemetery buried beneath all that dirt. She was still struggling with the concept that Momma no longer needed air to breathe. Without thinking, she scooted one step closer to Garrett.

It did not go unobserved. Garrett stifled a smile as he shut the door behind Mrs. Markham. All he needed was a little patience and time.

"That's the last of them," Garrett said. "I'm going to check on Doris to see if she's cleaned up the mess in the kitchen."

"I'm going to my room," Ellie said.

"Okay. When Doris leaves, I'm going to mine, too. I don't know about you, but the past four days have been exhausting. We're going to miss Momma like crazy, but we'll get through this, okay? I'll check on you right before bedtime just to make sure you don't need anything, but I won't come in. I promise."

Ellie squinted her eyes at him, wondering if he'd look as different as he was behaving, but he was already walking away.

"He's lying," Wyatt said.

Ellie nodded. She wanted to believe Daddy, but like Wyatt, they had too many years of betrayal behind them to take anything he said on face value.

They made a run for their bedroom, and the moment the door closed behind them, Wyatt shoved the slide bolt in place.

Ellie took off her good dress and hung it back up in the closet, then opted for her pajamas. She wasn't about to get undressed and bathe. Not tonight. Not until she saw if Daddy could keep a promise.

"Hey, Wyatt."

"What?"

"We can't live here forever with just Daddy."

Wyatt snorted. "It won't be forever. As soon as we get old enough, we're outta here, right?"

"Right, but in the meantime, we need someone to look after us."

"We're twelve. We don't need babysitters," Wyatt said.

"We don't have any grandmothers," Ellie said.

"I know. We don't have any grandfathers either, but what does that have to do with anything?"

"But we could have a nanny. One of the girls I know at school has a live-in nanny."

"That's because they have a little kid, too."

Ellie frowned. She didn't like to be thwarted.

"I want a nanny. If I had a nanny, Daddy would have to behave."

Wyatt shrugged. "And I wanna be six feet tall, but I don't think it's going to happen."

Ellie shrugged and reached for the remote.

A short while later they were readying for bed when there was a knock at the door.

"Ellie?"

"What?"

"I'm going to bed now, are you okay? Do you need anything?"

"I'm fine. Wyatt's fine."

"Then I'm off to bed. You know where I am if you need me. Good night."

"Night," she said, and then listened as he walked away.

Wyatt frowned. This didn't feel right, but he didn't have anything to add to what he'd already said. Besides, he was tired.

"I'm going to bed, too." Ellie aimed the remote at the television and turned it off. "Hey, Wyatt?"

"What?"

"Are you sad that Momma's dead?"

Wyatt shrugged. "I don't know how I feel. She didn't like me as much as she liked you, but then neither does Daddy."

"I love you."

"I love you, too," Wyatt said and turned out the light.

Ellie rolled over onto her side and closed her eyes. She was hanging on the verge of unconsciousness when Fern's face slid through her mind. She didn't look like she had the last time Ellie had seen her. Her face wasn't all mashed and purple, and she was smiling. Tears rolled out from under Ellie's eyelids onto the pillow.

Momma looked happy.

Ellie wished she could say the same.

Chapter Seven

A week had passed since they'd put Fern Wayne in the ground. Garrett kept asking Ellie if she wanted to go out to the cemetery with him to put fresh flowers on the grave, but each time she refused.

"Why don't you want to go?" Garrett asked as he stood in the doorway to Ellie's room, watching her paint her toenails. He was still holding to his promise not to cross the threshold, although there were plenty of nights he wanted to retract it.

"Wyatt doesn't want to go, so I'm not going," she said and dipped the brush back in the tiny bottle to reload.

Garrett frowned. He was losing his grip on her and wasn't sure how to regain it. The older Ellie got, the stronger she became. Even when Wyatt wasn't around, she was quicker to challenge him.

"Surely you could take a little time from your busy schedule and spend some time with your Momma," Garrett muttered, well aware that was a dig she wouldn't like, but again, Ellie surprised him.

"Momma never took time from her schedule to spend with me. Besides, she's not in that grave. Preacher Ray said so. Her spirit's in heaven with Baby Jesus. After all that praying she did to Him, she oughta be happy about that."

Garrett bit his lip and tried not to focus on Ellie's long slender feet and tiny pink-tipped toenails. "Fine. Then I'll go out there and see Momma by myself."

Ellie paused and looked up. The disdain on her face was impossible to miss. "I'm twelve. You and I both know you're not gonna *see* Momma anywhere. But just in case you do, tell her I said hi. And if you don't mind, close the door when you leave."

Garrett spun on his heel, slamming the door behind him. Within seconds, he heard the distinct click of the slide bolt. His eyes narrowed angrily, but he kept his tongue. He was a patient man. If he couldn't catch his little fly with sugar, he'd use force.

Ellie stood with her ear against the door until she heard him walking away, then exhaled slowly. Every time she challenged him, she feared it would be her last.

Then Wyatt came up behind her. "I heard you," he said. "Way to go."

Ellie shrugged, then went back to her nail polish and finished the job.

Wyatt, always curious about the *whats* and *whys* of how girls operated, said, "Are you going to do your fingernails, too?"

Ellie eyed the nails on her fingers then shook her head.

"Why not?"

"It would look weird. They're all uneven."

"Oh."

Finally Ellie screwed the cap back onto the bottle, then stretched her legs out in front of her and leaned back, bracing her arms behind her back as she waited for them to dry.

"I've been checking out nannies," Ellie announced.

Wyatt frowned. "Does Daddy know?"

"No. Why should he? He's not the one who's going to be spending time with her. That will be me."

"But, Ellie, you can't just hire someone like that. You're just a kid. How will you pay her?"

Ellie's eyes narrowed as she lowered her voice. "Last week I heard Daddy talking to the lawyer on the phone."

"So?"

Ellie's mouth curled up into a small, tight smile. "So he was mad."

"About what?"

"Momma changed her will before she suicided herself. She left it all to us and nothing to Daddy."

"Holy cow," Wyatt said. "So what does that mean exactly?"

"I'm not sure. I could only hear Daddy's side of the conversation, but I think Momma appointed someone besides Daddy to be the checker of her estate." Ellie frowned. "I don't think that's the right word, but I can't remember for sure. Anyway, the checker is the one who will control the money until we're twenty-one. So it seems to me I have plenty of money now to hire a nanny if I want one, and I'm going to tell the checker to pay her."

Wyatt grinned. "You're smarter than you look."

Ellie threw a pillow, but she was laughing.

"So what's this nanny's name that you like?" Wyatt asked.

"Sophie Crawford."

"Is she nice?"

Ellie shrugged. "She makes me feel safe."

"What's she like?" Wyatt asked.

"She's fifty-one. Older than Daddy. She's not very tall and her hair is gray and curly. Do you remember that Christmas cartoon movie about Santa and Mrs. Claus at the North Pole that we always liked?"

"Yeah."

"So her face looks sort of like Mrs. Claus. All round and happy."

"Where's she gonna sleep?" Wyatt asked.

"Doris will have to fix up Momma's room. I'll tell her today."

Wyatt gasped. "Momma's room? Really?"

Ellie shrugged. "Why not? Momma's through with it."

"You're not sad about Momma anymore, are you, Ellie?"

Ellie lightly touched the edges of her toenails, testing to see if they were dry, but they weren't. "I've cried all I care to about Momma. She wasn't crying about leaving us. I don't see a reason to cry because she's gone. I'm saving my tears for something that really matters."

"Like what?"

"That's a dumb question, Wyatt. How am I supposed to know what's gonna make me sad?"

Wyatt laughed, then threw the pillow back.

"Watch out for my toes," Ellie squealed as she rolled out of range.

"Hey, where are you going?"

"To find Doris. Sophie's coming tomorrow. We don't have much time."

Doris was still muttering to herself as she turned the mattress in Fern's bedroom, then put on a new pad. She felt sorry as all get-out for Ellie, but if anyone cared to ask her, she thought this was taking things a little too far. Doris knew the child had nearly died when she was first born. She'd heard the story more than once from Ellie. She also knew that for the first six or eight years of Ellie's life she'd been sickly. But that seemed to have passed. Doris guessed that the spoiling they'd done to her during her ailing times was pretty much set in stone, and there was little to be done about it now but go along.

Still, Ellie saying she needed a nanny at the age of twelve and then demanding this bedroom be turned out without much warning was aggravating. However, Doris knew she got paid the same amount of money no matter what she did, so it was no skin off her nose.

As soon as Doris finished making the bed, she went into the

bathroom to give it a good scrub. Hadn't much been done to the room at all since the funeral. She supposed it was about time, no matter who was coming to stay. But it occurred to her as she kicked off her shoes and got into the tub to scrub down the walls that if Ellie was going to start inviting people to come live in this house, Doris was going to ask for a raise. She hadn't signed up to work for no boarding house.

Garrett came home from work to find Doris setting the dining table with Fern's good china and silver instead of their everyday dishes at the table in the kitchen.

"What's going on?" he asked.

"Ask your daughter," Doris said and slapped another linen napkin into place.

Garrett's stomach did a flip-flop. These days, it was hard to tell what was going to happen next. He was halfway down the hall and heading toward Ellie's room when he heard laughter and talking coming from Fern's room. He hadn't been in there since they'd carried her out on a stretcher, covered from head to toe with a sheet. The door was already ajar. He pushed it open and walked in.

"What the hell's going on in here?"

Ellie looked up and frowned.

"You cursed. That is not a good example to set before your child, but I'm sure you won't do it again. Daddy, this is Sophie Crawford, my new nanny. She'll be staying in this room and she already said she doesn't mind all the angels and crosses, so you don't have to take them down. Sophie . . . this is my Daddy, Garrett Wayne. Daddy, meet Mrs. Crawford."

Then she beamed, obviously proud of herself for remembering the proper way to introduce.

Garrett took a deep breath as the aforementioned Sophie Crawford unfolded herself from Fern's rocking chair and came forward to shake his hand.

"Mr. Wayne, it's a pleasure I'm sure, and please call me Sophie as I've instructed Ellie to do. I find it makes it easier for children to confide in me, that way."

It was reflex that made Garrett clasp the hand in front of him, but he was still staring. The high-pitched voice and the slight stoop to her shoulders were going to take some getting used to.

"Uh . . ." He flinched as their palms touched. "I need to speak with

Ellie, please. Ellie. Out in the hall. Now."

"I'll come get you when dinner is ready," Ellie said and waved good-bye before following Garrett out.

Garrett shut the door behind them, then grabbed Ellie by the shoulders and gave her a shake. "What the hell's going on?"

She pulled out of his grasp. "I hired a nanny, that's what."

Garrett rolled his eyes and stared up at the ceiling as he shoved a hand through his hair. "Why do you persist in this?" he muttered.

"I hired a nanny because I've reached the age where female companionship is important. According to my health teacher, girls learn how to be women by watching the women in their family, but I don't have any now, do I?"

"No, but—"

"I like Doris and all, but she's already griping about being overworked. I don't think she'd take to having to teach me how to be a woman, too. So I hired myself a nanny. She's cheaper than you'd expect because Wyatt says he doesn't need her and doesn't want her here."

"First time I've ever agreed with Wyatt about anything," Garrett muttered, then did a double take as the other part of her statement soaked in. "And what do you mean she's cheaper? You actually think I'm going to pay her?"

Ellie's eyes narrowed and she took a step back. "No, I'm going to pay her."

"I am losing my fucking mind," he muttered, then turned in a circle with his hands over his face. He was hearing her words, but she wasn't making a bit of sense.

Daddy didn't often curse, so Ellie took a second step back, moving herself closer to her bedroom door just in case he planned to blow his top.

But he didn't. To her surprise, he was almost grinning.

"So you're going to pay her, are you? What with? Pink fingernail polish and those candy bars you hide that you think I don't know about?"

Ellie gasped. If he knew about the candy, that meant he'd been snooping in her room when she wasn't here. She shivered, but stood her ground. "I'll pay her with money from Momma's state."

Garrett's eyes widened. He must know she meant estate, but what he couldn't know was why she thought she could even do that. "What do you mean?"

"I know Momma left all her money to me and Wyatt and told

someone called a checker to take care of it for us until we're older. He's paying Sophie."

"Executor," Garrett mumbled.

"What?"

"The word is executor, not checker, and how the fuck did you find this out?"

Ellie frowned. "You're still cursing. What happened? Did you have a bad day at work?"

Before Garrett could answer, Doris appeared at the far end of the hallway. "Supper is ready," she said and stomped back to the kitchen.

"Doris is upset because I asked her to lay the plates in the dining room tonight," Ellie said.

"I saw. Why did you do that?"

"It's Sophie's first night here. I thought it would be nice if we started her job off in a kind of celebration."

Garrett felt like his brain was on fire. "Celebration? This is a celebration?"

"It is for me, Daddy," Ellie said. "You go wash up. I'll get Sophie and Wyatt."

She darted back into Fern's bedroom, then came out talking with Sophie on their way down the hall, pausing only long enough to open the door to her room.

"Wyatt. Supper's ready."

Garrett felt like he'd been punched in the gut. How the hell had he let Ellie spin this far out of control? He'd been shocked by her betrayal to Fern, then afraid she'd spill the beans to the cops, and now this. Was there any way of reeling her back?

Chapter Eight

School began in the last week of August, and except for Sophie, Doris had the house to herself again. Wyatt and Ellie began sixth grade in separate classrooms, but their lives were beginning to go in different directions as well, and Wyatt blamed it all on Sophie's arrival. Wyatt was still the same, but Ellie went to school with a new attitude, a different hairdo, and lipstick. According to Sophie, a little lipstick never hurt anyone, especially if it was a very pale pink. Even more intriguing to Ellie was the fact that she needed to go shopping for a different size bra. The changes in her appearance did not change her relationship with the other students. Now she was not only that odd girl, but also the one whose mother had committed suicide.

Garrett drove Ellie and Sophie to the mall, then waited for them on a bench outside a Victoria's Secret store, imagining how Ellie was going to look in the new lingerie.

Confident with Sophie's presence, Ellie marched into the store with cash in her purse and headed for a clerk.

"Hi," Ellie said. "I need to be fitted for a larger size bra. Can you help me?"

"Yeah, sure," the girl said. "Show me the style you like, and then I'll measure you for size."

Ellie sifted through the hangers until she found one that seemed intriguing. "This blue one fastens in front, doesn't it?"

"Yes."

"I like that, but I don't want blue. I need either white or ivory colors, please."

"Okay. Want me to see if we have it in your size?'

Ellie glanced at Sophie. Sophie nodded approvingly.

"Yes, please," Ellie said, and followed the clerk into a dressing room.

She felt a moment of sadness, remembering she'd done this before with Momma, then set the thought aside. There was nothing of her past she chose to revisit. She removed her bra and stood with her arms out to her side like she was about to take flight while the clerk measured her boobs. It felt a little weird to have a total stranger feeling her up like this, then she decided the stranger was preferable to Daddy.

"Looks like you're a 34B," the clerk said. "Wait here and I'll see if we have it."

Ellie smiled and gave Sophie a thumbs-up. "I went from barely a 34A to a 34B in one summer. Looks like I might have inherited more than blonde hair and blue eyes from Momma."

"What do you mean?" Sophie asked.

"Momma had really big boobs."

Sophie frowned. "Breasts. You should say *breasts. Boobs* is so common."

"Oh," Ellie said, and made a mental note.

A short while later they came out of the store carrying a pink shopping bag containing three new bras.

Garrett stood up. "Are you ready to go now?"

Ellie looked to Sophie for an answer.

"Yes, we're ready," Sophie said.

Garrett glared. "What the hell, Ellie? Have you also lost the ability to make a decision on your own?"

The pitch of Sophie's voice rose slightly. "Oh. I apologize for overstepping my bounds. I had no idea."

"You do not apologize to him for anything," Ellie hissed, and sailed past Garrett with her nose in the air.

Garrett cursed beneath his breath and palmed his car keys as he followed his daughter to the parking lot. She got into the backseat with her shopping bag in her lap and proceeded to glare at him in the rearview mirror all the way home.

At first Garrett was pissed. But the farther he drove, the more fascinated he became. He'd been intrigued by her shyness, but he was beginning to like the fiery side of her more. The next time she gave him an angry look, he winked.

Ellie froze. Something wasn't right. Why wasn't Daddy still angry? Confused, she looked away and began talking to Sophie, but the damage had been done. Once again, her fragile claim on stability had been rattled.

It took another month before Sophie's influence began to really get on Garrett's nerves. She'd set Ellie to reading an etiquette book and practicing place settings at the table, complete with all the forks, spoons, bread plates, and multiple glasses one would expect at a formal dinner. Doris had threatened to quit from all the extra laundry and dishwashing, and Garrett had had to raise her salary to appease her distress.

Every time Wyatt crossed swords with Sophie, she gave him a look that set his teeth on edge, followed by, "I had no idea," so his absence was not surprising.

Garrett was beginning to think he was the only one left with a brain and had ideas he would gladly share, but he knew it would get him arrested. He was so pissed about the ground he'd lost with Ellie that he finally made a demand she couldn't deny.

Ellie felt almost grown-up as she left the drugstore and started home. The air was chilly, and she was glad she'd worn her pink leather jacket and good denim jeans. At Sophie's instructions, she'd gone after pads so that she would be prepared when her next period began. Doris had taught Ellie how to keep track on a calendar, and Sophie added that it was always good to be prepared.

Besides the pads, Ellie had bought a new shade of nail polish and a Hershey bar and was eating it slowly one square at a time as she walked. It was one of those days when the world felt right—when it seemed like heaven was on her side. She was doing well in school. She felt pretty, and the chocolate melting on her tongue was about as good as it got. It didn't bother her that she had no friends her age. She was satisfied with just going about her business at school. Her life was far too complicated at home to get strangers mixed up in it.

As she turned the corner and started down the last block to get to her house, a car full of teenagers drove past, waving and honking like crazy people. She couldn't enjoy the attention because it reminded her of what happened the day Momma killed herself.

Ellie broke off another piece of chocolate and popped it in her mouth, then licked her fingers to make sure nothing had been left behind. As soon as she got home, she was going to take off her old nail polish and try her new color. It was called Sunset Coral—a bit darker than the pink she'd been wearing, but not enough to look common. Sophie said good girls should never look common.

But Ellie knew something that Sophie did not. It wouldn't matter how properly she spoke or how particular she was about her clothing and demeanor, it was going to take more than manners to offset being

Daddy's whore.

Whore was a new word she'd picked up at school this year. It was enlightening to Ellie. At least now she had a name to put to their relationship. Some girls pronounced the word as "ho," but Sophie said if you had to use the terminology, you should at least use it properly.

Ellie slipped the last piece of chocolate in her mouth and shifted her sack from her right hand to her left, then stumbled as she looked up.

Daddy stood on the front porch waiting for her, and she could tell he was mad. She wondered if he was going to get as pissed as Momma had about the boys honking at her. She shifted her stride to accommodate haste and hoped she could get past him without a situation.

It didn't happen.

The moment Ellie walked up the steps, Garrett moved in front of the door, blocking the entrance.

"What are you doing?" Ellie asked. "I had permission to go to the drugstore."

"From who?" Garrett snapped.

"It's from *whom*, not *who*, and Sophie said I could."

Garrett wanted to shake her, but opted for another time and place. Today, he had other fish to fry.

"I'm standing on the front porch of our house, in front of God and everyone so you'll feel safe enough to talk to me, and I will be heard."

Ellie paused, her heart thumping so hard it was difficult to breathe. "I'm listening," she said, and wished Wyatt or Sophie was standing beside her.

"You've been calling the shots around here for months. I've let you get by with a lot of it because of Fern's death, but you're turning into a tyrant."

Anger surged so fast Ellie forgot they were on the front porch. "Seriously? Do you really want to go there with me?"

Garrett knew he was taking a chance, but he pushed back.

"I'm not going to get into a shouting match with you, and I'm not going to stand here and take the blame for what's in the past."

"I didn't expect you to," Ellie snapped. "You never have. Why should I think you would suddenly change? Sophie says a skunk never changes its stripes."

Being referred to as a skunk by his own daughter was like throwing oil on a fire. Garrett was so mad he was shaking.

"I'm here to tell you that I'm sick of having Sophie thrown in my face—and you insisting either she or Wyatt go everywhere with us. We're never together like we used to be."

"There's a reason for that," Ellie yelled.

Garrett looked nervously toward the street, then shoved his hands in his pockets and took a step back.

"Here's the deal. I'm not asking for much. Just our Sundays like they used to be."

Ellie's head began to whirl, trying to decipher exactly what that meant. She could remember plenty of Sundays that had been hell on earth. Especially the ones when Momma had passed out. "What do you mean?"

"Either you agree to attend church with me . . . just me . . . like we used to, or I'm never taking you back there again."

Ellie gasped. He'd found her Achilles' heel. She liked the church even though her Momma's funeral had tainted it a bit. It was less of a castle now, but more of a sanctuary. She believed God could hear prayers better there, and it troubled her to think she'd lose that connection.

The idea of never going there again was almost worse than having to play Daddy's games.

She moved closer to him—so close they could feel each other's breath. "Just church. But if you hurt me again, I'll scream it to the world and take the consequences."

"Deal," Garrett said, and walked back into the house, stifling the urge to grin.

Ellie dragged her feet as she followed him inside.

Wyatt was waiting for her. "I heard. You're going to be sorry."

Her voice was shaking from the surge of anger she was trying to control. "Church doesn't mean the same thing to you that it does to me."

"Whatever. I'm just saying it's a mistake."

"Wouldn't be my first now, would it?" Ellie snapped.

Sophie slipped into the hall. "Here, here, you two shouldn't be fussing."

Wyatt turned on her. "You don't know anything about it," he said, and left.

"What's he talking about? What don't I know?" Sophie asked.

Ellie shrugged. "It doesn't matter."

But it did. When Sunday rolled around, the only one who walked out the door with Garrett was Ellie.

Chapter Nine

"You look very beautiful," Daddy said as they walked toward the car.

Ellie felt pretty in her pink skirt and white sweater with the pink embroidery around the yoke, but she didn't want to hear it from him. She stomped toward the passenger side of the car with her chin up and her eyes blazing, but instead of getting inside, she stood, waiting.

Daddy was already behind the steering wheel when he finally realized she was still outside. "What are you waiting for? Get in."

Ellie didn't budge.

With an angry exhale, he got back out. "What the hell, Ellie?"

"You're cursing on Sunday, and I'm waiting for you to open the door for me. Sophie says a gentleman always opens the door for a lady."

"Son of a holy bitch," Garrett muttered as he circled the car, opened the door, and moved aside for Ellie to get in. Ellie stepped in as carefully as if she were getting into a limo, then smoothed out her skirt, brushed a bit of dried grass from the toe of her white patent leather shoe, eyed her stockings to make sure they weren't twisted, and then buckled her seat belt as Daddy shut the door.

He was still muttering beneath his breath as he got back inside. Ellie had a small pink purse in her lap, one leg crossed over the other and one foot swinging as she waited for him to start the car.

He glared at her. "You're being rude."

"You wanted me by myself. I'm here, but you can't make me like it."

"That's not—"

"I'm doing exactly what you asked. You don't get to change the rules to get more."

"You've never had a spanking in your life," he said, "but there's always a first time for everything."

She turned to look at him then, hating even the sight of him. "You need to remember I'm not afraid of you. And you also need to remember to be a little bit afraid of me, because if you step out of line in front of Sophie, she will tell God and everybody what you've done. She's a nanny. She's been trained to protect and care for children. She doesn't know about the secret you have with me and Wyatt, and you better pray she never finds out."

Words froze in the back of Garrett's throat. Not once since Sophie's arrival had he thought of her as a danger to him, and the thought horrified him. The option to get rid of her like he did Fern did not exist. In a way, he and Ellie were trapped in webs of their own making.

He started the car and backed out of the driveway. The ride to church was made in silence. When he parked at the church parking lot and got out, he did a double take when he realized Ellie was still sitting in the front seat.

He bit his lip, retraced his steps, and opened the door.

"Thank you," she said primly, and walked beside him to the church.

Preacher Ray stood outside the doorway greeting the parishioners as they walked in—smiling at the grown-ups and patting little kids' heads. She remembered when he used to pat her head, but now she was too tall, and she wouldn't have liked him messing up her hair. It had taken her too long to get it fixed the way she liked it to have someone stirring up the top. But she liked Preacher Ray. She liked him a lot. She didn't often listen to all of his sermon, but it made her feel good to watch him standing up at the front behind the pulpit with all that thick white hair and his long preacher robes. She thought he looked like an angel. All he needed were some big white wings and a halo. Angels always had halos.

As they stopped in the doorway, he smiled benevolently and touched her shoulder. "Good morning, Ellie. It's always good to see your sweet face in my congregation."

Garrett beamed.

Ellie smiled back. "Thank you. I like church. It makes me feel clean."

Preacher Ray's eyebrows rose slightly. Garrett's heart skipped a beat. It wasn't good for the preacher to start wondering why a twelve-year-old girl would think dirty as a religious euphemism for sin.

"Come along, Ellie," Garrett said, grabbed her elbow and guided her toward their pew. His eyes narrowed warningly as they sat. "Don't talk like that to the preacher," he whispered.

Ellie put a finger to her lips and frowned. "No talking in church," she whispered back. "Sophie said."

Garrett grimaced, hoped it passed for a smile, and began studying the program.

Ellie took a slow deep breath, then leaned back and gazed up at the vast vaulted ceiling.

Are you here, God?

I haven't been praying much lately. I'm sorry. Is Momma happy? I hope so. Make sure she knows I'm not still mad. So the reason I'm talking to You with my eyes open and my mouth shut is because I don't want Daddy to hear, okay? The deal is, I'm scared. 'Course You already know that. I believe I've mentioned it before. But this is a different kind of scared. I got my period this summer. Oh. Sorry. You probably already know that too. Momma always said You were 'all seeing.' I thought it would make Daddy stop wanting to play the game. We haven't done it in a while cause Momma put a lock inside my bedroom door, but I don't think it's gonna work much longer. So my question is . . . what do I do?

That's all I need to know. Hope You have a nice day.

Satisfied that she'd put out the word, she looked down at her lap and smiled. There they were—the colors—spilling down the front of her dress and into her lap—yellows and reds, blues and gold, all running together like melted crayons. She looked up at the stained-glass window.

It was Jesus sitting in a garden with a whole bunch of little kids sitting around him. She remembered the verse, s*uffer the little children to come unto Me.*

She sure hoped some heavenly being had heard her prayer because she was a kid and she was suffering the worst kind of fear. She'd take guidance from Jesus or God or even one of those warrior angels—she wasn't picky.

Preacher Ray moved to the pulpit as the organ music suddenly swelled.

Ellie closed her eyes and inhaled as deeply as she could, then held her breath as the music rose throughout the sanctuary. The hair stood up on the backs of her arms and it felt as if every pore in her body opened to let in the music.

Tears sprang to her eyes, but she quickly blinked them away. She was still saving tears for something important, and while this music made her feel really, really good, she didn't think she should be crying.

Garrett laid a songbook in her lap with it opened to the proper page. She took it without thought. It was how church worked. He might be the monster in her house, but here he was just her Daddy.

Sunday dinner was a la carte. Garrett went through the driveway at Kentucky Fried Chicken for take-home.

"Wyatt likes extra crispy. I like original and Sophie would appreciate grilled. I don't believe I'd care for coleslaw but I would like macaroni and cheese. Wyatt will want mashed potatoes and gravy and—"

". . . and Sophie will be wanting baked beans, right?"

Ellie paused. "How did you know?"

"Because it's the only thing left on the menu that you have yet to mention."

"No it's not, Daddy. I think they have corn on the cob, too, but it always gets in my teeth, and Wyatt eats too much butter. Doris says."

Garrett almost smiled. "Doris? I was expecting a Sophie reference."

Ellie frowned. "Sophie doesn't cook for us. Doris does. Doris knows what we like to eat, remember?"

Garrett sighed. "I remember."

He placed the order, then moved forward in line. It felt good to be doing this again—just him and his daughter—the way it was supposed to be.

Rationally, he knew the laws of the nation condemned how he felt about Ellie, but they just didn't understand the love a man could have for his child. They had no idea. No idea at all.

A week had passed since Ellie sent up her prayer in church. She'd been waiting patiently, hoping for a sign that it had been heard.

She was also worried about Wyatt and Sophie. They weren't getting along and Ellie wasn't sure what to do about it. Every time she approached Wyatt about the issue, he just got mad. When it happened again, it was the following Saturday. The only good thing about the whole awful ordeal was that Doris hadn't been there to witness it, and it all started over pouring syrup on a waffle.

Daddy was at the grocery store. Ellie had overslept, which was good because he hadn't made her go with him like he usually did. He'd left her a note to make her own breakfast, so she'd chosen frozen waffles and popped them in the toaster.

"Wyatt, do you want one or two?" Ellie asked.

"Two for now," he said, and got plates out of the cabinet.

"Don't forget to set a place for Sophie," Ellie said. "I think she's up."

Wyatt got out a third plate, but she could tell he was unhappy.

"Why don't you like her?"

"She's bossy, always criticizing what we say and do."

Ellie shrugged. "But Momma and Daddy always told us what to do, too. What's the difference?"

"I didn't like it then, either, but they were our parents. That's what parents do. Sophie's not related. She's an employee."

"She's a nanny," Ellie muttered.

"Who happens to work for us," Wyatt said. "Not the other way around."

The waffles popped up. Ellie put one on her plate. Wyatt took two. They carried them to the table, then sat and began slathering them with butter while they were still hot.

Wyatt was in the act of pouring syrup on his waffles when Sophie's high-pitched voice broke the comfortable silence.

"Wyatt, that's too much syrup. You'll wind up wasting it. Waste not, want not, I always say."

Wyatt flung his fork down on the table. "You need to get something straight here. You're not my parent and you're not my nanny. You don't tell me what to do."

Sophie folded her hands in front of her, which made her look like she was getting ready to pray. "Somebody woke up on the wrong side of the bed this morning. My, my, I had no idea."

"Please, you guys, stop fighting," Ellie begged.

"Then call off your babysitter," Wyatt said.

"She's not my babysitter, she's my—"

"Oh hell, I know, I know. She's your damned nanny. You don't need a nanny. You just need to grow up."

Ellie stood, her heart hammering, her voice shaking with shock. "Wyatt Wayne. You cursed at me." She laid down her fork and left.

Wyatt was almost in tears. "See what you made me do. You don't belong here. Before you came Ellie turned to me for help. Now she doesn't need me anymore. It's all your fault that we fight."

Sophie sat, her chin quivering. "Oh dear. I had no idea."

Wyatt stabbed a fork into his waffles and took a big bite with syrup dripping, daring her to criticize him again. The food felt like sawdust in his mouth. He chewed angrily, swallowing the food in chunks.

But Sophie saw past the behavior to the pain beneath. "I never meant to come between you and Ellie. I understand how close twins can be. That's not what I want for her. She's a wonderful young girl on the verge of becoming a woman, and I just want to help her be the best she can be."

Wyatt chewed without looking at her. "I help her," he said.

"But you're a boy. You haven't the experience or knowledge to help her through this time in her life. I realize you've both lost your dear mother, but you still have your father to guide you. Ellie has no one."

Wyatt stifled a snort. For obvious reasons, he didn't want his father's guidance in anything, but he could hardly tell her that.

"I would like to make a suggestion," Sophie said. "Are you open to that?"

Wyatt shrugged then glanced up. "Maybe."

Sophie beamed.

Wyatt blinked, somewhat surprised to see that Ellie had been right. Sophie did sort of look like Mrs. Santa Claus.

"I think we can work together on this," Sophie said. "I'll help Ellie with all the girl stuff, and you continue to be her best friend and protector, which is something I could never be."

Wyatt thought about it. Ellie needed him for sure. But he had to admit he knew nothing about fingernail polish or using different forks for different foods, which he considered really stupid, but that was just him.

"So what do you think?" Sophie asked.

"I guess," Wyatt said.

"Marvelous. I'm going to eat breakfast now. Why don't you go find Ellie and you two make up. I'll do dishes."

Wyatt stuffed the last of his waffles into his mouth, washed them down with milk and then carried his plate to the sink.

Sophie was making herself some coffee when he left. He guessed where Ellie had gone and headed out the back door for the creek.

Ellie stumbled toward the creek with tears in her eyes. Not once in her entire life had Wyatt been cross with her. Not like this. All she knew was that he'd broken her heart.

She reached the creek bank then sat down on her favorite perch—a wide flat rock jutting out from the bank of soft green grass, and began to pick up little rocks and lay them in her lap. Some of the rocks were covered in a cushion of dark green moss. She thought about pulling off her shoes and wading in, but it was too cold.

After a few minutes, she stopped fiddling with the rocks and closed her eyes, trying to find peace. This place was usually their sanctuary, but there wasn't any peace to be had today. All she could feel was the knot in her belly.

She leaned back, opening her eyes and gazing up through the canopy. The leaves were beginning to turn, which meant winter wouldn't be far behind. She hated winter—short days with too many hours of darkness. The night was hard enough to get through as it was. Having it last longer only made her life more difficult.

She stood up and began tossing pebbles from her lap into the creek. They landed with tiny plops, startling a squirrel in one of the trees above. The scolding he gave her made her mood worse. Even the squirrels were mad at her today.

Too full of despair to really cry, she crawled over to the grassy bank, lay down on her belly and hid her face in her arms.

Unaware of passing time, she was startled when she heard Wyatt's voice near her ear. "I'm sorry."

Ellie didn't answer.

"Are you crying?"

"No."

"Oh. I thought you were sad or something."

"I am sad, Wyatt, awful sad. But it's the kind of misery when you're too sad to cry."

Guilt stabbed at his core. "Aw, Ellie, you know I didn't mean what I said. I was just jealous."

Ellie rolled over, then sat up, surprised by the admission. "Jealous of what?"

He shrugged. "Of the time you've been spending with her, I guess."

Ellie sighed. "I'm sorry, too. It's hard being this age, isn't it?"

"Yeah, but you don't need to worry about me fighting with Sophie anymore. We made a deal."

"What kind of a deal?"

"We're both going to take care of you, okay?"

Ellie smiled. "Yes, that's very okay."

Wyatt threw a rock into the water.

"You're going to get in trouble for that," Ellie said.

Wyatt frowned. "Why would Sophie care about that?"

Ellie laughed, as she pointed overhead to the squirrel that was having a little fit.

"Not Sophie . . . the squirrel."

Laughter rang out along the creek bank, and for a short period of time, Ellie's world was back on its axis.

It snowed the first day of Christmas break. Ellie was wild with excitement and flew out of bed, yelling at Wyatt to tell him the news, then she dressed in the warmest clothes she could find.

Garrett was sitting at the breakfast table when Ellie came running through. "Hey, hey, wait a minute," he called, as Ellie passed him on her way to the door.

"We don't want breakfast," she said. "Wyatt and I are going to play in the snow."

Garrett could remember his own youth and how exciting the first snow of the year could be.

"Yeah, okay, but you have to promise me something. You stay in the backyard. No going to the creek."

"Okay, Daddy, we promise!"

The door slammed shut. Garrett laid down the paper and walked to the window to look out.

Ellie was running in circles and throwing snowballs right and left at Wyatt, then squealing in wild abandon as they flew through the air.

He smiled to himself. He was going to have her to himself for the next two weeks—except of course for Wyatt and Sophie, but he already had a plan to take care of that.

Garrett waited until after dinner. Doris had already gone home. Sophie bid them good night when the meal was over, announcing that she was retiring to her room. Wyatt had followed that announcement up with one of his own, saying he was going to watch TV.

Ellie was finishing up the last of her cherry pie and seemed oblivious that she and Daddy were in the kitchen alone. She looked up. The expression on his face made her heartbeat stutter.

Oh no.

She glanced around for Wyatt and Sophie. They were gone. She hadn't noticed them leaving. Why had Wyatt left her alone with Daddy? He knew what Daddy was like. She jumped up, carried her plate to the sink and stuck it in the dishwasher. Doris had already put soap in the compartment. All Ellie had to do was turn it on.

"I'm going to watch TV with Wyatt," she said, and darted for the door.

Daddy grabbed her by the wrist before she could get past. "No. No, you're not."

Shock swept through her so fast she felt that familiar urge to pee. "I have to go to the bathroom."

He frowned. "You're too big to do that now."

"Let me go, Daddy. Please."

"Not yet. We need to get something straight between us."

There was a smear of red cherry juice on the floor near her shoe. Ellie focused on it to keep from looking at his face.

"I've given you all kinds of time to get over your Momma's passing. I've let you bring people into our lives that don't belong and paid Doris more money to keep her from quitting. I know you don't want Doris to quit."

The thought of Doris being absent from their lives was too shocking to consider. "I'll tell Sophie we don't need to practice setting the table anymore," Ellie whispered.

"That's good, but that's not all. You know I love you more than anyone, don't you?"

The cherry pie was coming up. It was in the back of her throat, burning like the tears she continued to swallow.

"I miss you, Ellie."

"No, Daddy. We can't play games anymore. I got my period. Remember?"

"There are ways of making sure nothing happens to you. You have to trust me. I would never do anything to hurt you, right?"

Ellie tried to pull away, but his hold was too tight. "Let me go. Sophie will hear. You don't want her to hear, remember? She will tell and then you'll be in big trouble."

This was the opening Garrett had been waiting for. "She's not going to hear, and neither is Wyatt, because you're not going to say or do anything to alert them."

"Yes I will, I promise I will. I'll scream. I'll scream so loud even the neighbors will hear."

"No, you won't, and I'm going to show you why. There's

something in my room that you need to see." He began dragging her through the house toward his bedroom.

"If you play the game, I'll scream."

"We'll see," he said, and locked the door behind them as he entered his room. He pointed to the cedar chest at the foot of his bed. "Sit there."

Then he grabbed the remote and aimed it at the VCR on the TV. "If you tell, and if Sophie calls the police, this is what they'll find when they come to take me away. The police will see. All the people at my trial will see. All the newspapers will put pictures in the paper and all the world will see. You watch this, and then what happens between us afterward is up to you."

Ellie couldn't breathe. She felt like she was going to faint. Daddy sat down on the end of the cedar chest beside her, but he didn't touch her. She could smell his aftershave, and the coffee he'd been drinking. When she heard the hitch in his breathing, she followed his gaze to the pictures dancing across the screen, and then froze. She never knew Daddy had been filming the game.

Ellie shuddered. "I am so little."

He was smiling. "You were three . . . such a beauty, even then. Look at that precious curve of your tiny cheek."

Ellie couldn't see her cheek for what Daddy was doing, guiding her little hand, putting candy in her mouth, urging her to keep playing.

She watched for almost an hour as she and Wyatt progressed in age and skill. The game got longer and more erotic. Sometimes it was her with Daddy. Sometimes it was Wyatt. Some of it she remembered. Most of it she did not. Then suddenly it was over and the room was dark. She heard a click.

Daddy had turned off the TV.

She could hear the rough, jerky sound of his breathing as he turned on a light. "So, what's it going to be?"

Her mind was in chaos.

Everyone would see. What do I do? Everyone would see. I have to protect Wyatt, like he's been protecting me.

She stared at her father's face, trying to figure out how it was possible to live with someone you hate so much and knowing God wasn't going to save her after all.

At that moment another piece of Ellie died. "I won't tell."

Garrett beamed. "That's my girl, now come to Daddy."

Chapter Ten

Memphis—April, 2005

Ellie reached for a towel as she got out of the shower and began to dry off. She had less than forty-five minutes to get to work at Franklin's Ice Cream Parlor—a place she'd been working after school and on weekends for almost two years now.

She didn't need the money. Momma's trust fund had turned out to be a good one. Truth was, Ellie wouldn't ever have to work a day of her life if she didn't want to, but that wasn't how Ellie wanted life to go. Work was her only opportunity to live like other kids her age, and she'd do almost anything not to lose her toehold in that world. She had access to computers at school, but they were blocked to any kind of social activity, and Daddy refused to allow one in the house. Everyone she knew was on Facebook, but all the social networks were off limits for her. She knew why. He wouldn't be able to control it or her. But it was maddening to be so isolated. The job was her lifeline to normalcy.

The full-length mirror on the back of the bathroom door was an aggravation. She knew what she looked like. She was seventeen, almost eighteen, with a pretty face that was going to get her nowhere. She'd grown taller than anyone would have predicted, topping out at five feet, seven inches tall. She was slim to the point of being skinny, except for her size 34D breasts. She wasn't proud of who she was, so why waste the time looking?

She kept her eyes averted as she continued to dry, then turned to the mirror, brushed her shoulder-length hair and put it up in a ponytail, applied minimal mascara and a little lipstick and called it done. Walking nude out into her bedroom, she began putting on the clothes she'd laid out earlier on the bed.

She would graduate high school soon and had stated she was going away to college, but Daddy wouldn't have it. There was a junior college within driving distance, and that's all he would allow. But she kept telling herself once she turned eighteen and was legally an adult, she was gone. She had it all planned out. One day when he left for work, she and Wyatt were going to get in the car and start driving and never look back. Daddy would never know where they went. She'd been making plans for a year, looking for a place where they could start over—a place where they could disappear.

She hated her father now with a passion more fierce than her need to breathe, but they were caught in a repetitive loop that went nowhere but to Daddy's bed. He had tutored her well. She knew how to make him happy, but the downside of that was that he knew how to make her body betray her, as well. She hated him for that most of all.

She put on her uniform, then stepped into a pair of slip-on tennis shoes and headed for the door. Once she would have called out to Wyatt that it was time to go, but there was a distance between them now that she couldn't bridge.

Wyatt had been gone since daylight. She had no idea where he went these days. He was absent from her life more than ever, and it was all her fault. When she'd let Daddy get to her again, Wyatt had been angry because she'd given in without a fight.

She had never told him about the movies Daddy had shown her that night and she couldn't tell him now. She knew Wyatt. He was already an angry young man. Learning that Daddy was harboring such an ugly secret and holding it over Ellie's head would have sent Wyatt over the brink. He would have killed their father without a second thought and spent the rest of his life either in prison or on the run. Ellie couldn't do that to him—wouldn't do that to him. It was ironic that in trying to protect Wyatt, she'd also driven him away.

Sophie was still in her life, but more family member than nanny now. She'd become very hard of hearing and was completely unaware of the undercurrents in the house. Even Daddy had come to accept the old woman as a fixture. Doris still cooked and cleaned for them, and she still had weekends off.

Ellie continued to attend church, but she didn't pray anymore. There were times when she doubted there even was a God. Either way, she knew for a fact He wasn't one bit interested in the hell into which she'd been born. Not much had changed in Ellie's world since her Momma's death, and wouldn't until she graduated.

Another glance at the clock and she began to hurry. She grabbed her purse and car keys and was out the door.

Since it was Saturday, Ellie was working the day shift with Randy

Parsons, the manager, and a girl named Tessa. Randy was an okay guy. He was short and pudgy, as Sophie would say, with a big bald spot at the crown of his head. He had a wife and three little boys who came in at least two or three times a week for treats. Ellie liked the kids. She thought the wife was mean. She was always belittling Randy in front of people. Ellie had experienced the same thing and felt sorry for him.

Tessa was nearly six feet tall and into Goth. She had black hair, black fingernail polish, and kohl-rimmed eyes with fake black lashes. Ellie was all for people doing their thing, but she privately thought the black lipstick was overkill and didn't like to work the same shift as Tessa because she was lazy.

Today Randy was taking orders and money while Ellie was in back, filling them from a computer screen. As she was filling up the strawberry syrup, a new order popped up. Two chocolate malts and a hot fudge sundae.

Ellie began scooping ice cream, adding malt and milk to the cans, then putting them under the mixers before moving on to the sundae.

Tessa was supposed to be cleaning tables and keeping all of the condiment bins full, but it wasn't happening fast enough. Ellie had already asked for a container of maraschino cherries and she had yet to get it.

"Tessa, I still need those cherries," Ellie whispered.

Tessa did a blink that might have stood for "oh yeah" and headed for the storage in back.

Ellie had been working here so long that she could make the orders without thinking. Her hands knew what was supposed to be happening, leaving her free to think. Sometimes thinking was good. Sometimes not so much. Today she was worrying about Wyatt, and just like that he walked in.

"Hey," he said.

Ellie turned. "Hey yourself," she whispered. "Where have you been?"

Wyatt shrugged. "Around." He could see they were busy, but he missed her. He eyed her curiously. He thought she was pretty and wished she had a real life like most of the kids their age, but doubted it was going to happen. He didn't know this Ellie as well as he'd known her younger self and hated that they'd grown apart as they'd grown older.

Tessa handed Ellie the container of cherries and gave her a strange look before going to bus tables out front.

Ellie set the two chocolate malts on the pickup counter and finished up the hot fudge sundae while Wyatt watched.

"You're pretty good at this, aren't you?"

"I guess. Are you going to be home tonight?"

"Maybe, why?"

"I thought we might go to the movies or something."

Wyatt frowned. "You know Dad isn't going to let you."

"I'll do it anyway," she said.

"No you won't and we both know it," Wyatt said and started walking away.

"Wait. Where are you going?"

"What do you care?" he said, and then he was gone.

Ellie wanted to call him back, but orders kept popping up and she kept scooping and dipping and pretending her heart wasn't breaking. The pain in her chest was so real that she wondered if she was having a heart attack. A part of her almost wished it were true. She might not mind dying so much. It would solve her problems. Even if she didn't go to heaven, she already knew her way around hell.

When Randy went on break, Ellie moved to taking orders and Tessa stepped in to fill them. She recognized a couple of the girls from her class and a few of the boys standing in line. One of the girls caught her eye and started to smile, then caught herself and looked away.

Ellie frowned. She wondered what they thought about her that made them behave that way. She knew they'd freaked out when Momma had committed suicide. The whole class had acted as if Ellie had been the cause. She knew why she was different, but she hadn't always believed that it showed. Obviously she'd been wrong.

Later, a group of boys from the football team came into the shop. As she began taking their orders, she caught one of them staring. When he saw he'd been caught, he blew her a kiss.

This time it was Ellie who looked away.

They laughed, but she just ignored it and told herself it didn't matter.

When quitting time finally came, she was more than ready to get away. She hung up her apron, grabbed her purse and her keys, and headed home.

She hadn't gone far when she felt the car pulling to the right. She stopped at an empty parking lot and got out, then kicked the tire in frustration. It was almost flat.

"Great. Just great," she muttered, as she got her cell phone out of her purse. Daddy to the rescue, which was just the way he liked it.

Garrett was watching the clock and pacing the floor while waiting for Ellie to come home. She'd insisted on taking a job, which he'd reluctantly agreed to, but only if she kept up her grades. With a 4.0 GPA, she'd given him no room to gripe.

Now she was talking about colleges and leaving home and he was in a state of constant panic. He couldn't think of one single way to keep her under this roof that wouldn't get him arrested.

When the phone rang, he ran to answer.

"Daddy, it's me. I have a flat. I'm at the parking lot in front of the old strip mall they're going to demolish—the one on Randall Avenue."

Garrett frowned. That wasn't the best neighborhood and it was getting close to dark.

"Get in the car and lock all the doors. I'll be there as soon as I can."

"Okay," she said, and climbed back inside and hit the locks.

It was nearing dusk and their house was on the other side of town. It would take him at least ten minutes to get here, maybe more depending on traffic. She hunkered down in the seat and told herself everything was alright. Daddy would change the flat and then they'd go home. No big deal. She just wished Wyatt had stayed with her. She wouldn't be scared if Wyatt was here.

When a shiny black car with tinted windows drove past, she hunkered down even further in the hopes no one could see her. Within a couple of minutes, the same car came past her again, only slower. Her stomach knotted.

"Keep going, keep going," Ellie muttered, then nervously watched in the rearview mirror to see if it made a third trip around.

When it appeared in her rearview mirror, she started to panic and this time when it rolled past, it didn't go far before the brake lights came on.

Her fingers tightened around the steering wheel. She thought about just starting the car up and driving away on the flat tire. But then both front doors opened and two young Latinos emerged. At that point Ellie got desperate.

"Okay God, You and I haven't had a conversation in about five years and we both know why, but I'm giving you one last chance to come through for me. Please don't let these people hurt me. Amen."

She watched them get out with their baggy blue jeans and long plaid shirts hanging nearly to their knees. They had matching bandanas tied around their heads and walked with a slight swagger as they stopped at her window. They didn't look much older than Ellie. One of them knocked on the window.

"Hey, pretty lady, are you having car trouble?"

Ellie could almost hear Wyatt telling her . . . *don't let them know you're afraid.* She made herself smile.

"I have a flat. My Daddy's on the way to help me change it," Ellie yelled, pointing to the right front tire.

They circled the car, pointed at her tire, then one of them tapped on the passenger-side window.

"Pop the trunk and we'll change it for you," he said.

Two things went through her mind. If she popped the trunk, they could steal the tools and spare tire. If she didn't pop the trunk, they might try going after her instead. She reached for the button.

The trunk popped up behind her and the two guys disappeared. She heard thumping and bumping. The car shook a couple of times, and then to her amazement they reappeared. One was carrying the spare, the other the jack and lug wrench.

"You don't have to get out. Just don't move around," he said.

Ellie nodded.

Within moments, she heard the hubcap pop. It fell onto the concrete with a clang. When the shorter one suddenly went out of view, she realized he'd squatted down beside the wheel and was loosening the lug nuts. She heard them dropping the nuts into the hubcap and closed her eyes in disbelief. This was exactly what Daddy would do. Oh my God, they were actually changing her flat.

When they began to jack up the front end of the car, it was instinct that made her grab the steering wheel to keep from sliding against the door. She was trying very hard to sit still—to not rock the car in any manner.

There was a loud thump as they dropped the flat tire to the side, and then the spare went on. In no time, the car was being lowered. One of them stayed behind to tighten the lug nuts and replace the hubcap, while the other one loaded up the flat. As soon as the last bolt was tightened, he put the lug wrench back in the trunk, then slammed it shut.

They walked past her, giving her a thumbs-up and a wink, and then got in their car and drove away.

Ellie was still shaking when she got her cell phone out of the purse. She counted the rings until Daddy answered.

"Hello? Ellie, I'm sorry. I'm at a red light. I should be there in about five minutes."

"It's okay. Some people stopped and helped me change the flat. I'm starting the car and heading home right this minute."

Garrett breathed a sigh of relief. "I'll pull in at the pharmacy parking lot until I see you drive past and then follow you home."

"Okay, and thanks. Sorry I had to get you out."

Garrett sighed. "That's what daddies are for."

When she hung up, it was with a heart was so full of joy she wanted to sing. But it wasn't because of Daddy, or even the two boys who'd stopped to change her flat. For the first time in her life God had answered a prayer.

By now, it was almost dark. She turned on the headlights before she pulled out of the parking lot.

"Thank you, God. Thank you very much. And if you see Momma anytime soon, tell her I'm doing the best that I can."

She drove home with a light heart, telling herself that things just might be turning around. She knew when Daddy pulled in behind her and followed her home, and for one of the few times in her life, didn't mind.

They pulled into the driveway, one behind the other and got out nearly at the same time. Ellie knew he was going to hug her. She stood her ground and let it happen, even though she would have preferred it not be the case.

"Sweetheart. I'm glad you're okay. Come inside. You must be chilled."

Ellie nodded as they entered the house. "They put the flat tire in the trunk," Ellie said.

"I'll drop it off at the garage on Monday on my way to work. I made tuna sandwiches. Are you hungry?"

"Yes, but I want to change out of this uniform first. I'll be right back."

She could hear him rattling dishes and glasses as she headed for her room. Even though she knew he was in the kitchen, she still locked her bedroom door before she stripped.

She would have liked to shower before putting on other clothes, but didn't want to take up too much time and have him come looking for her. She put on a pair of sweats and a long-sleeved T-shirt, slid her feet into some house shoes, then stopped by Sophie's door and knocked before poking her head inside. Sophie had the television turned up to what Wyatt called blastoff.

Ellie ran over to the rocker. "I'm back from work. Daddy has sandwiches in the kitchen. Come eat with us."

Sophie hit the mute button on the remote. "What did you say?"

"I said come eat."

Sophie nodded. "Be right there."

Ellie was almost skipping as she headed for the kitchen.

"Just in time," Daddy said. "Do you want soda pop or iced tea?"

"Tea, please and make another one for Sophie. She's on her way."

A shadow passed over his face, but he didn't comment. Instead, he filled a third glass with ice and tea, added another plate and then set the sandwiches on the table.

Sophie took a seat at the table with Ellie.

Garrett sat across the table.

Ellie looked up. He hadn't set a place for himself.

"Aren't you eating?"

"I already ate a sandwich when I was making them. Help yourself."

Ellie served sandwiches to Sophie and herself, then dug a handful of potato chips from the bag and divided them on their plates.

"So who were the people who stopped to help you?" Garrett asked.

Ellie shook her head as she reached for a napkin. "I don't know. I did like you said and got in the car and locked myself in. They stopped, asked me if I needed help. I popped the trunk. They did the rest."

He frowned. "You say you didn't know them."

"Right." Ellie popped a chip into her mouth and washed it down with a drink of iced tea.

"What's right?" Sophie asked.

Ellie laughed. "I was talking to Daddy."

"Oh," Sophie said then promptly dropped part of the sandwich in her lap. "Oh no."

"I'll get it," Ellie said, and jumped up to get a paper towel.

"Were they old or young?" Garrett asked.

Distracted by Sophie's mishap, Ellie had lost track of the conversation. "Um . . . I'm sorry, Daddy, what were you saying?"

Daddy's jaw visibly clenched. "It doesn't behoove you to play stupid, Ellie."

Ellie's heartbeat skittered before it caught back up in rhythm. What had she done wrong?

"I'm sorry, Daddy. I was talking to Sophie and—"

He slapped the table. "You were talking to me."

Ellie felt the tuna coming up. "Yes. Sorry."

Sophie got up, making no attempt to hide her disapproval of his behavior. "It appears I am in the way, so I'll be leaving. Sorry, Ellie. I had no idea."

The joy in Ellie's heart vanished—just like that. She laid her sandwich back on the plate and then sat with her eyes on her glass, watching a cold drop of condensation make a run for the tablecloth.

"The people who changed your tire, were they old or young?"

The condensation hit the cloth, then slowly soaked into the fabric, leaving a small tear-shaped stain.

Ellie's voice trembled, and no matter how many deep breaths she took, she couldn't make it stop. "They were two Latino guys who looked like they might be my age. I was a little nervous at first because I thought they were wearing gang colors, but they didn't say or do anything that made me think they meant to hurt me. They just changed the tire and left."

She watched her father's face flush. This didn't feel right.

"You're asking me to believe you didn't know them, and that they just stopped? Bullshit! Boys like that don't do anything for free. They didn't ask for money?"

"No, Daddy. I told you, they just changed the tire and left."

"They didn't want anything from you?"

The storm was coming closer. She could feel the heat from his anger and no matter what she said, she couldn't make it stop. It made her angry as well. Was there never going to be a day of peace in her miserable life?

"Like what? What are you getting at?"

"I know what boys like that want from a girl like you."

Ellie started to shake. "Boys like that? A girl like me? What the hell are you trying to say?"

He stood up, towering over her where she sat. "I'm talking about lowlifes like them."

"And what do you call a girl like me? Your daughter or your whore?"

He slapped her.

Ellie fell backward. The chair hit the floor, taking her with it.

Their gazes locked in a moment of shocked silence and then Ellie rolled onto her knees and bolted, but he was right behind her, running in an all-out sprint.

Ellie heard the roar of Sophie's television and realized that even if she called for help, Sophie wouldn't hear a thing. She hit her bedroom door with the flat of her hand and slid sideways before grabbing the doorknob. Her heart was pounding, her breath coming in short frantic gasps as she slammed the door shut. She shoved the slide bolt into place and ran backward until she reached the wall. The bones were melting in her legs. She was going to die. The door reverberated from the first kick.

Ellie screamed and started to move backward, only to realize she was already against the wall.

"Wyatt!" she screamed. "Wyatt help me!"

The adjoining door didn't open. Wyatt wasn't here. No one was going to come to her rescue.

The door reverberated again and Ellie watched in horror as the frame split away from the wall, taking hinges and the rest of the door with it.

Ellie shuddered, and then everything began to happen in slow motion. Rage changed Daddy's face from a man to a demon with its mouth wide-open in a roar she couldn't hear—the floor was quaking beneath her feet from the impact of his stride—his hands turned into claws—reaching for her throat.

And then he grabbed her. "Did you fuck those boys? Did you? Did they crawl between your legs?"

She spit in his face.

Garrett hit her with his fist then seemed surprised when she went limp. It didn't stop his rage, he just threw her over his shoulder, jumped the broken door and carried her to his room and locked them in.

She was seemingly lifeless when he threw her onto his bed and began tearing at her clothes, ripping them in pieces until she was naked. He wanted to see for himself. He had to know if she'd been with them.

"Wake up," he shouted, and slapped her cheek again.

She didn't blink as her head lolled to one side.

"Wake up, damn it," Garrett yelled, and shook her by the shoulders.

She dropped back onto the mattress without making a sound.

"Have it your way," he muttered, and then ripped off his clothes and climbed onto the bed.

Chapter Eleven

Ellie woke up flat on her back in her bed. Every fiber of her body was a solid ache and she wondered if she was getting sick. She couldn't remember going to bed, or why she would be hurting, but when a yawn sent pain ricocheting through her head and out her eyes, she groaned and pressed her fingers against her lids until the pain eased.

It wasn't until she sat up and saw the gaping hole where her door had been that she remembered.

Oh my God, oh my God.

She slapped a hand over her mouth to keep from screaming, then frantically shoved back the covers. There was blood on her thighs. Horror seeped through her in shock waves.

"Wyatt! Wyatt!"

The fact he didn't answer shocked her. He hadn't even come home last night or he would have hit the ceiling when he'd seen the missing door. He'd always been the constant she could depend on, and now he had abandoned her, too.

Damn you, Wyatt Wayne.

She crawled out of bed, clutching her belly and moaning with every step as she dragged her battered body into the bathroom. The moment the door closed behind her, she turned the lock.

The distinct click was a virtual tap on the shoulder that she'd done this once before and it hadn't stopped him. If he wanted, he could kick that in, too.

Afraid to look at herself, Ellie staggered toward the vanity then braced herself against the counter. Her legs were shaking and she was struggling with the urge to vomit. The smell of him was in her nose and on her skin. She turned her back to the mirror and began stripping off her clothes, then got into the shower and turned the water on full force.

It was cold when it first hit her body, but she welcomed the bitter sting, and when it began to warm, she stepped beneath the spray and closed her eyes.

The force of the water hit the top of her head, spilling down her face to her breasts, onto the flat planes of her belly, then the valley between her thighs. She kept turning the tap, making the water run hotter and hotter until her skin was burning. She was desperate to wash away the shame. The longer she stood, the more resentment began to build. She was mad at God for ever letting her be born—at Momma for abandoning her to a fate truly worse than death—and at Wyatt for turning his back on her when she needed him most.

She had not directed anger toward Garrett, because you had to love someone before their betrayal hurt. She didn't know if she'd ever loved her Daddy, but she knew how she felt about him now and love had nothing to do with it.

When she began to hear hammering above the rush of water, her first thought was that he was back and coming through this door. But when she stepped out from beneath the spray to listen, she could tell the sounds were inside her room, but farther away.

Bam! Bam! Bam! Bam!

What was he doing? Oh my God, couldn't Sophie hear anything anymore? Ellie slid to the bottom of the tub, her heart hammering against her chest as she hid her face against her knees.

The water kept running.

The hammering didn't stop.

She stayed in the tub until the water ran cold. When she finally turned it off the silence was startling. Even the hammering had stopped.

Her body was so sore it was a struggle to get up. As she was reaching for a towel, she accidentally caught a glimpse of herself.

Shock swept through her in waves.

There was a spreading purple bruise on her jaw and another one on her neck. One eye was nearly swollen shut and there were bite marks on her breasts and scratches on her thighs. She didn't remember what had happened, but she knew—she knew.

Shock shifted swiftly to rage. Why hadn't he gone ahead and killed her? She would have preferred it.

When she realized she was standing on her pajamas and had gotten them wet, she kicked them in a corner. No way would she put those back on. His scent was on them, too.

She needed clean clothes, but they were all beyond this door. Did she dare look? What if he was sitting on the side of her bed, waiting for her to come out?

Suddenly, it occurred to her that there was nothing left that he could do to her that he hadn't already done. The recognition of that horror turned her fear to rage . She had no one left to depend on but herself. To hell with hiding. To hell with being afraid. The only thing left was to kill her, and she wasn't afraid to die.

She started to wrap a towel around herself then decided it was too much like closing the barn door after the horse was out. In a gesture of defiance, she dropped it on the floor and walked out completely nude, only to find herself alone. There was a new door on her room and with a new lock like the one she'd had before. She slid the bolt into place then went to get dressed. It was Sunday and there was a strong and growing need within her to be washed in the blood.

An hour passed, and when she came out dressed and ready for church, she found a note taped to the outside of her door.

Went to get your flat fixed. Daddy

She stared. Was that how it was going to play out? Just like that they'd move on? No, I'm sorry—no, are you okay—just, I'm just off to do a chore? She ripped the note from her door, wadded it up and dropped it on the floor.

She glanced toward Sophie's room. There was no sound coming from inside. Either she was sleeping in, or she was gone for a walk. Sophie liked to take walks in the neighborhood when the weather was good. At this point, Ellie didn't much care. Having a nanny hadn't helped her last night.

Her footsteps echoed on the hardwood floor as she walked down the hall. She remembered Momma's heels making the same sound when she dressed up, but just thinking about Momma made Ellie pissed. Momma had been a coward, going off to live with Jesus and leaving Ellie alone with the Devil.

In the living room, she paused to check her appearance before leaving the house. It was going to raise questions and she was still uncertain what she would say.

The mirror had been Momma's favorite. It had been a wedding gift from Ellie's grandparents. They'd died when she was too young to remember them, but it was huge, spanning more than three feet across and four feet long, with a burnished gold frame decorated with bas-relief carvings of ribbons and angels.

When Ellie was little, she'd pretend she was Sleeping Beauty and stand before it, reciting the phrase from Beauty's story. *Mirror, mirror on the wall, who's the fairest one of all?* Once Daddy had heard her and scooped her up into his arms and said she was the fairest.

She wondered what he'd say now.

She looked at herself with a judgmental eye as Sophie had taught her. Her hair was hanging in soft waves, framing her face and hanging just below her shoulders. Her makeup was perfect, as were her nails. The springtime weather had been unusually warm, so she'd chosen a pink linen sundress with a matching jacket and wore white strappy sandals. The only thing wrong with the picture was the bruise on her throat, her swollen eye and purple chin.

Rationally, she knew it would have been smart to stay hidden until she healed and all the bruising had faded, but that wasn't possible. She had school tomorrow, and six weeks later, she would graduate. She wasn't going to miss the last six weeks of her education just because her father had lost his mind. She still had to cope with life and she couldn't do it by hiding.

Bracing herself for the morning ahead, she dug the car keys out of her purse and left the house.

Fifteen minutes later, Ellie sat in the church parking lot, trying to get up the nerve to get out of the car. She imagined Daddy was probably at the house by now and freaking out because she was gone. He would go through her room to see if she'd packed any clothes—to see if she was running away. She didn't care what he thought. He didn't know it, but in a way, what had happened to her last night had been freeing. Short of murder, he couldn't hurt her anymore.

She could see Preacher Ray standing in the doorway like always, shaking hands and greeting his parishioners. Beyond that opening was her redemption. She'd come here with a need for solace. All she had to do was get out and walk in.

Preacher Ray saw her coming up the walk. His first thought was that Ellie Wayne had come alone. He didn't think she'd ever done that before. The smile was still on his face from the child he had just greeted, but when he saw her condition, it froze. He extended his hand in greeting, just as he did to all who entered, when in reality he wanted to wrap his arms around her.

"Good morning," Ellie said, and shook his hand firmly.

"Ellie. Child. What happened?"

Ellie paused. There were all kinds of excuses she could have given, but it didn't seem right to lie to a man of God.

"I've been raped."

"No, no, dear Lord, no." His eyes filled with tears. "How can I help you?"

"I want you to pray for me."

He kept looking at her face, imagining what she had endured. "Consider it done."

"And not to mention what happened to me to anyone else."

"Of course."

He assumed she'd already dealt with hospitals and police. It never occurred to him that she'd faced it all alone.

"Where's your Daddy?"

"Getting a flat fixed."

The answer was as incongruous as his absence in the face of such a trauma.

Ellie could hear the sounds of approaching footsteps. Unwilling to involve herself in a more in-depth conversation, she headed straight for the pew where she and Daddy always sat—in the spot where the sun came through the Jesus window.

She scooted past a couple on the end of the pew, pretending not to hear their shocked gasps, ignoring the tentative touches and murmurs of concern as she slid into the patch of light.

The news of her condition spread through the congregation in hisses and whispers. Ellie heard them, but couldn't invest herself in shame when she'd come here to find peace.

Ellie's car was gone.

It was the first thought that went through Garrett's mind as he came up the driveway. The second was that she'd run away. He parked in a panic and ran into the house, then down the hall to her room. His note was wadded up on the floor and the door was standing ajar.

"No, no, no."

He headed for the closet to see what she'd taken. To his relief, her clothes were still there. He moved to the bed and tore off the covers. When he saw the blood spots staining the sheets, his stomach rolled. He'd done that. He'd done that to his precious love.

He went into the bathroom next, looking for clues, and saw that she'd taken a shower, but frowned when he saw the clothes and towel still on the floor. That wasn't like Ellie. She was always neat, especially after she'd brought Sophie into their world.

He picked everything up and put it all in the hamper, then went back through the house in long anxious strides, looking for anything that would tell him where she'd gone. It occurred to him that she might have had to work, then remembered it was Sunday. The ice cream shop didn't open until after church.

Church?

His stomach rolled. She wouldn't. She couldn't have.

Son of a holy bitch.

He was running when he got to the car, then tore off down the street to see for himself if she had indeed taken herself to church.

He could hear the swell of organ music as he pulled into the parking lot. Services were already in progress. He glanced at his watch. It was after eleven. Maybe he'd jumped the gun. Maybe she wasn't here after all. And then he saw her car parked in the shade of the great oaks lining the curb and felt like throwing up.

Her eye and lip had been a little swollen when he'd put her in bed around midnight, and there was the beginnings of a faint bruise on her face. Maybe she'd covered it with makeup. Surely she wouldn't show her face if it was bad.

He thought about going inside to join her, then realized he wasn't dressed properly—and there was that fear of the unknown. How would she have excused his absence?

Still, it was comforting to know she hadn't run away, that she was simply in the house of God like all good girls should be.

Relieved that his worst fears had not been true, Garrett decided to go home and make them a good dinner. He would apologize for not believing her and everything would be alright.

Convinced that he'd panicked for nothing, Garrett drove away from the church, unaware Ellie had taken the first step in unraveling their world.

The last notes of organ music still hung in the air as Preacher Ray walked up to the pulpit. Ellie watched him lay his Bible down, but instead of opening it up to a passage upon which he intended to preach, he gripped the sides of the pulpit then looked out into the congregation—straight into her eyes.

All the hair rose on Ellie's arms. For a moment, it felt as if he was pouring his love and energy into her. She held her breath. Then he looked away and the feeling was gone. A few moments later he began to preach.

Ellie closed her eyes, waiting for the hollow feeling in her belly to go away, but it didn't happen. She looked down into her lap. The colors that had been there only moments before were gone. The sun must have gone behind a cloud. She tried not to take it as an omen, but nothing was going the way she'd planned.

She'd come to church expecting to be healed in spirit, if not in body, but she was getting mixed signals. Even though she chose not to panic, she wasn't getting a good feeling about this. Now might be a good time to pray.

> *God, You know what Daddy did. I wish one of us was dead. Personally, I don't care which one of us You take. Amen.*

After that, she sat quietly, waiting for the sun to come back, but it never did. Even God had turned His face away.

When church was over, she had no option but to walk along the aisle with all the others as they made their way to the exit. She'd known these people all her life. It stood to reason they would be concerned. One after the other, the same question was asked.

"My goodness, Ellie Wayne, what on earth has happened to you? Are you alright?"

And one after the other, she ignored the first part of their question, and answered the last. "No, I'm not."

By the time she got to her car she was exhausted. The sky was dark and threatening rain and she didn't feel restored in any sense of the word. Just as she started the engine, the heavens opened. No little drops to signal what was coming—just a sudden downpour. Depression settled over her as she turned on her windshield wipers and started home.

The thought of going back into that house seemed impossible. She'd been shocked to her core by her Daddy's rage. There was no way for her to know how he was going to react when she got home, but it was something of a relief to realize she didn't care.

She remembered Momma telling Ellie when she'd become scared of a storm that rain was only angel's tears. She didn't put much faith in that being the case, but if it was so, then she would like to think the angels might be crying for her, because she was holding too much hate to do it for herself.

Garrett was in the kitchen putting the finishing touches on their meal when he thought he heard the front door open.

"Ellie, is that you?"

Ellie set the umbrella on the covered porch to drip dry and was closing the door behind her when Garrett entered the room.

"Dinner is nearly—"

She turned around.

The words died in the back of Garrett's throat. His mind went blank.

Ellie took off her muddy shoes at the doorway. "I can't chew, so unless it's soup, you've wasted your time."

"Oh shit. Oh, Ellie. I'm sorry. I don't—"

"Shut up, Daddy. Just shut up. The only thing you're sorry about is that what you did to me left marks. I'm going to my room to get out of these wet clothes."

Garrett swayed as if she'd just punched him in the face. "You went to church looking like that."

She managed to smile, even though it hurt. "Ahh . . . so you did go looking for me. Did you check my room first to see if I'd run away?"

The look on his face gave him away. "Did anyone ask you what . . . did they say any—"

"Preacher Ray asked me what happened."

Garrett started to shake. "What did you tell him?"

"That I'd been raped."

Garrett grunted. "No you didn't."

"Yes, Daddy, I did. You taught me not to lie. Too bad you didn't remember that last night. I told the truth then, just like I'm telling it now."

His mind raced. Should he make a run for it, or stay and face arrest?

Ellie could almost hear the wheels turning in his head, trying to figure out how to handle what she'd told him.

"I didn't tell him that you did it, but only because he didn't ask," Ellie said.

Garrett shuddered, then staggered toward a chair to keep from falling. "What did he say to you?"

"He asked how he could help. I told him to pray for me. I also asked him not to tell what happened."

Garrett's head felt like it was going to explode. He had underestimated his daughter in every way. "Oh my God . . . what did the others say? All our friends and neighbors? What must they have thought?"

Ellie threw a shoe. It missed his chin and hit his chest.

"What the hell?"

"You are one sorry son of a bitch. You're worried about what people are thinking, but you haven't once asked about me. You didn't ask me if my breasts hurt where you bit them. You didn't ask if my lily was still bleeding, or if I could see out of this eye. You are disgusting, and if you ever come near me again I will wait until you are asleep and then I will kill you. I will cut you up into so many little pieces that they'll have to bury you in a sack."

She threw her other shoe for punctuation and walked away.

Bile rose at the back of Garrett's throat. He stood up, but he didn't follow. She'd made her feelings plain. He retraced his steps into the kitchen and then turned off the stove and got his car keys and jacket. Walmart opened at noon on Sundays and he was going to need a lock for the inside of his door or he'd never be able to close his eyes again.

Chapter Twelve

Being an outcast at school had its advantages. Ellie didn't have any best friends running up to her on Monday morning asking her what had happened. She didn't have a boyfriend to have to explain herself to. She didn't even have the ear of the school counselor who saw her in the hall but kept on walking.

She got her books out of her locker and headed to first hour. And then she got a surprise.

Her homeroom teacher, Mrs. Smith, took one look at her and put her arm around Ellie's shoulder. "Ellie. What happened? Did you have a wreck over the weekend? Are you alright?"

"No, ma'am, I didn't have a wreck, but I'm not feeling so great."

It was obvious to the teacher that Ellie Wayne wasn't giving out any more information, which didn't surprise her. She'd known Ellie for years and knew nothing about her other than that her mother was dead and her father worked at Strobel Investments.

Ellie took her seat and opened her book without paying any attention to the page. She just needed to be doing something besides fielding stares.

The boy who sat behind her had never said a word to her all year and yet within seconds of sitting down, he tapped her on the shoulder. "Hey Ellie, uh . . . sorry you got hurt."

Ellie's heart skipped a beat. The sympathy was unexpected. She nodded without turning around.

The girl who sat at the desk across from her was one of the popular girls. Her daddy was vice president of a bank and her mother was president of the PTA. They had not exchanged so much as a glance—until today.

From the corner of her eye, Ellie saw the other girl lean toward her. "Ellie . . . are you okay?"

Once again, Ellie nodded, but kept staring at her book. The sympathy was getting to her. If she wasn't careful, she just might cry, and she'd made a decision years ago that she wasn't wasting tears unless it was for something that really mattered. She should be able to handle a little sympathy, even if it was unexpected.

All through the day, people she only knew by name kept coming up to her, or stopping her in the hall to speak. She'd expected ridicule, not this. It was ironic that she'd spent all these years in school without being noticed, and now everyone was being nice. It made her bitter. It shouldn't have taken being raped and beaten to have someone get the manners to just freakin' say hello.

When school was over, she raced home and then met Sophie in the hall.

Sophie grabbed her heart. "Ellie. Dear child. What on earth happened to you?"

Ellie sighed. "I fell in the shower last night. I'm going to be okay. I promise."

Sophie was in tears. "I'm so sorry. Bless your heart, I'm so sorry. Is there anything I can do? Do you need help getting your clothes off?"

Ellie could only imagine what Sophie would have to say about the bite marks on her breasts, so she quickly rejected the offer. "No, really. I can handle it," she said. "I don't have much time before I'm due at work, so I have to hurry. See you later."

She left Sophie in tears. She hated lying, but if she'd wanted the police in her business, she would have gone to them herself. She knew how it would work. She wasn't eighteen until next month. The court would take her out of her home and put her in foster care. She'd have to start a new school—the whole shebang. It was better just to let it go, because as soon as she graduated, she was gone.

After changing into her uniform, she headed to Franklin's Ice Cream Parlor. She worked until closing tonight, which was fine with her. The less time she spent at home, the better.

As soon as she got to work, she approached Randy, the manager. Like everyone else who'd seen her today, he was shocked.

"Hey kid, what the hell happened to you?"

"It's a long, ugly story that you don't want to hear, believe me."

"Are you sure you're up to working? I can call someone to fill in for you?"

"No, no. I'm fine. Just maybe keep me off the register for a while until the worst of this goes away. I don't see so great out of my swollen eye. I'd be more comfortable filling the orders, if it's alright with you."

"You got it, kid." He started to say more, then looked away, unwilling to get involved in her business.

Satisfied that she wouldn't have to face too many curious eyes, she put on an apron and got to work.

Tessa came to work an hour later and once again, Ellie had to go through the whole discussion.

"Dang girl, what happened to you?"

Ellie shrugged. "Nothing good."

Tess frowned. "My face looked like that once. My old man caught me smoking a joint and beat the crap out of me."

Ellie eyed Tessa curiously. On the outside, they couldn't have been more different, but it appeared they had more in common than she would have thought. "Really?"

Tessa nodded. "I told him if he ever did it again, I would shoot him dead."

Ellie shrugged. "It's a good thing I didn't have a gun, or I might have used it."

Tessa was quiet for a bit as she began filling syrup bottles and getting out new paper cups and bowls. When there was a lull in business she sidled up close to Ellie and whispered, "If you're interested, I know where you can get a gun. Cheap."

Ellie's heart skipped a beat. "Where?"

Tessa lowered her voice even more. "This guy I know."

"How much?"

"I don't know . . . maybe a hundred dollars."

Ellie had that and more. "I don't know how to shoot a gun."

"He'd show you."

It was worth considering. She needed backup, and everyone she'd thought she could depend on had let her down. A gun would definitely even the odds. "I might be interested."

"Do you work Friday night?" Tessa asked.

"I work from three thirty to six."

"He might be stopping by around six, if you want to hang around a little longer."

Ellie's heart raced. This was a scary thing she was doing, but her life was scary. What was the difference?

"I could do that," she said.

"I'll tell him."

Then Ellie added. "Tell him I don't want anything complicated, and it needs to be small enough that I can carry it home in my purse."

"Okay," Tessa said.

Now that the deal was done, they were both a little ill at ease.

"Oops, another order coming up. Better get busy," Ellie said.
"Right. Busy," Tessa echoed, and the evening passed.

Chapter Thirteen

Wyatt showed up for supper just after Ellie got home. She was in the bathroom when she heard him going into his room. There was a moment of panic, wondering how he would react when he saw her, but she was still hurt that he hadn't been here when she needed him. If things had gone a little differently, she'd be dead and there would be no way of finding him to let him know.

She hated that he'd removed himself from the house without giving her well-being a second thought. Besides that, she didn't need Wyatt fighting her battles after the war was over. She was going to get a gun and take care of it herself.

Wyatt was gone by the time Ellie came out of the bathroom, but when she walked into the kitchen, he was there.

He heard her footsteps and looked up to say hello, then forgot to breathe.

Ellie glared. She wouldn't let herself be swayed by the sudden tears in his eyes.

"Ellie. My God."

"She fell in the shower," Sophie said, as she walked around the table laying place settings of their everyday cutlery.

Ellie knew he didn't buy that but now was not the time to elaborate—and then Daddy walked in.

Wyatt felt Ellie's instant disgust, which answered his question. She hadn't fallen anywhere except into their father's clutches.

Wyatt grabbed Garrett by the arm. He knew Ellie didn't want Sophie alerted, but he couldn't just ignore it. "If you ever touch her again, I will kill you."

Garrett blinked. "You're about a day late and a dollar short. And by the way, Ellie's version was more original."

Wyatt didn't know what that meant and there was no way to ask without giving themselves away.

Sophie continued to set the table and Wyatt continued to glare. Garrett stood in the doorway, watching the people Ellie had drawn into her world and wishing there was a do-over button to life.

It wasn't until the meal was over and Ellie was back in her bedroom that Wyatt confronted her.

"Is this door new?" he asked, as he shut and locked it behind him.

"Yes."

"Why?"

"That would be because he kicked the other one in."

Wyatt shuddered. The matter-of-fact tone in her voice was the exact opposite to what she must have felt when it happened.

"I don't get it. You were still letting him . . . I mean you guys were still . . ." He sighed. "Why did he freak out?"

Ellie was so mad she was shaking. "Seriously? You're asking *me* that question? You know how it works."

"But he never . . . I mean, it wasn't . . ."

When he reached toward her, she stepped back. "If you were ever here anymore, you'd know that he's getting more and more paranoid about graduation. He's trying to keep me here when he knows I don't want to stay."

Wyatt touched the side of Ellie's face with the tip of his finger. "But why hurt you?"

She pushed him away. "I had a flat, Wyatt. I got raped and beaten because two guys stopped and changed it for me before he got there. He assumed I paid them with sex."

Wyatt felt sick. He'd let his personal feelings interfere with his duty to protect her, and Ellie had suffered the consequences. "I'm so sorry."

"So am I."

She turned her back on him and went into the bathroom, locking the door behind her. The distance between them was too great to bridge now. All her focus was on getting through the next six weeks of school, and then getting the hell out of Memphis.

Ellie was a bundle of nerves by the time Friday arrived. She went to work after school with a hundred dollars in cash, telling herself she was doing the right thing.

Tessa was already at work when Ellie arrived and instantly gave her a questioning look.

Ellie nodded.

Tessa gave her a thumbs-up.

Ellie felt stupid—like they were playing spies or something, only this wasn't a game and by buying this gun, she was committing a crime. It wasn't what she'd ever expected to do when she'd gone to work in an ice cream shop.

She worked with one eye on the clock and the other on the computer screen, making sundaes and malts and dipping cones in all flavors and sizes.

Tessa seemed energized by the drama and actually worked at a decent pace. They stayed busy until Ellie's quitting time. She was hanging up her apron in back when Tessa popped in the doorway and gave Ellie the word.

"He's out back in the alley—skinny white guy driving a red Dodge truck."

"You swear he's okay? That he won't try to hurt me?"

Tessa eyed Ellie's face then shook her head. "He's a business man, not a hood, and anyway, Honey, someone else has already done that, remember?"

Ellie was nervous as she slipped out the back door, her purse clutched against her breasts.

"Damn, bitch. Someone did a number on you."

Ellie blinked. If the kid standing in front of her was old enough to drive, then she was a virgin and she didn't like his attitude.

"Do I look like a dumb-ass?"

The kid frowned. "You look like shit, that's for sure."

"I already know that, but if you think I'm gonna stand here and let you call me a bitch and then give you money, you're dumber than you look."

The kid shifted nervously, moving back and forth on his feet like he was trying to dance. "Whatever . . . do you want it or not?"

"Do you want my money?"

He glared. "You got the dough?"

Ellie nodded. "She said you would show me how it worked."

He frowned. "I didn't sign up to give no lessons. Besides, it's a .38 Special. You don't need lessons. You just point and shoot."

"Show me."

He glanced around the alley, then opened the truck door, got a sack out of the console and dumped the contents onto the seat.

Ellie picked it up. It fit the palm of her hand. "Is it loaded?"

"No, but I'll load the cylinder for free. Holds five rounds."

"Five?"

"Yeah. Got a snappy recoil, but I'm guessing you're not gonna use it for long-distance shooting."

"A hundred dollars, right?"

"Yeah, and you're getting a bargain. They go for four or five hundred."

"I'm getting a stolen gun, not a bargain at Walmart."

When the kid grinned, he flashed a mouthful of bad teeth. "You're alright. Show me the money."

Ellie handed it over.

He stuffed it in the pocket of his pants and then loaded the gun and handed it to her. "Aim and shoot. Aim and shoot."

Ellie dropped the gun into her purse as he drove away. She walked out of the alley to the employee parking lot, got in her car and headed home.

All the way she kept telling herself to drive slowly. Don't do anything that would get her stopped. She didn't breathe easy until she got home, then chose the back door rather than the front, only to come face to face with her father.

Garrett was frying potatoes at the kitchen stove when Ellie walked in the back door. "Supper is nearly ready."

Ellie walked past him without comment. Once she got to the hall, she ran to her room and locked the door. She took the gun out of her purse, then stood in the middle of the room, trying to figure out where to hide it.

Daddy prowled her room all of the time. No matter where she hid it, he would eventually find it. She glanced at Wyatt's door. Maybe she'd hide it in his room. Daddy didn't mess in Wyatt's room. He didn't care what Wyatt did anymore.

She didn't think he was home, but she checked anyway. "Wyatt?"

No answer. She slipped inside his room and began going through closets and shelves, then the bathroom, then behind his bed, but everywhere she thought about, either Wyatt or Doris might run into it.

Then she remembered his bed had slats underneath the box springs for added support. She got down on her back, then shoved the gun between the slat and the springs that was nearest the headboard.

She didn't know Wyatt was watching, or that when she came out from under the bed, he made himself scarce. As soon as Ellie left, Wyatt got down on his belly to see what she'd been doing. It took him a couple of minutes to find the gun, and when he did, he was shocked.

Whatever Ellie had endured at their father's hands must have been worse than he thought, but at least he knew what was on her mind.

The gun gave Ellie an odd sense of power. She hadn't spoken to her father in days and he wasn't pushing the issue.

Wyatt began showing up every evening and spending the nights in his room like he used to. Ellie was still mad at him, but she didn't deny that she liked knowing he was within shouting distance.

It wasn't until Ellie came home from work with a friend that Garrett knew fate was taking him down a road he'd never wanted to go. Sophie was intrigued, and Wyatt was horrified. Not once in Ellie's seventeen years had she ever brought a friend home from school, and then she showed up with a girl named Cinnamon.

Doris was making dinner as Ellie came in the back door, dumped her book bag on the floor and headed for the refrigerator.

"Doris, this is Cinnamon Hardy. She's a friend of Tessa, the girl I work with at the shop. Cin, do you want something to drink?"

"Any kind of pop as long as it has caffeine," she said, then waved her index finger at Doris. "Hey."

Doris stared at Ellie for a moment, and then sighed. She'd been here too long to be shocked anymore. "Nice to meet you, Cinnamon."

The redhead laughed. "You can call me Cin . . . as in committing one, which I have most certainly done."

"Yes, well," Doris muttered, and went back to her cooking.

Ellie handed Cin a Pepsi. "Wanna see my room?"

"Yeah, sure, why not?" Cin said, popped the top on the can and then took a long swallow before following Ellie.

"Heaven help us," Doris muttered, and kept on stirring.

Ellie opened the door, then came to a stop. She hadn't expected to see Wyatt. "I didn't know you were home," she said.

"Obviously."

Ellie shrugged. "So, meet Cinnamon. She's my new friend. You can call her Cin. Cin, this is my twin, Wyatt."

Wyatt didn't bother to hide his distaste. He didn't like Cin's skanky smile or the way she stood, like she was purposefully drawing attention to her big boobs.

Wyatt nodded.

Cinnamon winked.

Wyatt rolled his eyes and disappeared.

Ellie giggled. "My brother can be a little antisocial, sorry."

Cinnamon smiled. "It doesn't matter. He's cute."

"I know, but he knows it too."

"Girl . . . don't they all?" Cinnamon drawled, and then plopped down on the side of Ellie's bed and downed the rest of her Pepsi. "So what's the scoop on all the bruises on your face? Got a boyfriend who likes it rough?"

"You could say that," Ellie muttered, and changed the subject. "Wanna stay for supper?"

"Yeah, sure. I don't have anything better to do."

It wasn't the most genuine comment she could have made, but at least she was honest.

Ellie led the way back to the kitchen and she and Cinnamon began helping Doris finish supper and set the table.

Wyatt hovered without getting involved, and when Sophie appeared and was introduced to Cinnamon, it was all he could do not to laugh. He could see the wheels turning in Sophie's head. Cinnamon would be a serious reconstruction project.

At that point, Garrett came home.

The silence that followed his entrance was telling.

Cinnamon gave Ellie an "introduce me" nudge. Ellie had no choice but to comply. "Daddy, this is Cinnamon Hardy, a new friend of mine, and she's staying for dinner."

Garrett was speechless.

Cinnamon was not. "Ellie, you don't look a thing like him. I guess you took after your Momma."

"Thank God," Ellie muttered.

"What's wrong, Dad . . . cat got your tongue?" Wyatt asked.

Garrett looked at Doris, who shrugged. "Supper is ready."

"I'll wash up."

Ellie moved her plate to the far end of the table. If she was going to have to eat with him, she wanted to be as far away as she could get.

The meal was strained, to say the least. It was the first time Garrett and Ellie had shared a meal since *that night*, and he didn't know whether to be happy or nervous. As it turned out, he didn't have to worry. Ellie kept up a running dialogue with everyone but him. He just listened as he ate without inserting himself into the conversation.

When the meal was over, Cinnamon glanced at her watch and got up. "Thanks for the chow, but I gotta run. See you tomorrow, Ellie?"

"Absolutely," Ellie said.

And just like that, she was gone.

Wyatt breathed a sigh of relief.

Garrett gave Ellie a strange look then made himself scarce.

As soon as she'd cleaned up the kitchen, Doris was the next to depart. “See you tomorrow,” she said and locked the door behind her as she left.

“So that just leaves us,” Wyatt said.

Ellie eyed him curiously. “What did you think of Cin?”

“You don’t want to know.”

Ellie glared. “I should have known you wouldn’t like her.”

“I can’t imagine why you do,” Wyatt snapped.

Ellie shrugged. “She knows the score and she doesn’t lie, and she likes me.”

Wyatt sighed. “I like you, too.”

Ellie bit her lip. She didn’t want to feel guilty, but this was Wyatt, the other half of her soul. “I like you, too,” she said.

“I know you do. Despite everything that’s gone on between us, I’ve never doubted that.”

Ellie’s vision blurred. “I’m going to my room to watch TV.”

“Want some company?” Wyatt asked.

She shrugged.

“I’m right behind you,” he said softly.

Ellie wasn’t going to get all giggly, but it felt right to be doing this again.

Ellie’s eye returned to normal size within a week, but it took two weeks for the last of the bruises to fade.

The following Sunday Garrett found something else to do when it was time for church. He’d lost faith in Ellie’s ability to stay quiet about personal business and wasn’t going to put himself in the position of being outed.

Ellie went alone, but the magic was gone. Even when she sat in the sunlight with a lap full of colors—even when the choir sang *Washed in the Blood*—even when she managed to find the words to pray—it wasn’t the same. She felt a growing sense of doom but didn’t know how to fight it. If she only had a clue as to what might be wrong, she could be making a plan.

As the date neared for Ellie and Wyatt’s eighteenth birthday, she wondered if her dread was connected to the event.

Daddy was sitting at the breakfast table when Ellie came in to eat. Startled by his presence, she was about to go back to her room when he stopped her.

"Wait, Ellie. Don't leave."

Ellie sighed. *Why was she always alone when no one else was around but Daddy?*

"What?"

"Weren't you coming to eat breakfast?"

"Yes."

"Then eat, damn it. I'm not going to hurt you." His voice shook. "I realize you have no reason to believe that, but I can promise it's safe to eat a bowl of cereal in my presence."

"But that's the problem, Daddy. I don't *want* to be in your presence. Why would I? You're asking me to sit down with my rapist. You're expecting me to pour milk on my cereal and have a nutritious little breakfast with the person who hurt me in unspeakable ways."

Garrett paled. He set down his coffee cup and walked out of the kitchen without looking back. She didn't move until she heard his car start.

"That was cold," Wyatt said.

Ellie turned. "Where did you come from? I thought you were gone."

"Not far." He moved to the pantry. "Rice Krispies or Raisin Bran?"

"Rice Krispies, please."

"You get the bowls and spoons. I'll get the rest."

Ellie smiled. It was good to have Wyatt back.

"Do you know where Sophie is? She wasn't in her room."

"The day is warm and sunny. I'd bet she's out on one of her famous walks."

Ellie laughed. "Remember how mad you were when she came to live with us?"

"Oh yeah."

"It turned out okay, didn't it?"

Wyatt smiled. "Yeah, Ellie. It turned out just fine."

Ellie glanced at the clock. "I have to be at work in an hour, but I'm off early today. Wanna hang out afterward?"

"Don't take this wrong, but not if Cin's going to be with you, okay? She gives me the creeps."

Ellie sighed. "She probably has a crush on you."

"Ellie, girls like Cinnamon don't have crushes. They devour the guys they want, and I'm not on the market or in the mood."

"For obvious reasons, I get that. Sorry she comes on so strong."

He shrugged. "I can handle her."

Wyatt poured milk on his cereal then passed the carton to Ellie. They carried their bowls to the table and sat down. After the comfortable silence of sharing food with a loved one, Ellie paused.

"What's going to happen to us, Wyatt?"

"What do you mean?"

Ellie couldn't stop the tremor in her voice. "We're broken . . . so broken."

"Yeah. I know."

Ellie pushed her cereal back and leaned forward. "Why do you think bad things happen to some people, when others live their whole lives without a single day of harm?"

"I don't know."

"Even when people pray for mercy, why do you think God lets bad things keep happening?"

"I don't think God lets it happen, Ellie. But I think He's there to help us through it when it does."

Ellie sighed. "I never knew you felt like that. You never went to church with Daddy and me when we were little. I didn't know you believed much in God."

Wyatt grinned. "Maybe I'll be a preacher someday."

"Then you'll have to stop cussing."

"Or maybe not," Wyatt said.

They both broke into laughter—a sound that wasn't heard much where they lived.

Later, Wyatt rode part of the way to work with Ellie before she dropped him off.

One day ran into another and then they turned eighteen. The magic number that was going to set them free.

Chapter Fourteen

Cin was lounging against the headboard of Ellie's bed, sucking on a lollipop as Ellie came into her bedroom carrying a load of towels she'd taken out of the dryer.

"Where's your hunky brother?"

Ellie fired back. "Where did you come from?"

"Sophie let me in. I repeat, where's Wyatt?"

"You make him nervous."

Ellis tossed the towels on the bed then started folding them.

Cin laughed. "He makes me nervous too, if you know what I mean."

Ellie frowned. "Can I ask you something?"

"Sure, whatever."

"Why are you so—"

"Blatant? It's what Sophie called me."

Ellie gasped. "Oh my gosh, I'm sorry. Sophie's getting up there in years, you know. She's hard of hearing and getting pretty blatant herself."

Cin's smile widened. "It's no big deal. Besides, you can't be mad at the truth."

Ellie folded another couple of towels, wondering why Cinnamon Hardy was wired the way she was. "Can I ask you something personal?" Ellie asked.

"Sure, why not?"

"Why are you so up front about what you think and feel? How do you get that way? Most people hide what they're thinking and feeling."

"And they're all fucked up, too, aren't they?"

"Oh. Okay. I get it." She grabbed another handful of washcloths and continued folding. "I wish I was like that. I guess it's why I like you. I'm envious."

Cinnamon threw a towel at Ellie's head, but it missed and landed on her shoulders. "Shit. Don't be envious of me. My life is messed up. Pretty much like yours, I'm guessing."

"What do you mean?" Ellie asked.

"So, we've been hanging out long enough now that I know you don't have any boyfriend, and Wyatt worships the ground you walk on, so I'm thinking Daddy dearest was responsible for the beating you got."

Ellie's shoulders slumped. "He's responsible for a lot of bad stuff."

Cin's eyes narrowed thoughtfully. That had been a very telling statement. She wondered if Ellie knew that sometimes it's not about what you say, but what you don't that tells the story.

"Then why are you still here?"

"I won't be much longer. Wyatt and I turn eighteen tomorrow. We graduate in a couple of weeks after that. That's all I'm waiting for—a diploma and being legally recognized as an adult."

"What do you want to do with your life?"

"I always thought I'd go to college and figure it out there," Ellie said. "What about you?"

Cin rolled her tongue around the sucker then yanked it out of her mouth with a soft popping sound. "I never much think about my future."

Ellie frowned. "Why not?"

"I just never imagined myself growing old."

Ellie shivered. "You mean you think you're going to die young?"

"Sooner or later, everyone dies."

Ellie didn't know how to respond to that, so she kept folding towels until she was through, then put them in the linen closet.

"So are you through playing Martha Stewart?" Cin asked.

Ellie grinned. "Yes, why?"

"Let's plan what you're going to do for your birthday. Eighteen is a big deal, right? Is your dad going to throw you a big party?"

"No."

Cin frowned. "Why not?"

"I don't associate with Daddy."

The stark expression on Ellie's face was startling.

"Sorry I stepped in the shit again. You'd think one day I'd learn to mind my own business."

"Don't worry about it."

"Then I won't." Cinnamon laughed, and did a little dance in the middle of the floor.

Ellie laughed, which she knew was Cinnamon's goal.

"Now that I've fucked up your day," she said. "I gotta run. Maybe I'll see you tomorrow, and in the meantime, don't do anything I wouldn't do."

"Yeah, see you," Ellie said.

The day ended without note. As soon as supper was over, Ellie snuck back to her room and wrapped Wyatt's birthday present, then hid it in her dresser.

Later, as she lay on her bed watching TV, she could hear Daddy's footsteps out in the hall. When he paused in front of her door, her gaze shot toward the lock. It was undone.

She flew out of bed and slammed the slide bolt into place, then leaned her forehead against the door, her heart hammering so hard that it hurt.

The silence outside was almost as frightening as if he'd been kicking it in. She knew he was there. She could hear him breathing.

Then to her surprise, he spoke. "Ellie."

She held her breath.

"I know you're listening, so I'm just going to say what I came to say. Tomorrow is your birthday. I know I've messed up, but I am so sorry. You are the light of my life. You have always been Daddy's girl. Please don't shut me out. Please forgive me."

Ellie went back to the bed, grabbed the remote, and turned up the volume.

Later that evening, she went to the kitchen to get a snack. She was getting cookies when Wyatt returned.

"Aha. Caught with your hand in the cookie jar," he said.

Ellie giggled. "Want one?"

"No, but I'll take two."

"Help yourself. My hands are full," Ellie said, and together they went back to their room.

Wyatt walked in last.

"Lock the door," Ellie said.

Wyatt slid the lock into place then turned around. "Why? Something happen while I was gone?"

"Daddy begged for forgiveness outside the door."

"What did you say to him?"

"Nothing. I just turned up the volume on the TV."

"Just be careful," Wyatt warned. "We know now that he can lose it big-time. Don't push your luck."

"Luck? I don't have luck, Wyatt, and neither do you. If we did, God wouldn't have put us in this place."

"I'm sorry. You know what I mean. Come on, Ellie, let's eat, drink, and be merry for tomorrow we will be officially old."

She smiled.

For Wyatt, it was enough.

"Good morning, Ellie. Happy birthday."

Ellie smiled as she rolled over onto her back to see Wyatt standing by her bed.

"Happy birthday, Wyatt."

"That never gets old, does it?" he asked.

"You mean being twins?"

"Yeah. It's pretty cool to be linked with another life."

"That's a weird way of putting it," Ellie said.

Wyatt laughed. "Are we gonna have cake tonight?"

"Doris is making strawberry cake with cream-cheese icing."

"Oh man, my favorite."

"And mine, which is why she's making it."

"Yeah, but I like it because of the strawberries. You like it because it's pink."

Ellie laughed. "True. Did you get me something?"

"Wait a minute and I'll get it."

As soon as he left, Ellie sprang out of bed and ran to the dresser to get his gift out of hiding.

He came back carrying a small box wrapped in pink paper with a bow bigger than the box, which made Ellie smile. "This is great."

"You haven't seen what's inside it yet. Open it."

Ellie pulled off the lid. "Oh, Wyatt."

He watched her pick up the stained-glass piece by the hook and chain.

"It's called a suncatcher. You hang it in the window and—"

". . . all the colors spill onto the floor," Ellie said, finishing his sentence. "Just like the Jesus window in church. Oh, Wyatt . . . how did you know?"

"Come on, Ellie. I'm your other half, remember?"

Ellie ran to the window, shoved the curtains aside and hung the suncatcher on the curtain rod. Within seconds, flashes of pink and green and violet and yellow were spilling onto the floor at her feet.

She poked a toe into the colors, then stepped all the way in and danced. It was just one little step, but for her, it might as well have been a waltz. "Oh, Wyatt, I love it. I love you. This is the best birthday ever."

"Thanks."

"Now you." She handed him a small oblong box covered in dozens of little gold stars.

"Gold stars?"

She laughed. "Remember how happy you always were when Mrs. Rutherford would give you a gold star for good behavior?"

"Yeah. Good call. Kindergarten was great."

"So open it," Ellie urged.

Wyatt tore through the paper then removed the lid. "Oh wow. Oh, Ellie . . . wow."

"Do you like it?"

Wyatt lifted the silver key chain from the tissue then held it up to the light. The angel hanging on the other end looked like she was flying. "She's beautiful, Ellie, just like you."

Ellie's eyes filled with tears, but again, she wouldn't let herself cry. Not about this. This was a time for joy.

"Let's get this birthday in gear. We'll get dressed and go eat breakfast, then spend the day together at the mall. We can eat junk at the food court or maybe go to a movie . . . whatever we want."

"What about that birthday cake?"

"That's for tonight. I'm not willing to spend any more of this day with Daddy than I have to. What better place to get lost than the mall?"

"Sounds like a deal."

Garrett came back from running Saturday errands to find the house empty. Doris had obviously come by with the birthday cake because it was in the refrigerator when he put up the milk and butter. She'd left two cards on the counter. He checked the names on the envelopes—one for Ellie and one for Wyatt. He frowned, then shook his head and walked away.

When he poked his head into Ellie's room, he saw the remnants of wrapping paper and bows, then the suncatcher hanging on her window. He didn't know the significance it held for her, but it made him sad he hadn't bought any gifts. It was fairly obvious after their last conversation that she'd throw anything he came up with in his face.

He walked across the hall to Fern's old room, then changed his mind about going inside and went to his room instead. All he wanted to do was go to bed and sleep until this nightmare was over.

He was so sick at heart that it hurt to breathe and the thought of food made his stomach turn. He kicked off his shoes, stretched out on the bedspread, then closed his eyes. He was drifting toward a semiconscious state when he thought he heard Ellie's voice.

". . . cut you up in so many pieces they'll have to bury you in a sack."

He flew out of bed and shoved the slide bolt in place, and then crawled back in bed, rolled over onto his side and cried himself to sleep.

It was just after 1:00 p.m. when Ellie and Wyatt stopped window-shopping and headed for the food court.

"What are you going to have?" Ellie asked, as she scanned the assortment of options. "Ooh, look, Red Wok. How about Chinese?"

"Not in the mood, but you can. I'm looking pretty hard at that pizza," Wyatt said.

"Umm, works for me. What kind—cheese or supreme?"

"Supreme. You want one or two slices?"

Ellie giggled. "Two. It's our birthday."

"I'll get the food. You find a place to sit."

Ellie nodded.

Wyatt headed for Pizza by the Slice and got in line. Within a few minutes, he was weaving his way through the crowd toward the table Ellie had chosen.

Ellie took a big bite of the hot pizza, then picked up a string of cheese from her plate and popped it in her mouth.

"So good," Ellie said as she looked up. "Hey! Look who's here!"

Wyatt rolled his eyes.

Ellie grinned. "Cinnamon! Are you eating?"

"Already did. I'm just hanging out."

Ellie glanced at Wyatt, who gave her a "whatever" look.

"So hang with us for a while," Ellie said.

"Sure brother won't mind?"

"If I did, I would have already told you to get lost," Wyatt said.

Cinnamon grinned. "Ha. A chink in the armor. I knew I could break him."

"Don't get too cocky," Ellie said. "He's just humoring me because it's our birthday."

"Like I already knew that," she said. "I would have gotten you guys gifts, but no dough. You know how it goes."

"We don't need presents, just friends," Ellie said.

Wyatt groaned. "Dang, Ellie. You need to go to work writing verses for Hallmark. That was seriously corny."

It made everyone laugh and was the needed icebreaker that carried through the rest of the afternoon. When they finally left the mall for home, Cin was with them.

Garrett saw the car pulling up into the driveway. He took the cake out of the refrigerator and quickly poked eighteen candles he'd already counted out into the icing and lit them as the door opened.

As they entered the kitchen, it was the first thing they saw.

"Cool," Cinnamon said. She snuck a quick peek at Garrett when he wasn't looking.

The man was obviously on edge. She'd seen happier men at a funeral.

"Doris brought your cake over this morning . . . the traditional strawberry," Garrett said.

"I love strawberries," Cin said. "Ellie? Wyatt? Come on guys. Somebody blow out the candles so we can eat."

Garrett watched without comment, wondering if Ellie would crumble. To his surprise, it was Wyatt who pulled her in.

"Come on, Ellie. We can't disappoint Doris. She made it on her day off, right?"

"She left cards for you, too," Garrett said. "They're on the table."

"For both of us?" Ellie asked.

Garrett nodded.

Ellie picked hers up. When she opened it, a ten-dollar bill fell out.

"Wow. Doris is cool," Ellie said.

"Seriously," Wyatt echoed as his produced the same.

Cinnamon sidled closer to the table. "Now the cake?"

Ellie sighed. "Now the cake. On the count of three, Wyatt."

"One. Two. Three." They blew until all the candles were out.

When Garrett began to cut the cake, the skin crawled on the back of Ellie's neck. She watched him absently licking a bit of icing from his thumb and shuddered. Just the thought of him touching anything she was going to eat was disgusting.

"Easy," Wyatt whispered.

"I'm fine," Ellie muttered, then picked up a piece of cake and a fork and sat down at the table to eat.

"Oh my God, this is so good," Cin gushed.

Sophie entered the room, frowning. "God is not responsible for that cake. Doris is."

Cinnamon choked on her bite. "Oh, yeah, my bad. Sorry about that."

"Cut a piece of cake for Sophie," Ellie said.

Garrett did as she asked, and knowing Sophie's proclivity for manners, added a napkin with the fork.

"Enjoy," he said.

"Hey! Aren't you having any?" Cin asked.

"Wasn't invited to the party," Garrett said.

Wyatt sighed. "Don't make a big deal out of this. Just get a piece of cake."

Garrett served himself some cake, started to sit down at the table, then caught the expression on Ellie's face and walked out of the room carrying the plate.

"What was that all about?" Sophie asked.

"Who wants something to drink with this?" Ellie asked.

"I'll take anything with fizz," Cinnamon said, and Sophie forgot her question had gone unanswered.

After a second piece of cake, Cin carried her plate to the sink.

"I'm outta here, guys. Thanks for letting me hang with you today."

"Don't you need a ride somewhere?" Ellie asked.

"I'm good. See you when I see you," she said, blew Wyatt a kiss and waved at Ellie.

Sophie frowned. "She's very forward, that girl."

"But she's my friend," Ellie said.

Sophie smiled. "Yes, dear, I know. I was simply making an observation. Times have certainly changed since I was a girl. My, my, I had no idea."

"I'll clean up," Ellie said, and began loading the dirty plates and glasses into the dishwasher.

Sophie set her plate on the counter. "I believe I'll retire for the evening."

"Good night," Wyatt said. "Thanks for helping us celebrate our birthday."

Sophie smiled. "It was my pleasure." She started toward the door, then stopped and turned around. "You know, Wyatt, there were times when I had my doubts about you, but you've turned into quite a nice young man."

Once she was gone, Wyatt and Ellie looked at each other, then burst into laughter.

"I'm going to jump in the shower," Wyatt said. "I'll see you in the morning."

"Want to go to church with me?" Ellie asked.

"Sorry, but I'm not *that* nice."

Ellie flicked water at him.

He was still laughing when he left her.

Garrett sat in the living room with the uneaten cake in his lap and listened to the chatter coming from the room behind him.

There was a part of him that wondered if this was his penance for what he'd done to Fern. He'd killed to keep his daughter, then ruined everything because of unjustified rage.

He wanted Ellie back, but was beginning to accept that it was never going to happen. Heartsick, he set the cake aside and went to his room.

He paused to lock the door, put one of his favorite tapes into the VCR, crawled up on the bed, and hit *Play*. When three-year-old Ellie Wayne danced onto the screen in fragile innocence, he took a deep shuddering breath. He watched as she walked toward him. On the screen, he took her tiny hand and put it on what was hanging between his legs. When she looked up, the trust on her face was there for the world to see.

Ellie didn't know when Garrett had left, but all that mattered was he was gone.

After a thorough sweep of the house, she paused in the hallway by the night light. As she did, she noticed they hadn't turned the calendar from April to May and stopped to flip the page. She scanned the month, counting down the days until she was officially a high-school graduate.

"Ten more school days and then I'm gone," Ellie muttered, and started to turn away, when a thought skidded sideways through her mind and struck her dumb.

She grabbed the calendar and flipped back to April.

April Fool's Day had been the last day of her previous period. Today was May eighth. She'd never been late one day in her life, and now she was ten days late?

The rape.

She moaned. "No. Please God, no."

"Ellie. I'm out of the shower." Wyatt's call, so ordinary in the face of new horror, seemed obscene.

"Yes . . . alright, I'm coming."

Wyatt was already in his room when she walked in, pausing long enough to lock the door. She got ready for bed on autopilot, turned out the light and crawled between the covers.

The room was quiet.

The night was dark with an absence of moon.

She stared up at the ceiling, unable to form a complete thought.

Chapter Fifteen

Ellie woke up feeling the same way she'd felt the morning after Momma committed suicide. When she'd died, so had Ellie's hope for rescue. She'd managed to survive by keeping her eye on the future and graduating high school—the one thing that would facilitate her escape.

Then this, with graduation in sight and escape on the horizon . . . She felt like God had slapped her down one more time just to see what would happen. In church, Preacher Ray talked about sacrifices and how during Lent you gave up something you really liked in the spirit of an offering to God. So she skipped breakfast as a sacrificial gesture and slipped off to church before Daddy knew she was gone.

The air felt heavy. Sophie would have called it sultry. Ellie felt like she couldn't breathe, but that might have been from the panic. When she got to the church, she parked in her usual spot and then sat, watching Preacher Ray shaking hands, just like he did every Sunday. Later, she knew he'd go inside, stand behind the pulpit and lift his arms to heaven, signaling the choir to begin. People would sing and pray to God then go home to Sunday dinner and an afternoon nap. It didn't seem fair that other people's lives continued all happy and calm, when someone else's was coming undone. She waited until nearly everyone was inside then got out and walked toward the church.

Every Sunday since Ellie's assault, Preacher Ray had kept her in his heart and thoughts. He felt that she was burdened, but she didn't offer an explanation, or ask for anything more than a prayer, so he continued to pray. It was the least that he could do.

When he saw her coming from the parking lot, his first thought was that someone had died. She walked with slow steps and slumped shoulders—her gaze down at her feet instead of where she was going.

He said a silent prayer for her and then smiled and extended his hand.

"Good morning, Ellie. It's always a blessing to see your sweet face."

Ellie clung to his hand like it was her lifeline, then got embarrassed and quickly turned loose. "Preacher Ray, did you pray for me?"

"Why, yes I did, Ellie."

Her chin quivered slightly, and then she took a deep breath and looked up. "If you don't mind, would you do it again, only louder? I don't think God's paying attention."

Before he could question her, she moved past him. His heart hurt for the child. He looked toward the parking lot. Her father's continuing absence seemed strange, but it wasn't his place to judge.

Ellie moved into the sanctuary, but instead of immediately sitting down, she paused to look down the aisle at the altar and the big statue of Jesus on the cross hanging on the wall behind it.

Blood dripped down his cheek from the crown of thorns, and from his feet and hands that had been nailed to the cross. Ellie studied the expression on his face. He was suffering, just like they said. But what Ellie couldn't figure out was if He'd died for all their sins so that they could be saved, then why wasn't someone saving her?

The first notes of organ music sounded, signaling for the services to begin. She slipped into her pew and scooted down to the place where the sun came in. The colors that spilled into her lap seemed sad and faded, partly muted by the haze between earth and sun. Considering she felt sad and faded too, it fit the mood she was in.

The choir began to sing, but Ellie didn't join in. Instead, she sat with her head down and her eyes closed, willing God to feel her pain—begging Him for mercy—praying with every fiber of her being not to be pregnant with Daddy's child.

Two hours later, church was over. Ellie slipped out a side door and got into her car. She had one stop she needed to make before she went home for dinner—to the pharmacy to get a pregnancy test—but she had to drive to the far side of town where she was unknown. If she went to the pharmacy near her house and any of the girls from high school were working the registers, it would be all over school before she went home tomorrow.

If that wasn't enough pressure, driving farther would make her later getting home, which would light Daddy's fuse. As Wyatt would say, she was already fucked, why make a big deal out of a little more?

Garrett had a sausage and rice casserole in the oven that Doris had fixed for them on Friday. He'd made salad and iced tea and got out the leftover birthday cake for dessert. He set the table, put ice in the glasses and then waited.

When she was thirty minutes late, he began to panic. He'd already looked in her room and nothing was missing, although he'd pretty much figured out she wouldn't bolt until after graduation. But there were accidents happening every day. What if she'd gotten in a wreck? What if she was unconscious and unable to tell anyone who to call? What if she didn't tell them to call him because of what he had done?

He'd worked himself up into a fine mess by the time she finally got home. When she walked in the house, the first thing out of his mouth was a mistake, but having said it, it was too late to take back.

"Where the hell have you been? I was afraid you'd had an accident."

Ellie fired back before she thought. "What happened to me was no accident, and the car is fine."

"What?"

"Never mind," Ellie muttered.

"I made dinner. Are you going to eat?"

"I'll get a plate after I change."

"You're not going to sit at the table with me ever again?"

"Not by choice."

Garrett's composure died. "Ellie. Please. Don't do this."

She paused at the doorway then turned around. "Hey, Daddy."

"What?"

"Did you just say, don't do this?"

"Yes."

"Did I ever ask you that? Did I ever say, 'Daddy don't'?"

He grunted like he'd been punched, then looked away.

"That's what I thought."

She walked out, and when she heard the sound of breaking glass behind her, she knew he'd thrown something at the wall. She ran to her bedroom, locking the door behind her. Once inside, she checked to see if Wyatt was around. After seeing she was alone, she went into the bathroom and opened the kit. The directions were simple.

Pee. Drop of urine on the test strip. Spend the longest two minutes of your life waiting to see the result.

Once the procedure had been done, she laid the strip down on the counter and walked out. Her heart was hammering against a racing pulse. It felt as if her body could explode. This was worse than waiting for the monster, worse than the first time Daddy had quit using his fingers, worse than the rape and beating. What if the Devil had planted his seed?

Unaware that her fingers had curled into fists, she started to shake. She looked up at the clock. Another thirty seconds and she'd have an answer.

Breath stopped. The minute hand was moving in slow motion. Twenty seconds. Fifteen seconds. Ten. Five.

She lifted her chin, her voice shaking. "Okay God, it's me again. I hope You know that if You let me down again, You and I are done." Ellie shoved her fingers through her hair and went into the bathroom.

A siren sounded somewhere outside the house, then slowly faded. The wind was coming up, like the weather had finally worked itself into a storm.

Ellie flushed the toilet and came out of the bathroom and put on her nightgown.

"Coming in," Wyatt called out.

Ellie turned around. "Hi."

"What's going on?"

The corner of Ellie's mouth turned down, but just for a moment. "Not much. I'm getting ready for bed."

"Yeah, me, too. Got a history final this week and then we get to pick up our caps and gowns. Are you excited?"

"Out of my mind."

"Okay, see you in the morning."

"Yeah, good night."

"'Night, Ellie."

Ellie turned out the light and then crawled into bed. The storm was closer now. Even when she closed her eyes, she could still see the flashes. Thunder rumbled in the distance, then as time passed, came even closer.

She rolled over on her side and pulled the covers up over her head like she used to do when she was little. But Wyatt had his own room now. He wasn't beneath the covers with her anymore. And no matter how much she squinted, she couldn't make the lightning look like fireflies. She thought it had something to do with getting older or maybe a loss of innocence and faith.

She heard Wyatt's footsteps as he passed her bed on the way to the bathroom. "Sorry. I'll be quiet."

"It's okay," Ellie said.

A few minutes later he passed the bed again. Ellie felt him poke her leg.

"'Night again. Don't forget to say your prayers." And then he was gone.

Ellie wanted to cry—really, really wanted to cry but was too numb for tears. She wouldn't be saying prayers or talking to God ever again.

Chapter Sixteen

Doris was in the kitchen making breakfast when Ellie and Wyatt came in.

"Good morning," Doris said. "How hungry are you—one egg or two?"

"Toast and juice," Ellie said.

"Two eggs, scrambled, and thanks," Wyatt added.

Doris smiled. She'd been feeding the pair for so many years she was somewhat territorial about it now.

"Thank you for our cake and the card and money," Ellie said.

"Yeah, thanks a bunch," Wyatt added.

Doris beamed. "I always make your cake."

"It was a hit, but we have leftovers. You need to be sure and have a piece for yourself today."

"I'll probably do that," Doris said. "Now sit. I'll have your food in no time."

Daddy came into the kitchen carrying his briefcase and a coffee cup. He'd obviously been in here earlier because he was topping off his cup.

"Thanks for breakfast, Doris. I have an early appointment so I'm off. Have a good day everyone," he said quickly and was out the door.

Ellie stared blankly at a spot on the wall. Have a good day? Not likely.

Wyatt dug into his food.

Ellie spread butter on her toast just like Momma used to do for her, spreading it generously all the way to the crusts. Then she ate it without tasting, washed it down with her juice and carried her dirty dishes to the sink.

"See you this evening," Ellie said.

Doris smiled. "Bless your heart. Eighteen years old. I can hardly believe it."

Ellie turned around and wrapped her arms around Doris's neck. The gesture was so unexpected that Doris almost forgot to hug her back.

"Well now," she said, and patted Ellie on the back like she was burping a baby.

"You've really been good to us," Ellie said.

Doris frowned. "And I hope to do so for at least a few more years. I'm not ready to retire. Now you run along. Have a good day."

Ellie laughed, and then left before it turned into a scream. It was ironic that of all days, everyone seemed to feel the need to tell her to enjoy it.

Wyatt followed her out. "Are you alright?"

Ellie handed him the car keys. "Do you mind driving this morning? I don't feel so good."

"Do you think you need to stay home?"

"No. I need to get through the next two weeks of school."

"I hear you," he said. "Hop in."

Ellie had turned in her resignation at the Franklin Ice Cream Parlor the previous week and was going to pick up her last check. She would miss this part of her life. Other than school, it was the only normal thing that she'd done.

She parked in front of the store instead of in employee parking and got out. Blinded by the glare of the sun, she reached back inside for her sunglasses. It made her feel like she was already in hiding, which had yet to happen. When she walked into the shop, the cool air and sweet smell of ice creams and toppings pulled her to the counter. The place was empty except for Tessa and Randy, but it was early in the day.

Randy waved when she walked in. "Hey you. Couldn't stand to be away from us, right?"

Ellie smiled. "I came to get my check."

"Got it right here," he said, taking an envelope from the drawer beneath the register and handing it over. "How about an ice cream on the house?"

"That would be great."

He grabbed a scoop. "Aren't you the strawberry girl?"

"Yes, thank you."

He made her a double dip in a waffle cone and presented it with a flourish. "We're going to miss you around here. I want you to know that I wish you every kind of success and happiness."

It was a bittersweet wish. "Thank you, Randy. You were a good boss."

He beamed. "So sit, eat. As hot as it's getting these days it's gonna melt fast."

Ellie slid the paycheck into her purse and sat down at a table. It felt weird to be where the customers sat, but in a good way. Tessa came out and slid into the other chair. She had white skulls painted on her black fingernail polish and a new piercing in her ear. Ellie counted seven earrings on that ear and four on the other. It looked very unbalanced, but she didn't care enough to ask why.

"So you graduate tonight, right?" Tessa asked.

Ellie nodded as she took another bite of her cone.

"Are you excited . . . about leaving home and stuff?"

"What do you think?" Ellie muttered.

"I think yes."

"Then you'd be right."

Tessa watched Ellie's face, thinking to herself that Ellie Wayne didn't seem to know how pretty she was, or how good she was built. She knew Ellie was smart. She lived in a nice house in the good part of Memphis. But something was off. She couldn't put her finger on it, but in all the years she'd known Ellie, she'd never seen her laugh. She'd smiled, even occasionally giggled, but never a real belly laugh. What happens to people to make them sad that way? Then she shrugged off the thought. There was enough shit going on in her own life without worrying about someone else.

"So have you decided where you're going after graduation?"

"Not for sure."

"Yeah, you've got all summer to figure that out," Tessa said. Then the bell over the door jingled as a group of customers came in.

"Oops! Gotta get to work. Take care of yourself."

"You, too," Ellie said.

She left as Randy began taking orders, dropping what was left of her ice cream in the trash on the way out the door, then got in the car and drove off.

Next stop was the bank, but instead of depositing her paycheck as she usually did, she cashed it, pocketed the $401.50 and drove home. She still had to press her dress, wash her hair and make sure the battery was good in the camera. She had all of the graduation expenses covered, but the Gates Abortion Clinic required cash and an appointment.

She now had both.

"What time is it?" Ellie asked, as she hurried out of the bathroom in her bra and pantyhose.

"You have to be out of here in thirty minutes," Sophie said, and gave Ellie's hairdo a last squirt of hair spray. It had been years since Ellie needed her like this and she was enjoying it immensely.

"Where's Wyatt? Why isn't he getting dressed?" Ellie asked.

"He's here and already ready to go. I expect he's waiting in the living room."

"Or in the kitchen, eating."

Sophie laughed. "Well yes, there's that. Now let's get this dress on and pick out which shoes you're going to wear."

The dress had been hanging in her closet since the end of March. The fabric was pink with tiny white polka dots in a retro-style that suited Ellie Wayne—cap sleeves, a square neckline, and a tulip-shaped skirt. At the time it had seemed the perfect choice for her send-off to adulthood only to have it turn out she should be wearing black.

"You look like a picture," Sophie said, as she zipped up the back of Ellie's dress. "And speaking of pictures, don't forget your camera."

"Daddy has it."

"You know he's going to ride with us," Sophie said.

Ellie's jaw tightened. "Yes."

"I don't know what's going on with you two, but at times like this I think a cease-fire is called for. It's not every day a person graduates high school, and it's a parent's right to be there . . . if, of course, they've done their parental duties."

"Oh, he's been a very hands-on parent," Ellie muttered.

Sophie beamed. "Then it will be fine. You'll see."

Ellie shrugged. "It doesn't matter. It will all be over soon."

Sophie frowned. "That sounds so permanent. You need to be thinking of the future, not ending one."

"I'm thinking all the time," Ellie said.

"Okay. You're zipped. Your hair is perfect. All you need is the cap and gown."

"On a hanger by the door."

"Then we're ready to go. My, my, this has been quite an event to get ready for. I had no idea. Did I remember lipstick? Is my hair okay?"

"You look perfect," Ellie said.

Sophie's lips pursed. "Well, not perfect, I'm sure. Now let's go find Wyatt and your Daddy."

When they got to the living room, Daddy was wearing his best suit with camera in hand. He stood the moment he saw Ellie. "You look beautiful."

"She does, doesn't she?" Sophie said. "Where's Wyatt?"

"I'm here."

Ellie retrieved her cap and gown. "We need to leave. I don't want to be late."

Obviously keeping his distance, Daddy opened the door then stepped back. "After you."

Ellie stopped, fixing him with a pointed look. "Wyatt and I are sitting in the back. Sophie will ride up front with you."

His nostrils flared. "Whatever you want." It was the only sign he gave of his displeasure.

The gymnasium was decorated with blue and gold, the school colors. Banners were draped along the sides of the bleachers while the floor had been set up for the graduating seniors. A temporary stage was at the far end of the gym where the school personnel would be sitting during the ceremony.

The energy inside was so high it felt like the air was buzzing. Memphis High School was about to eject another set of seniors out into the world with a pat on the back and a diploma that guaranteed nothing without some initiative to go with it.

Ellie had incentive, but her goal had been sideswiped. The lobby of the gym was awash with young girls on the verge of being women. Some wore their finery well. Others appeared awkward, as if they were playing dress-up and at any minute someone was going to call them on the charade.

Ellie felt like she was in a play and everyone around her were actors. Any minute someone was going to pop up and yell "Cut" and it would all go back to normal. She'd seen Cinnamon once on the other side of the gymnasium. She'd waved and then disappeared in the crowd. Ellie guessed it was a little awkward for Cin to be here. If she'd stayed in school she'd be graduating with them tonight.

But for Ellie, an even stranger event than graduation was taking place. Classmates who'd never passed the time of day with her were pulling her into their group photos, and then jumping into the shots Daddy was taking of her. It was surreal. Where had they been when she'd needed them? Her life was finally coming together while she was physically coming apart.

On top of everything else, there was a glitter in Daddy's eye that made her nervous. She couldn't help but remember the videos he was fond of making and wondered what he was thinking as he took pictures now. Finally, she called a halt.

"That's enough, Daddy. We have to be seated. Come on, Wyatt. The program is about to start."

"I'll be right up there on the fourth row," he said, pointing to the seat another parent was saving for him.

"And I'll be with him," Sophie said.

Ellie didn't care where Daddy sat as long as it was a good distance away from her.

Within moments, the chaos out in the lobby began to wane. Students lined up in alphabetical order. When the processional began to play, they filed into the gym and took their seats.

Ellie stood tight-lipped with her head up and her eyes open as the class president opened the ceremony with a prayer. She wasn't praying and no one could make her. She and God had already had a parting of the ways. It had taken a lot of years for her to accept that she was on her own.

The class valedictorian and salutatorian gave their speeches, talking about bright futures and looking onward and upward and how they would always value the bonds they had made at Memphis High. Ellie listened, but connected with none of it. It was as if she'd spent her entire educational experience in an alternate universe, popping in to this one now and then to take tests and move on to the next grade. Their voices began to drone. She was getting hot and a little sick at her stomach and wished this would be over. When she heard Wyatt sigh, she realized he was feeling the same thing.

When the presentation of diplomas began it was none too soon. Ellie wondered if anyone had ever thrown up on the stage and hoped she made it through without becoming the first.

"How many seniors are there?" Wyatt whispered.

"Two hundred and twenty-three."

Wyatt groaned. Diplomas were presented alphabetically and with the last name of Wayne, they'd be here a while.

"Dad's looking at us."

"Let him look."

"Sophie waved."

"I can't look, Wyatt. Stop pushing it."

"Hang tough, Ellie. It's almost over."

Not quite, Ellie thought, but wouldn't let herself go there. She could only handle one traumatic event at a time.

After a while, her mind began to wander from how she was going to get out of the house tomorrow without waking anyone up, to the color of the girl's hair in the row in front of her. The red was so shocking and obviously artificial that she kept wondering if it came off on the pillow when she slept. She tried to remember her name but couldn't, which was pathetic.

At that point Ellie had another revelation. She had no right to be pissed at her classmates for ignoring her existence when she didn't know them any better. What was it Sophie always said about karma? Oh yes—everything you give out in life will be returned to you twofold. Since she'd made no attempt to befriend anyone, they'd definitely returned the favor.

Whatever.

"Hey Ellie, it's time."

Wyatt's warning reset Ellie's focus. She fussed with her gown as they stood up and filed into the constantly moving line. That was when she tuned in to the names being called.

"We're almost there," Wyatt said softly.

Ellie felt his presence as surely as if they were holding hands. Being twins was amazing—the ability to tune in to each other without a physical connection—a gift.

Ellie reached the steps to the stage.

Only two students ahead of her.

She began walking up the steps. Now only one more ahead.

Then she was standing on the stage, watching Principal Warden's mouth forming the words that said her name.

"Elizabeth Ann Wayne."

As she began walking toward him, everything around her faded away. She didn't hear the crowd's applause or even hear them call Wyatt's name. The only thing she saw was the diploma Principal Warden was holding.

It was physical proof that Garrett Wayne's tenuous hold on her life was almost over. She had Momma's money, her education and Wyatt. All she had to do now was get rid of her last tie to Daddy and start over.

Chapter Seventeen

To Garrett's consternation, Sophie chattered all the way home. He wanted to talk to Ellie, to hear what she thought about this milestone in her life, but Ellie wouldn't look at him.

"Didn't Ellie look beautiful?" Sophie asked. "I swear pink is certainly her color. I suppose it's her fair complexion and blue eyes, but it does complement her nicely. I hear Ellie and Wyatt got their complexions from their mother. It's obvious they didn't get it from you with your red hair and green eyes. Not that there's anything wrong with red hair and green eyes, you understand. Wyatt and Ellie have your height, though. I know we're not supposed to envy, but I always wanted to be taller."

Garrett nodded in all the right places and kept on driving when in actuality, he wanted to tell her to shut the fuck up. Finally, they were home. He pulled into the drive and parked.

Sophie gasped. "Well my goodness, we're already here. I had no idea."

"And none too soon enough," Garrett muttered.

"What was that?" Sophie asked.

"Nothing. I was just talking to myself."

"Oh. Well, I'm hard of hearing now, you know."

"So I've heard," Garrett said, and got out.

Ellie bolted from the backseat with her door key in hand and was in the house before Garrett could lock the car. He cursed beneath his breath as he hurried to catch up. She was on her way out of the kitchen when he got inside.

"Ellie. Wait."

She had a don't-mess-with-me look on her face when she turned around.

"I have a graduation present for you."

"I don't want it. I don't want anything from you."

Garrett shoved a hand through his hair in frustration. "I know that, but if your Mother was still alive, she would have been the one doing this now and not me."

That was the last thing Ellie expected him to say. "Doing what?"

Garrett took a small box from the top of the refrigerator and handed it to her.

"Nothing for Wyatt?"

"It's a girl thing. When you see it, you'll understand."

"It's okay, Ellie. Open it and see what it is," Wyatt said.

Ellie gave Garrett a suspicious look.

"I swear this has nothing to do with me," Garrett said, and took yet another step back. "Just look at the damned thing."

Sophie clapped her hands. "Oh Ellie, hurry. I can't wait to see."

Ellie tossed her cap and gown over the back of a chair and then took the lid off the box. She recognized it instantly. The diamond ring that Momma always wore on her right hand.

"Your momma said it was a family heirloom and that her grandmother sewed it into the hem of her coat and smuggled it out of Poland just before World War I broke out in Europe. Ever since, tradition was to pass it down to the eldest daughter on her eighteenth birthday. If you remember, I was persona non grata on that occasion, so I saved it for graduation. You can have it sized if it doesn't fit."

Ellie slipped the ring onto the finger of her right hand and stifled a gasp when it fit. There was a moment of emotional connection to her mother that was so strong she wanted to weep, and then she remembered why Momma was no longer here.

"It would have been nice if Momma had been thinking of me before she swallowed that butt load of pills. I could have used her back-up instead of a three-carat diamond, but I appreciate the sentiment and will treat it with the reverence it deserves."

Garrett didn't know whether that was a thank you, or a brief lesson in parental failure. "Well, then that's that." He opened the refrigerator and pulled out a bottle of champagne. "I thought we would celebrate this night with some bubbly."

Shock was evident in Ellie's voice. "Seriously, Daddy? That's illegal. I'm too young to drink."

Wyatt hesitated. "I might try—"

"Indeed you won't," Sophie said, giving Garrett the evil eye. "I'm sorry, Garrett, but offering your own children alcohol is not appropriate."

Having said her piece, Sophie exited with Ellie and Wyatt in tow.

"Right," Garrett said, then turned around and popped the top on the bottle, grabbed a glass and walked out of the kitchen, leaving them all behind.

He stomped all the way down the hall while his sense of injustice continued to build, locked himself inside his room, poured a glass of champagne, popped in a video of Ellie and Wyatt at the age of ten and proceeded to get shit-faced drunk while Ellie lay wide-eyed and sleepless in her bedroom, waiting for morning.

It was just after daybreak when Ellie tiptoed out of the bathroom. She didn't want to wake Wyatt and explain why she wasn't sleeping in, but according to the checklist she'd gotten from the abortion center, there were things that had to be done before she arrived.

1. Shower.

Check.

2. Shoes with socks and a two-piece loose-fitting outfit.

Check.

She got the loose-fitting outfit, but the need for socks seemed odd. She supposed it would

all become clear after she got there.

3. Proper underwear for a sanitary pad.

Check.

That meant the thong underwear she didn't own wouldn't have worked. Goody for her.

4. Do not eat or drink anything for four hours before procedure.

Check.

No problem. At the moment, food was not a priority in her life.

5. You may bring a support person with you, but NO CHILDREN ARE ALLOWED.

Except for the one she was bringing with her.

Ironic, but logical. No children allowed, alive or dead.

6. You may bring a book to pass the time, which will extend from two to three hours.

Not so much.

So what kind of reading should one take to an abortion? War and Peace? To Kill a Mockingbird? Maybe Treasure Island because she definitely felt deserted.

Ellie got her purse, checking again to make sure the needed cash was still there. It was going to cost exactly $395.00 to remove her last tie to Daddy. Ellie had decided years ago that it wasn't safe to be a child, and the easiest way to protect them was not to bring them into the world.

The first thing she heard when she opened the door was the sound of snoring coming from the end of the hall.

Good. He was sleeping in.

She walked quietly through the house, and then to her car. After the dry run she'd made last week, she knew the way and didn't want to be late. The abortion clinic operated on a first-come, first-served basis and the sooner this was over, the better.

It was six minutes to eight when she pulled into the parking lot. When another car pulled in to the space beside her, Ellie got out and headed to the entrance. She hadn't planned on standing outside for everyone to see, but she wanted to be the first in line. As soon as that became fact, she relaxed. She'd done her job just by getting here. The rest was up to the people inside.

She heard footsteps coming up behind her before being swarmed by the cloying scent of a very sweet perfume. At that point she caught a glimpse of the woman's reflection in the front door glass. She had painted-on eyebrows giving her a look of permanent surprise, yellow-blonde hair tied up in a ponytail and lips that looked like she'd bitten into a hive of bees. A serious case of collagen overload, but Ellie knew it wasn't proper to judge others so she looked away. She would have liked to spend these few minutes in silence, but it appeared that wouldn't be the case.

"Hey sugar, how's it going?"

Instead of turning around to speak face to face, Ellie looked at the reflection. "Doesn't the fact that I am here already answer your question?"

The woman laughed. "Sorry. Nervous chitchat and all that. So I'm Bev. What's your name?"

"Alice. My name is Alice."

Bev laughed. "As in Wonderland, I guess."

"As in Wonderland."

Bev stepped sideways, obviously to get a better view of Ellie's face. "Wow, you're young."

"Yes I am."

"Are you nervous?"

Ellie sighed. "Not anymore."

"So I guess this is your first time?" Bev asked.

The question startled Ellie, enough so she actually turned around to face her inquisitor. "It's not yours?"

"Naw. Third. Maybe third time's a charm and all that."

"Did you never hear of using protection?"

Bev arched an eyebrow. "Where do you get off asking me that? You obviously fucked up, too, or you wouldn't be here."

Anger shot through Ellie so fast it was all she could do not to hit her. "No. I didn't fuck up. I was raped. Stop talking to me." She turned around and unconsciously hunched her shoulders, trying to make herself as small as possible.

"Sorry, kid."

"So am I."

The last few minutes were passed in an uncomfortable silence. When they finally opened the doors, Ellie made a beeline for the check-in desk.

They wanted an ID and the cash before sending her to the lab. She wanted a life do-over so she supplied what they needed.

When she finished at the lab, she was sent to view the "informative video" about what to expect. After a few moments of viewing, she decided they had understated *informative*. She had an actual moment of shock at how the procedure would take place, but it didn't lessen her intent. It did occur to her that the person who needed to be watching this was Daddy. He was the one who needed to live with this on his conscience, not her. She remembered Momma telling her once that in life, it was always the women who carried the burden because Eve had sinned in the Garden of Eden. Ellie mentally added Eve to the list of people who'd screwed up her life.

From there, she was taken to a counselor. The first thing Ellie noticed was the woman's pink blouse, and that even though she wasn't smiling, she had kind eyes. In made Ellie relax.

"Come in, have a seat," the lady said. "My name is Mrs. Cashion and you're Elizabeth Wayne, is that correct?"

"Yes, ma'am," Ellie said, sat down, crossed her legs at the ankles and folded her hands in her lap as Sophie had taught her to do.

"My job is to make sure that you fully understand your decision and to make sure you've weighed all your options, okay?"

"Yes, ma'am."

"Elizabeth, had you been on any birth control?"

"No, ma'am."

Mrs. Cashion frowned. "So you were sexually active without protection?"

Ellie frowned. While she understood why she'd asked, she didn't like the woman's tone. "I was raped."

Mrs. Cashion sighed. "I see. I'm sorry."

"Yes, ma'am, so was I."

The counselor eyed Ellie closer. Something was off about this young girl's manner, but it wasn't something she could put her finger on. Maybe it was because she was so matter-of-fact. There were no tears, no embarrassment—just a cold statement of facts.

"Did you ever consider carrying the baby to full term and putting it up for adoption?"

"No."

"May I ask why?"

"Is what I tell you confidential, like between a lawyer and client . . . or a doctor and patient?"

"No, but—"

"Then it stays with me. I'm eighteen. This is my decision."

The counselor nodded. "I can recommend a couple of kinds of birth control protection for when—"

"Mrs. Cashion—"

"Yes?"

"We can save ourselves some time right now if I tell you where I'm coming from. I won't be using birth control because I don't plan to ever get married. I don't intend to have children, nor will I be in a relationship, sexual or otherwise."

"My dear, it's obvious that the rape has traumatized you to the point of shutting down. I would hate to see you waste your life in this manner. With guidance and therapy you can learn to move past this and live a full and productive life."

Ellie leaned forward. Her tone hovered on angry—her words firing in rapid succession. "You don't know anything about me, and I can assure you that no amount of counseling—not even until the Rapture comes down—will change anything about me. I am broken. It happened years ago—long before the rape, and there's not enough glue in the world to put me together again. I understand there is some information I need to know about my aftercare?"

Mrs. Cashion's cheeks were burning, so she knew she was flushed. She'd been doing this service for several years and thought she had long ago learned to control her emotions, but for some reason, she had an overwhelming urge to cry.

"Yes. I'll go over the details with you and then you'll be ready. You do know they'll do an ultrasound before the actual procedure is done, don't you?"

Ellie's voice was flat, her face expressionless. "Lady, I don't care what it takes, as long as they get this out of me."

"Elizabeth? Can you hear me? The procedure is over. You need to wake up."

Ellie heard, but she didn't want to come back. She and Wyatt were playing in the creek, wading and chasing each other up and down the water until they were both soaked to the bone. If they went back now, Momma would know where they'd been and she'd specifically told them not to get wet.

"Elizabeth. Wake up. Wake up."

Ellie moaned. She hurt. She must have fallen on something. Momma was for sure going to be mad now.

"Elizabeth, wake up."

Ellie opened her eyes. She wasn't at the creek. She wasn't even in her house. Then she saw the uniform and remembered. "Is it over?" she mumbled.

"Yes. How do you feel?"

"Relieved."

The nurse sighed. "No, I mean physically, how do you feel?"

"Dizzy. Thirsty. Hurts."

"The dizzy part will wear off. You can have ice chips in a little bit, and we'll give you something for the pain."

"When can I go home?"

"In an hour or so . . . just as soon as the nitrous oxide wears off and you're steady on your feet. Did you come alone?"

"Yes."

The nurse patted her arm. "It won't be long."

Ellie nodded.

It was over. She closed her eyes and took a deep breath. Just knowing that the last remnants of the rape were finally gone was all she needed to hear.

About forty minutes later, she walked out of the clinic, past the curious stares of the women still waiting, lighter in body and spirit than when she'd gone in. She got into her car and went through the drive-through at McDonald's, ordered breakfast burritos for three, hash browns and a Pepsi, which she drank on the way home.

The sanitary pads she'd bought yesterday were still on the floorboard. They were her alibi. She knew women used their monthly period for a multitude of excuses. It should serve her needs as well.

She was shaky by the time she finally arrived and grateful the drive was over. Grabbing her breakfast and the sack with her pads, she went inside. It was just after ten thirty.

Garrett was running water into the coffeepot when she walked in the back door. Miserable from a hangover, he snapped.

"Where the hell have you been?"

"Getting breakfast and Kotex. I can tell by the snotty tone of your voice that you feel like hell, but don't take your hangover out on me. I have my own shit to deal with, okay?"

Garrett groaned. The sharp tone in her voice felt like nails on a chalkboard.

"Don't fucking shout," he mumbled.

Sophie entered just as the curse word left his mouth.

"I had no idea you were just getting up, but it appears from your bad behavior that you should have stayed in bed. Do not curse in front of your children."

Wyatt slipped in behind Sophie. "Do I smell food?"

Ellie smiled. "I brought burritos and hash browns from McDonald's."

When she opened the sack, Daddy gagged and bolted from the room.

Wyatt laughed. "Guess the smell of food didn't agree with him."

Ellie ate most of her burrito then washed it down with juice. "You guys finish the rest between you. I'm not feeling so great so I'm going back to bed."

Sophie frowned. "Are you getting sick, honey?"

"No. Just getting my period."

Wyatt held up a hand. "TMI. TMI."

Sophie's frown deepened. "What does that mean?"

"Too much information," he muttered, then grabbed the rest of his food and disappeared.

Ellie sighed. "Sorry."

"You pay him no mind," Sophie said. "You lie around all day if you need to. In fact, you can spend all the time in bed that you want right now, so enjoy. No more school or job—just a summer to get your head into a mode for the future."

Ellie was too weak and shaky to think about the future, so she took herself to bed.

Ellie's weekend was a blur. Cinnamon came by Saturday afternoon long enough to find out Ellie wasn't well and didn't stay. Sophie hovered, coaxing her to eat some soup and plumping her pillows.

Ellie woke up off and on during Sunday to find Wyatt sitting in a chair by her bed.

"What are you doing here?" she muttered.

"You're sick."

"Not sick, just tired," she said, and rolled over and closed her eyes.

The next time she woke, Wyatt was gone and Cinnamon was there. "Hey. It's Monday, your first official day as an unemployed high-school graduate. Wanna go listen to some music? There's this band playing in the park and the lead singer is seriously hot."

"No, thank you."

Cinnamon leaned forward, staring intently into Ellie's face. "I see secrets," she whispered.

"Everyone has secrets," Ellie muttered. "Go listen to your band and let me sleep."

Garrett got home from work that evening and was concerned when Doris told him Ellie hadn't gotten out of bed all day except to eat soup and crackers at noon.

He went straight to her room and knocked. "Ellie, it's me. Are you alright? Do you need anything?"

She was sitting up in bed with the television on mute, staring blankly at the screen without a notion of what was playing. When he shouted, she wished her remote had a mute button for his voice, as well. "I'm fine. Go away."

"Doris said you've been in bed all day. Do you need to go to a doctor?"

Ellie sighed and closed her eyes, willing him to disappear.

"Ellie. Damn it. Open this door so I can see you face to face if for no other reason than to assure myself you are alright.'

Ellie threw back the covers, dragged herself across the room and unlocked the door.

Garrett was surprised when it suddenly swung inward, but was shocked at Ellie's appearance. Her hair was lank and clinging to her head—her skin color almost ashen. The dark circles under her eyes made her face gaunt.

"Oh my God. You look terrible. You need to see a doctor. Get your robe and house shoes. I'm taking you to the emergency room."

Ellie pointed across the hall at Sophie's room. "Keep your voice down unless you want her in the middle of this conversation."

Garrett glanced over his shoulder, then caught himself and groaned. "Stop it with the Sophie business. You need to see a doctor. Now."

Ellie grabbed him by the arm, yanked him into the bedroom and quickly shut the door. He had no time to process the fact that he was suddenly inside her inner sanctum, and at her bidding, when she blindsided him.

"I look like this because I don't feel good. I don't feel good because I went to an abortion clinic on Saturday and had an abortion. I had an abortion because you got me pregnant. You got me pregnant because you raped me. You raped me because you're a sick, controlling pervert." She opened the door and physically shoved him back outside. "For obvious reasons, you make me sick to my stomach. I am not going to the doctor. Don't bother me again."

She slammed the door shut in his face and punctuated it with the sound of the slide bolt.

Garrett shuddered. All he could think about was getting to his room before he came undone. As he turned, he caught a glimpse of himself in the hall mirror, and froze.

The man looking back at him was a stranger. He had not set out in life to become a murderer. The first time he justified it by telling himself it was for the love of Ellie. But this time, there was no justification. What he'd done to her had been in the name of jealousy and rage, not from love, and in the long run, had ended yet another life. There were no words for what he felt—only a final acceptance that there was no going back to the way it was. Not after this.

Chapter Eighteen

A strange thing was happening to Ellie that she didn't understand. Her body was healing, but it didn't feel the same. Instead of feeling lighter as she had when she'd first left the clinic, she began to feel weighted down. If she hadn't seen for herself that she was actually losing weight, she would have assumed she was gaining. Her movements were lethargic—even her thought process was slower. She wasn't sleeping well, and when she did, her dreams were tormented. She attributed it all to the trauma of the abortion, and assumed it would eventually pass.

The first time she heard the baby crying, it was in a dream. In the dream, she was running from room to room inside an unfamiliar house, but no matter how many rooms she searched there were no babies, just that long, frightened wail. After she woke, she felt sick.

Every time after that when she slept, she relived the same dream—a baby crying and crying with no one to tend it. When the dream became a constant waking nightmare she feared she was losing her mind. Momma hadn't been right by the time she committed suicide. Maybe craziness was in the blood.

The high-pitched wail with a little catch of breath in between was like a knife to Ellie's heart. She could feel the pain and the panic in that cry with every fiber of her being. The video she'd seen at the clinic became a running loop in her mind. They'd sucked the fetus from her womb as surely as if they'd shoved a vacuum cleaner hose in her body and turned on the power. She hadn't considered what was in her as anything more than a foreign object Daddy had left behind, but it appeared she might have been wrong.

After forty-eight hours, the constant dirge of that mournful cry convinced her she was hearing the ghost of the baby she'd killed, and she was being haunted on her way to hell.

Sophie and Wyatt knew she was suffering, but didn't know why. It was making Wyatt crazy, seeing Ellie becoming more and more fragile. They took it upon themselves to monitor her every move, and when they lost track of her, it wasn't unusual for one or both of them to panic.

"Have you seen her today?" Sophie asked.

Wyatt nodded. "She looks like hell, excuse my language. But she won't talk to me. She won't even look at me anymore."

Sophie blotted a tear and then wadded the tissue up in her lap. "I think we need to have an intervention."

"That's for addicts and alcoholics—people who are addicted. Not Ellie."

Sophie persisted with the notion. "Then a confrontation. That's it, a confrontation. We need to make her tell us what's wrong."

"You can't make Ellie do anything she doesn't want to do. Believe me, I know."

"Then maybe we could ask Cinnamon. She might know something we don't."

The thought that Ellie would share something with that skanky redhead before sharing with him made Wyatt angry. "I don't believe it. If something was really bad, Ellie would come to me. We share everything."

"That's not true," Sophie said. "You don't share what you do when you're not with her."

Wyatt shifted nervously. "That's different."

"No it's not. I don't care how close people are, there will always be things that must remain private. It's how we're made. Anyway, the next time Cinnamon comes, I'm going to ask her."

"Whatever," Wyatt muttered. "But count me out."

"Even if it's for Ellie?"

"That's not fair."

"Life's not fair," Sophie stated, and the subject was closed.

Doris was running the vacuum in the back of the house and had taken advantage of the beautiful weather to open the windows and air out the rooms. Ellie sat curled up on the window seat in the living room, watching traffic and trying to ignore the constant wail of the ghost baby's cries.

It seemed that everything around her was amplified. The buzz and chirp of cicadas and grasshoppers, the birds up in the trees beyond the window, even the sound of her own breathing was a steady roar inside her head. She rubbed her hands up and down her legs, feeling the prickle of leg hair. The last time she'd tried to shave her legs she nicked the skin and made it bleed. The constant seeping of big red drops had turned into ladybug beetles crawling out of her skin. She didn't know if she was losing her mind, or really had bugs, but just in case she wasn't shaving anymore.

The baby shrieked, and Ellie covered her ears, focusing on the scent of lilacs filling the room. They reminded her of the days when Momma was still alive and how she had kept a vase of cut flowers in every room. She'd called it bringing the outside in.

Back then, Ellie would sit on a stool in the kitchen without making a sound, watching her mother arrange flowers while keeping up a running commentary about why she trimmed the stems on an angle and how adding an aspirin tablet to the water would keep them fresh longer. She didn't know if it worked, but it had been her Momma's way and so she'd do the same.

The baby hiccupped and paused.

Ellie's heart skipped a beat. Maybe this was it. Maybe the crying had finally stopped. But the moment the notion went through her head, she heard a wail. About that same time, she spied a hummingbird dive-bombing the blossoms and hoped the baby's cries didn't scare it off.

Momma had planted the lilac bushes near the house on purpose to draw in the tiny birds, and she and Ellie made a game of counting how many they could count feeding at one time. Ellie had learned early that it was the small things in life that mattered. She wished she had Momma here now. She needed someone to tell her how to make that baby go away.

Ellie wasn't the only one living with ghosts.

Garrett was languishing as well. He thought he might be dying—that he was rotting from the inside out. No matter how many showers he took, the scent of his body offended him. Despite Doris's attempts to encourage his appetite, he couldn't get down more than a few bites at a time and began taking sick days from work. The last time he'd missed work had been the day he'd buried his wife, so he knew whatever was wrong had to be bad. After a visit to the doctor he was given a clean bill of health, but he knew that wasn't true. There wasn't a single thing about him that was clean—certainly not his soul.

He and Ellie lived under the same roof with Sophie and Wyatt, and during the daytime, even Doris, but they were as far apart as if they were at opposite ends of the earth. He couldn't look at her and bear the accusation in her eyes. His only resolution was to pretend she wasn't there. What had once been an existence of constant turmoil between them had turned into a cold war.

It was the middle of the morning when Sophie caught Ellie walking the hall. She stopped to visit, but Ellie would have moved past in what looked like a trance had she not caught Ellie by the arm.

"Ellie, darling, it's so good to see you getting up and about again. Have you eaten anything today?"

Ellie rubbed her hands over her face in a rough, scrubbing motion then suddenly jerked and tilted her head.

"Do you hear that, Sophie?"

Sophie frowned at Ellie's blank stare. "Hear what, dear?"

"That baby. I hear a baby crying."

"No, but you know how hard of hearing I am," Sophie said. "I'm going to make myself a bite to eat. Come sit with me and have something to eat."

"I can't. I have to find the baby."

Worried about Ellie's strange behavior, Sophie hurried off in search of Wyatt.

Ellie was still standing in the hallway when Doris came out into the hall. "Well, hello, Ellie. I'm finished in your father's room and was about to do your room, but if you're planning to take a nap, I can wait."

Ellie shuddered. The thought of sleep made her panic. "No, no nap."

"Then why don't you get out of the house? Maybe go for a walk?" Doris asked.

The notion clicked. "I might go for a walk."

"Whatever you want, dear, but I won't be long in your room."

"Doris?"

Doris paused on the threshold to Ellie's room. "Yes?"

"Do you hear a baby?"

Doris's heart skipped a beat. She'd lived too long in this house to ignore anything out of the usual order and this was definitely one of those times. "No, Ellie, there's no baby here."

"But I can hear it cry."

Doris frowned. "There's no baby. Maybe it's a bird. You know how those mockingbirds are."

"Bird?"

Within moments, the vacuum was going again, and Ellie left. She couldn't abide the sound of vacuum cleaners anymore. When she took her purse and left the house, the tiny, high-pitched wail went with her.

Outside, Ellie paused and lifted her face to the sun. It was warm on her skin with just enough of a breeze to keep from being uncomfortable. There was a loose thread on the fringe of her jeans—the ones she'd cut off at the knees last summer. They'd fit fine last year, but now they were hanging loosely on her hips. She pulled the loose thread until it broke off and tossed it away. Her yellow T-shirt seemed too large as well, but it couldn't be helped.

The decision to get out of the house was a good one. It felt natural to be doing something ordinary, even if she was hearing ghosts. About halfway down the block, a kid on a bike came pedaling up behind her.

"Coming through," he yelled, and swerved onto the grass to miss her, then swerved back onto the sidewalk once he was past.

Ellie's heart twisted painfully. He reminded her of Wyatt at that age—blonde hair and a smattering of freckles across a sunburned nose. Life had been simple then. It hadn't been perfect, but it was something they'd understood.

The light was red when she reached the crosswalk. As she waited for it to turn, she saw Cinnamon walking up from the other side of the street. Her red hair was short and spiky and her black shorts and cropped T-shirt were too tight, but Ellie envied Cinnamon's ability to thumb her nose at what society deemed appropriate. It was obvious she was comfortable in her own skin.

Cinnamon saw Ellie and smiled and waved.

Ellie waved back. When the light turned, she walked across to meet her.

"Hey, good to see you out and about," Cin said. "Where are you going?"

"The pharmacy. Come with me?"

"Sure. I was coming to see you anyway. I'd just as soon see you out here as in that house."

"What do you mean?"

Cin shrugged. "That house sort of freaks me out."

"Really? You never said anything before."

"Well, why would I? That would be rude. Can you imagine? Like, uh, Ellie, I like you and all, but your house gives me the creeps."

Ellie understood, although she'd never thought about what went on behind closed doors actually giving an inanimate object like a house a bad vibe, she supposed it was possible. She'd gotten so used to living with the Devil she hadn't known he would rub off onto someone else. Of course it was probably worse now that it was haunted, too. She couldn't blame Cinnamon for not wanting to be there.

Cin cut a glance at Ellie, trying to read her expression. "Did I make you mad?"

"No, I'm not mad."

"Good. You got so quiet you scared me."

"I was just thinking."

"About what?"

"Stuff."

Cin grinned. "What stuff?"

Ellie thought about telling her, but they were at the pharmacy. "We're here." She walked in, pausing a minute to scan the aisle signs, then headed for the one that shelved sleeping aids.

Cin followed, then frowned when she saw what Ellie was getting. "Sleeping pills? What do you need sleeping pills for?"

"I haven't been sleeping. I thought they might help."

Now Cin was concerned. Those secrets she'd seen when Ellie was sick were getting bigger. She knew about secrets like that. They ate you up from the inside out.

Ellie took a couple of bottles toward the register, pausing at the candy aisle to pick up two Hershey's bars.

"One of those for me?" Cin asked.

"Sure. Want a cold drink too?"

"Pepsi?"

"I'll get it," Ellie said, then suddenly paused and turned her head. "Do you hear that?"

"Hear what?" Cin asked.

"There's a baby crying. Someone needs to pick it up. You shouldn't let a baby just lay there and cry."

"I don't hear a baby."

Ellie turned around. She was smiling, but there were tears on her face. "I do. It won't go away. I don't know how to make it go away."

Shock shattered the smart remark Cinnamon had been going to make. Something was really wrong with Ellie. "Here, honey. We'll go pay for your stuff and then go home, okay?"

"I don't want to go home," Ellie whispered. "There's a ghost in the house."

Cin started to shake. She tried to laugh, but it was obvious Ellie was serious. "Now you're scaring me."

"I'm scared, too," Ellie whispered. "I did a bad thing and God wants me to suffer."

"That does it," Cin muttered, and grabbed Ellie by the hand. She led her to the register, paid for her stuff, and dragged her out of the pharmacy.

"Where are we going?" Ellie asked.

"I'm taking you home."

Ellie started to cry. "It's sad there."

"That's what I'm figuring out, but we can't fix what's wrong until you tell me, and we're not playing twenty questions out here in front of God and everybody."

"It's okay. Haven't you heard?"

"Heard what?" Cinnamon asked.

Ellie whispered in her ear. "There is no God."

"Oh shit, shit, shit," Cinnamon muttered, and started walking Ellie home.

"Want some candy?" Ellie asked, and broke off a square of chocolate and handed it to Cinnamon. "Hershey bars are my favorite. Don't you just love the way they melt on your tongue."

Cin put the candy in her mouth and ate without tasting it as she continued to pull Ellie along. "We're almost there. It won't be long now."

"Have another piece," Ellie offered.

Cin put it in her mouth like a dose of medicine, chewed and swallowed.

Ellie frowned at her. "You're not doing it right. You're supposed to let it melt on your tongue. Here, try again, and this time don't chew, let it melt."

"Yeah, okay . . . sorry."

Cinnamon could see the house now and would have walked faster, but Ellie wouldn't comply. The closer they got to her house, the slower her steps became.

"I'm going in with you," Cin said, and gave Ellie's hand a tug to remind her she was there.

Ellie's eyes filled with tears all over again. "You'll hear the baby soon. It's louder there."

Ellie was turning into a stranger, and Cin had a horrible feeling the Ellie Wayne she'd grown to love was disappearing.

"Don't go anywhere, sweetie," Cinnamon whispered. "I need you to stay with me. You're all I have."

When they walked in the front door, Doris was dusting. "Back already?"

Ellie pointed. "Cinnamon brought me home. I need to go lie down now."

Doris frowned but didn't comment.

As soon as they got inside, Cin locked Ellie's bedroom door. "Is your dad at work?"

Ellie shrugged. "I don't know where he is. It doesn't matter. He'll never bother me again."

"Where's Wyatt?"

Ellie waved her arm up in the air, as if he'd disappeared.

"Somewhere . . ."

"Come lie down on the bed with me. We can talk while you rest."

"I've got to go to the bathroom first," Ellie said.

"Okay, but remember I'm waiting."

"Listen for the baby. You'll hear it any time now."

She waited as Ellie asked, but when Ellie finally came out, she seemed to have forgotten Cinnamon was there. Instead of sitting down to visit, she crawled up onto her bed and rolled over onto her side.

"I'm going to sleep now."

Cin crawled up beside her. "Talk to me, sweetie. Tell me what's wrong."

"Promise not to tell," Ellie mumbled.

"I promise."

"Daddy raped me and made a baby. I got rid of it and now its little ghost won't let me sleep."

Oh my God. "Did you tell?"

"Wyatt knows about the rape, but not the baby. Everyone else saw my bruises, and I said I fell in the shower."

Cin groaned, remembering the swollen eye and all the bruises on her face. "Why didn't you tell the police?"

Ellie's eyes were closed, but she put a finger up to her lips and then lowered her voice to a whisper. "I can't tell. If I do, Daddy said they'll arrest him, and when that happens they'll find the movies—years and years of movies. He knows I don't want anyone to see them. Wyatt doesn't know about the movies."

"What movies, sweetie? What movies would they find?"

"All the bad movies. The ones Daddy made when he made me and Wyatt play the game."

Cin was suddenly sick to her stomach, realizing that Ellie and Wyatt's entire childhood was nothing but a sham. "Have you seen them?"

"Daddy made me watch so I would understand. I was Daddy's special girl. That's why we couldn't tell."

Cin felt like throwing up. She'd had a hard life, but nothing like this.

"Oh Ellie . . . sweetie."

"Do you hear the baby yet?" Ellie asked, and then choked on a sob.

Cinnamon put her arms around her and held her close. "No, sweetie. The only baby I hear crying is you."

"Don't tell. You promised."

"*Sssh.* Just close your eyes and sleep. I'll be here when you wake up."

It was near suppertime when Ellie opened her eyes and saw Cinnamon sitting at the foot of her bed.

"You're still here?"

It sounded more like a question than a statement, but Cinnamon didn't press the issue. "I'm not leaving you. Doris knocked on the door a few minutes ago. She said supper was ready. Go wash up and we'll eat."

Ellie squeezed her eyes shut and clasped her hands over her ears. "I can't eat. I don't want to eat. I just want to go to sleep and never wake up. It's too hard to live. I'm tired. I wish I would die."

Cinnamon grabbed Ellie by the shoulders and shook her angrily. "Don't say that. Don't ever say that again."

Either Ellie didn't hear her or she was ignoring her. She swung her legs off the side of the bed then got up. "Where are my sleeping pills? I need to find my pills. Then I can go to sleep like Momma did and never wake up again."

"No!" Cinnamon made a dash toward the bathroom, grabbed the open bottle of sleeping pills and dumped them all in the toilet and flushed. Then she remembered Ellie had bought two bottles and dug through the drawers in a panic until she found that one as well.

"Don't do that," Ellie begged. "Please. You don't understand. I can't do this anymore. Daddy won. He beat me. I don't want to be here anymore."

Cin pushed her away and flushed the second bottle as well, then pushed Ellie aside and ran out the door. She needed to find Sophie or Wyatt. Someone needed to get her to a hospital before she took herself to the morgue.

"Help, help, somebody help," she screamed.

She ran through the house, looking in every room. Doris came out of the kitchen, wiping her hands on a towel and frowning at the noise.

"What's going on?"

Cinnamon grabbed her by the shoulders. "I need to find Wyatt. Have you seen him?"

Doris sighed. "Not in a while. He doesn't like you, you know, so he may be ignoring you."

"Crap. I didn't think of that. Sophie. I'll find Sophie."

"Maybe she's in her room. Ellie says she's hard of hearing."

"Right." Cin dashed back down the hall, shouting Sophie's name.

Sophie opened the door then peered out. "Is someone calling me?"

Cin was in a panic. "Ellie tried to kill herself. You need to find Wyatt. She needs help."

Sophie gasped and began calling Wyatt's name as she ran toward Ellie's room. But by the time they got back into the bedroom, Wyatt was already there.

"Where's Ellie? What's all the shouting?" he asked

"Oh my God," Cinnamon screamed and ran to the bathroom, but it was empty. "Where did she go?"

Wyatt frowned. "What the hell's going on?"

"Ellie tried to kill herself by taking a bunch of sleeping pills. I flushed them down the toilet then ran to find you, but now she's gone."

All of a sudden, Wyatt thought of the gun. He bolted for his room with Sophie and Cinnamon on his heels and found Ellie on her hands and knees by his bed. The only thing that had saved her was her lack of physical strength. She was too weak to crawl under.

He pulled her to her feet then sat her on the side of his bed. "What's the matter with you? You don't quit. We're tough, Ellie, we're tough. Together we can get through anything, remember?"

Ellie looked at him with a blank expression. Not only did she not recognize Wyatt, she didn't appear to even know where she was.

At that point, Wyatt crawled under his bed and pulled the gun out from its hiding place.

When Ellie saw the gun, reality surfaced. "Give it to me. It's mine."

Wyatt shoved her backward. "What's wrong with you?"

She hit the bed with her fists and started weeping, which frightened Wyatt even more. Ellie hadn't cried in years. She'd been saving them for something that mattered. So what the hell had happened that he didn't know about?

"I know what's wrong with her," Cinnamon said.

Wyatt turned in disbelief. "Why do you know that? I don't."

"It has something to do with protecting you, I think," Cinnamon said.

"You promised not to tell," Ellie mumbled.

"But I didn't say I would let you kill yourself."

Wyatt snapped. "Damn it. Someone better tell me something."

"Your Daddy has been molesting both of you for most of your life, hasn't he?"

Wyatt reeled as if he'd been slapped. "She told you that?"

Sophie clasped her hands over her mouth in disbelief. "No! Why didn't you tell me? I would have stopped that in an instant."

"Ellie said her dad had movies of the game you used to play. Lots of movies."

Wyatt flinched. All of a sudden the past began to make sense. Why Ellie went back to playing the game after she'd made Garrett stop—why she wouldn't explain anything to him.

"Ellie, Ellie, I didn't know. I'm so sorry. Is that why you quit fighting him? To protect me?"

"That's not all," Cinnamon said. "You know all those bruises on her face?"

The shock of this revelation was almost too much for Sophie to comprehend. Her chin was trembling and she was beginning to shake. "When she fell in the shower?"

"No, when Garrett raped her."

Sophie moaned. "I'm calling the police this minute."

"She got pregnant, had an abortion, and now she hears a baby crying all the time. She calls it her ghost baby. She said she wants to die."

Pregnant? The son of a bitch got her pregnant? Rage shot through Wyatt so fast he forgot to breathe. He grabbed the gun and ran out of the room.

Ellie moaned. "No Wyatt," but it was already too late.

Chapter Nineteen

Garrett was on his bed, staring blindly at a video of him and Ellie after she'd turned thirteen—so pretty and already a little woman. He'd promised to take care of her.

What had he done?

He heard shouts in the hall outside his room but couldn't draw enough interest to go see what was happening. Whoever it was would come to him if the need arose.

His face itched. He thought about shaving and taking a shower, then discarded the notion as a waste of time. No amount of soap could get him clean.

His focus shifted back to the screen as Ellie turned toward the camera, naked as the day she was born. He held his breath, knowing what came next. She stood there without moving—her eyes closed and her hands across her breasts as he picked her up and carried her to the bed.

"Look at me. Look at me," Garrett begged, as he had that day, but she still wouldn't look.

Someone screamed. It took him a few moments to realize that wasn't part of his movie. They didn't have any sound. So if he heard a scream, then what he was hearing was happening now and under his roof.

At the sound of footsteps running down the hall toward his room, he glanced at the door to make sure it was locked. And it was. But when the doorknob turned and the door wouldn't open, he expected to hear a voice, not the gunshot that blew the doorknob into his room.

He screamed—a high-pitched shriek that popped his ears. Even as he watched Wyatt bound into the room with a gun, Garrett was still processing the fact he had screamed like a girl.

"What are you doing?" Garrett fumbled for the remote, anxious to turn it off before Wyatt saw, but it was too late.

Wyatt burst into the room, stopping suddenly to stare at the images on the screen.

"You bastard! You sorry, perverted son of a bitch!" He swung the gun toward Garrett's face.

"What are you doing? No, Wyatt, don't! Don't do this!" Garrett tried to get up, but his legs were tangled in the sheets.

Wyatt waved the gun like a maestro with a baton, punctuating every word. "You got Ellie pregnant and she had an abortion. You ruined her life, you destroyed her joy and now you've killed what was left of her. Say your prayers, Daddy. You're next."

Wyatt heard Doris screaming in another room as he pulled the trigger. The first shot hit Garrett in the belly. He grunted—grabbing his gut in disbelief as blood gushed between his fingers.

Wyatt fired again, hitting Garrett high in the shoulder. He fell back against the headboard with his mouth agape, his eyes wide with growing horror.

Garrett groaned. He thought he was screaming again, when in fact he wasn't making a sound. Pain was radiating from his gut throughout his body and Wyatt's face was fading when he saw Fern standing off to one side in the corner.

I must be dying.

Wyatt pointed the gun again.

Fern came closer.

Doris ran into the room. "No, dear God, no! What have you done?"

Wyatt spun her toward the television. "Have a look at Daddy's home movies and you'll know what I've done. I've killed the Devil."

Doris saw Ellie's frail naked body and the redheaded man manipulating her every move, then looked at Garrett in disbelief. She'd never suspected. Not once.

Garrett grunted then choked. "Wait . . . confess."

Wyatt laughed, but the sound was closer to a sob. "Confess? Confess to what? I already know what you've done. I was there, remember?"

"Fern . . . tried to take Ellie. Had . . . stop her."

Wyatt's entire focus was on making sure Garrett strangled on the blood bubbling up his throat and missed the implication of what Garrett was trying to confess.

Garrett lifted his hand toward Wyatt, oblivious to the horrified expression on Doris's face. "Gave sleeping pills. Didn't wake up."

The words finally sank in, and when they did, Wyatt felt like he'd been kicked in the gut. "You killed Momma?"

Doris couldn't believe what she'd just heard. "Oh dear Lord."

Garrett blinked. Fern was standing beside Wyatt now, looking at him with that accusing stare. "Yes . . . I needed—"

Wyatt put a bullet between his eyes.

Garrett's head popped back against the headboard as Doris ran screaming from the room.

Wyatt felt nothing but relief. The rage was as spent as the last bullet he'd put in his father's head. He turned his back on the dead man, dropped the gun on the bedroom floor and walked out. In the distance, he could hear the sound of sirens. The police were on their way. Might as well wait for them and get this over with.

Sophie was in the hall outside Ellie's bedroom. "Oh Wyatt . . . what did you do?"

"He won't hurt her anymore."

"Where are you going?"

"The police are here."

"What's going to happen to us?"

"It doesn't matter anymore. Daddy killed us all."

"Wait, we'll go with you. Ellie, get up. You're going to have to help us explain what happened or they're going to charge your brother with murder."

"Leave her alone," Wyatt said. "I did it. There's nothing she can say that will change the truth."

"I'll get her," Cinnamon said, and led Ellie out.

Lee Corbett had come on duty at the Memphis Police Department battling a summer cold and had been short-tempered and miserable most of the day. When he and his partner, Allen Paul, got a "shots fired" call, they were the first to arrive on the scene. Officers Fredericks and Stanton were in the second cruiser. As they pulled up to the residence, they saw a middle-aged woman standing in the yard in a state of hysteria. She came running toward them as they got out.

"Someone's dead inside the house," she said, then covered her face with her apron and continued to sob.

"Who are you?" Lee asked.

"The housekeeper."

"Is the shooter still inside?" Corbett asked, as he quickly pulled his weapon.

"Yes, but—"

Wyatt walked out with his hands in the air.

"There's a dead man in the last bedroom down the hall on the left. His name is Garrett Wayne. The son of a bitch was my father and I just killed him."

Startled by the shooter's appearance and the instant confession, it took Corbett a moment to react. He was reaching for his handcuffs when Sophie jumped in.

"Wait. You don't understand. There were extenuating circumstances. Garrett Wayne was molesting them. I only just found out about it myself, but it's been going on for years."

Cinnamon came forward, dragging Ellie with her. "This is Ellie. She and Wyatt are twins and have been molested by their father ever since they were babies. A couple of months ago Garrett Wayne raped Ellie and nearly beat her to death. She got pregnant and then had an abortion. When Wyatt found out, he sort of lost it."

Wyatt pushed them aside. "Shut up, Cinnamon. You don't have to tell the ugly story to the whole world—and leave Ellie alone. She can't cope with this and we all know it."

Doris stood by, her heart breaking for Ellie and wondering what the police were going to make of all this.

For a moment, Lee Corbett thought his cold medicine was causing hallucinations, then saw that his partner, Allen Paul, looked as confused as he felt.

"Turn around," he said shortly, and handcuffed his shooter. Now they could talk all they wanted. "Fredericks . . . you and Stanton go look for the body." He caught the housekeeper's gaze. "Ma'am, what's your name and relationship?"

"Doris Bailey. I'm the cook and housekeeper for the family. I've worked here for almost fifteen years."

"Officer Paul will get your statement," he said, then pushed Wyatt down on the top step. "I don't know what's going on here, but I need you to sit down while I sort all this out."

Sophie felt responsible. The children had been in her care and she had missed every warning sign. Guilt raised her normally high-pitched voice a good octave.

"You can't arrest Wyatt. He was just protecting Ellie."

Corbett shoved a hand through his hair. "Look, lady, I—"

Cinnamon interrupted. "Find the movies. Garrett Wayne made dirty movies of everything he ever did to them. You'll see. He deserved to die."

Corbett felt like he'd walked into the Twilight Zone. He pointed at

Doris. "Mrs. Bailey, what the hell's going on here?"

Ellie blinked. It was the word *hell* that made her focus.

"Sophie says you shouldn't curse, but hell is real, Daddy showed me."

Ellie began to cry again, huge silent tears. "Do you hear that? Listen. The ghost baby's crying."

Corbett's head was swimming again. Had to be the cold medicine.

"Ma'am, if you would just—"

"My name is Elizabeth Ann, but you can call me Ellie. I'm tired. I need to go lay down now. Cinnamon, what did you do with my pills?"

"I flushed them down the toilet."

Ellie leaned against the porch post. "I just want to sleep and never wake up." She looked up at the officer. "Make her give me my pills."

Doris had enough. They would never make sense of this unless she said what she knew.

"Officer Corbett, I can help straighten all this out."

At that point, Fredericks and Stanton emerged from the house. Both of them were pale. One glanced at Ellie, then quickly looked away.

"We found the body," Fredericks said. "And videos. A lot of videos."

"That does it," Corbett muttered. "Paul, get the captain over here ASAP."

"Please, you have to listen to me," Doris said. "Ellie can't help it. She's always been this way."

Corbett squatted down in front of Ellie. "Miss, what's your name?"

"Who are you talking to?" Cinnamon asked.

"I think he means Ellie," Sophie said. "Officer, did you want to talk to Ellie? If you do, we'll have to get her. She doesn't know how this works, but we do."

Doris patted her shoulder. "I've got this Sophie. Let me explain."

Ellie put her hands over her ears and began to rock back and forth. "I still hear that baby. Somebody needs to make it stop."

Doris took a deep breath. "The only person who's real is Ellie. The others are people she's made up in her mind. I read up on it once. They call it multiple personality disorder."

"I'm as real as I need to be," Cinnamon snapped.

Corbett stood abruptly and took a step back as Doris continued to explain.

"That's Cinnamon. She's a friend who's Ellie's age. Wyatt is her twin and Sophie Crawford is her nanny. Ellie got the nanny after her mother committed suicide when she was twelve."

"It doesn't freakin' matter," Wyatt said. "All he needs to know is that Daddy's dead and I'm the one who killed him."

Stifling the urge to curse, Corbett grabbed Ellie's arm.

"Stand up, miss. You're going to the police station."

Wyatt did as he'd been told and started walking toward the cruiser when all of a sudden he stumbled. By the time he caught himself, Ellie was back and trembling violently.

"Keep moving, kid."

"My name is Ellie."

Even though he was sympathetic to what she'd been through, he still hadn't bought into this multiple personality crap.

"Keep moving, Ellie."

But Ellie wouldn't budge. "Wait. What are they going to do with Daddy?"

"You don't need to worry about that. You've got enough trouble of your own."

Panic spread so fast Ellie could barely breathe.

"No! You don't understand. Tell them. Tell them Doris. Tell the people at the funeral home. Tell the police. Tell whoever needs to know that they can't bury him by Momma. She does not deserve to spend eternity beside the man who murdered her." She began talking louder and louder until her words were a scream. "Does anybody hear me? Do not bury him. I am his daughter. I am telling you. I do not want him to be buried."

Corbett flinched. He got her point. "Look, Ellie, I'll pass your message along. I promise."

"Tell them to cremate him and keep the ashes."

"Yes, I'll pass that along, too. Now get in the squad car."

"Come on Ellie. We have to go," Wyatt said.

Corbett put Ellie in the back of the squad car and then shut the door.

Ellie flinched when the door slammed shut. "Where are they taking us?"

"To jail."

"Oh Wyatt . . . what have you done?"

"Something I should have done a long time ago."

"Is he really dead?"

"Yes, he's really dead."

Ellie exhaled slowly, then leaned against the seat and closed her eyes.

"Maybe that ghost baby won't follow us to the jail. I'm so tired. I just want to sleep and never wake up."

Chapter Twenty

It was all over the evening news. By the next day, the story had gone national.

> In Memphis, teenage girl with dissociative disorder kills abusive father. Sixteen years' worth of videos depicting her molestation found in his room with the body.

Preacher Ray heard the story and rushed to the police station to see if they would let him talk to Ellie, but she had already been booked and was in a holding cell awaiting arraignment. No visitors allowed—not even her preacher.

He left the jail with a heavy heart and the feeling that once again, he'd somehow failed her. All the way home he kept remembering her asking. *Did you say a prayer for me, Preacher? Would you say it louder? I don't think God heard.*

When Tessa from the ice cream shop realized she'd helped Ellie buy the gun that had been used to commit a murder, she quit her job and moved to Nashville, hoping no one would be able to connect her to the crime. The manager, Randy, was in tears. He kept remembering Ellie's battered face and swollen eye and wishing he'd followed his instincts to interfere.

As her teachers and classmates heard the news, their reactions were varied, but their guilt was the same. Everyone had seen that she was different, but no one had ever stopped and asked her why.

Mrs. Cashion, the counselor from the clinic, was interviewed by the police. She confirmed the fact of the abortion, but went home that evening with a sense of having failed someone who'd been in dire need of rescue.

Ultimately, it was Doris's statement to the police, confirming her knowledge of the number of years Ellie had lived with alternate personalities, that was the turning point in keeping charges from being filed, and the fact that she'd personally witnessed Garrett Wayne's deathbed confession of killing his wife.

The District Attorney sat down with Ellie Wayne and her court-appointed attorney, thinking he was going to see a young girl who'd had a fight with her father playing the insanity defense. But her mental condition was fairly obvious and after reviewing the tapes confiscated from Garrett Wayne's bedroom, he knew there wouldn't be a jury in the nation that would find her guilty. The only obvious issue at this point was that she was a danger to herself. After refusing to prosecute, the court ordered her to Mind and Body, a psychiatric hospital on the outskirts of Memphis.

Ellie was finally safe from prosecution—safe from the abuse that she'd endured all her life—but she was still broken, still hearing her ghost baby and still wishing she was dead. She didn't know it yet, but her future was now in the hands of Doctor Aaron Tyler, the Chief of Psychiatry at Mind and Body.

Ellie's arrival at the hospital was all a blur. By the time she was taken to her new living quarters, she was numb. It was nothing like her room at home. No soft carpeting. No television. Nothing personal. Just a bed, a dresser and a bathroom with a shower. Ellie noted the changes without comment. The only thing she wanted in life was for the baby to stop crying.

As soon as the aide left her alone, she sat down on the side of the bed, testing the mattress, and realized it lacked comfort as well as style. Her head throbbed from the noise and she put her hands over her ears and closed her eyes, willing the room to silence, but the baby still cried.

She got up and poked around the bathroom, then flushed the toilet to see if it worked. The water ran slowly and sluiced around and around in the bowl for a very long time before it finally went down, which didn't bode well for future visits.

Ellie couldn't imagine what she was supposed to do in this place. She heard Cin and Sophie talking, saying it was like jail for crazy people.

What had Wyatt gotten them into?

The aide who'd brought Ellie to her room had left her suitcase by the door. When she dragged it to the bed to unpack, she was surprised to find a note from Doris.

Dear Ellie,

Don't worry about anything here. I'll take care of the house for you until you come home. The executor of your estate has taken your Momma's jewelry into safekeeping for you, especially your ring. Your Daddy was cremated according to your wishes, and his ashes are being held at the funeral home until you come to claim them.

I want you to know how dear you are to me, and how sorry I am that I never knew what was happening. I wish you had told me. I would have helped.

You are a good girl, Ellie. Never doubt that.

Do what the doctors tell you to do and get well soon. I sent some of your favorite clothes. If you need more, send word.

Love, Doris

Doris was Ellie's last link to her past, and she wasn't sure she wanted to retain that connection. She laid the letter aside and began putting her clothes in the dresser.

"It's too bad there's not a rug," Sophie said.

Ellie glanced at the gray and white tiles. "I guess."

Sophie wasn't through with her critique as she eyed the walls and the curtainless windows with obvious disdain. "I had no idea there was a shade of green this color. What would you call it . . . *puce*?"

"Don't you mean *puke*?" Cinnamon asked.

Sophie frowned. "I don't particularly like the word *puke*. It's so common. The proper term is vomit, you know. And I swear I don't know where they think we're supposed to sleep. There's only one bed."

Cinnamon laughed. "Get real, Sophie. You know we don't need separate rooms." She fell backward onto the bed with her arms outstretched and then noticed a water stain on the ceiling that looked a little like a giraffe.

Sophie frowned. "I've always had my own room."

Wyatt felt Ellie's panic welling. "Shut up, both of you."

They both looked at Ellie and quickly apologized. She was trembling again.

"We're sorry honey. It doesn't matter. Wyatt and I are still here for you," Sophie said.

"Absolutely," Cinnamon said.

Ellie put her hands over her ears, crawled onto the bed and rolled up into a ball. She didn't care where she was or where she slept. She just wanted it to be quiet.

Wyatt sat down beside her. "You have an appointment with a shrink named Tyler in a couple of days."

Ellie rolled over onto her back. Wyatt was always the voice of reason.

"You go, Wyatt. You're the one who shot Daddy."

Wyatt sighed. "That's not how they're going to see it."

Sophie patted Ellie's leg. "He's right. We love you, but they don't know us."

Ellie persisted. "But they will if you go with me to the appointment."

"So we'll all go with you at first. If we're lucky, he'll be cute," Cin said.

Sophie frowned. "Seriously, Cinnamon, you need your head examined."

Cin burst into laughter. "Then we're in the right place."

"I can't believe I'm stuck in here with three women," Wyatt muttered. He felt Ellie's shock, and quickly added. ". . . with the exception of Ellie."

Aaron Tyler had read Elizabeth Wayne's file and was ready to begin therapy, but he liked to give patients a couple of days to settle in before he began. A part of him felt guilty that he was looking forward to meeting this patient. He'd never met a multiple before, although he'd certainly studied them. He'd requested the videos the police had confiscated, to understand what she had been enduring for the past eighteen years. It would be necessary in order for him to be able to help her heal. But when the tapes arrived, it didn't take long for him to see that no amount of studying could have prepared him for this.

Viewing the abuse and degradation she had suffered from such an early age made him considerably empathetic. He was going to have to keep himself focused on the issues and not be swayed by the trauma of her life.

When the day of their first meeting arrived, Aaron kept a close eye on the time as he made rounds. He didn't want to be late. Trust was imperative. He got back to the office, poured himself a fresh cup of coffee then set up a camera to video their sessions.

When she was finally escorted to his office, he was ready. Although he'd seen her file photo, it was immediately obvious it had not done her justice. Except for the fact she was too thin and her eyes seemed haunted, she was what society would have called a beautiful young woman. Classic features, long blonde hair so light it was almost white, blue eyes shimmering with unshed tears and a manner of deportment that he'd seen only in young women from the finest of finishing schools. Not what you'd expect with her history.

"Come in, Elizabeth. Have a seat. My name is Doctor Tyler. I have a note in your file that says you prefer to be called Ellie. Is that correct?"

"Ellie's here but she doesn't want to talk. I'm Wyatt."

"So, Wyatt, have a seat and we'll get started."

Sophie tugged at Wyatt's sleeve. "Wyatt, introduce me."

Wyatt frowned. "Yeah, okay. Uh, Doctor Tyler, this is our nanny, Sophie Crawford, and I'll tell you up front she's hard of hearing."

Sophie smiled and quickly shook Aaron's hand. "It's a pleasure to meet you. My, my, I had no idea I'd ever have my own therapist. This is so exciting."

Aaron was so interested watching a beautiful young girl go from the masculine mode to an older woman with rounded shoulders and a higher voice, he almost forgot to speak. "Um . . . nice to meet you, too."

"Hey, don't forget about me. I'm Cinnamon." Cinnamon's deep throaty laugh took Aaron aback. "Even though I'm really a good girl, you can call me Cin."

"Nice to meet all of you," Aaron said. "Shall we begin?"

But Sophie had gone into nanny mode and took it upon herself to organize Ellie's seating arrangements. "Ellie isn't well. She probably needs to lie down? Ellie, why don't you lie down, dear? It will be more restful that way."

"She's fine," Wyatt said. "We'll take the chair."

Aaron pointed to a brown, pillowback chair. "This chair will be fine. Have a seat . . . all of you."

Wyatt sat and slid forward, his knees slightly apart, his hands folded over his belly.

Aaron made a note, then looked up and smiled.

"Are you going to write everything down?" Sophie asked.

Aaron frowned slightly. "Am I speaking to Sophie?"

"Well yes, who else would I be?" Sophie asked, and then clasped her hand over her mouth and giggled. "Oh. Right. Sorry."

"Would it be alright with all of you if Ellie answered some of the questions?"

"You'll have to ask Ellie," Wyatt said.

"Ellie? Do you think you would be okay with answering questions?"

Aaron watched the defiant Wyatt turn into a trembling child with her hands over her ears. He thought she didn't want to hear him until she spoke to him in a shaky voice. "You'll have to speak louder. I have a hard time hearing over the baby's cries."

Aaron leaned forward. "You hear a baby crying?"

Ellie tilted her head a little to the side. "Can't you hear it? I think it's the ghost of the baby I killed."

"Are you talking about the abortion?"

She nodded.

He hadn't intended to get into this so quickly, but she'd opened the door. He felt it necessary to pursue the topic since it had been introduced. "Were you sad about doing that?"

She frowned. "No. When you get a splinter, you take it out. When you have a bad tooth, a dentist will pull it. Daddy left something in me that didn't belong. The doctor just took it out."

"You felt no attachment to it in any way?"

"No."

"Did you ever think about having the baby and then giving it up for adoption?"

The moment Aaron asked, Ellie looked at him as if he'd lost his mind. "Why would I do that?"

"Why wouldn't you? Make me understand."

"It's not safe to be a child."

"Do you ever want to be a mother someday?"

"Never. I'm really tired of living. It would be easier to be dead."

Aaron made a few notes about a suicide watch then looked up and caught Ellie whispering. "Who were you talking to?"

"She's through talking today," Wyatt said. "If you have questions, I'm answering."

Aaron didn't want to give them the impression that they were in charge of the session. "We'll see where it takes us."

"Whatever."

"So, Wyatt, what's your earliest memory?"

"That's easy . . . listening to Ellie cry."

"Cry? Do you know why she was crying?"

Wyatt shrugged. "Ellie nearly died when she was born. She was sick a lot the first three years of her life, then she started to get stronger."

"So you remember being three?"

"I think younger. I remember crying when we didn't know how to talk. Ellie cried all the time, and then she found me and didn't cry so much anymore."

"Can Ellie remember that far back?"

"I don't know. You'll have to ask her that, but not today. She's still too sad to talk."

"Why is she sad?"

Wyatt frowned. "I'm gonna pretend you didn't ask that question, because I'd like to think you're smarter than that."

Aaron made another note. *Wyatt is smart and protective and doesn't trust me.*

"This is Cin and I know a reason Ellie's sad."

Wyatt jumped back in. "Damn it, Cinnamon, if Ellie wants her business told, she can do it."

Cinnamon snapped back. "We're here for Ellie and this man is a doctor. If anyone can put Ellie back together again, it would be him."

Aaron pushed her to continue. "Tell me, Cin. What do you know?"

"When Ellie was twelve, her mother died. Everyone thought she committed suicide and Ellie felt abandoned and got real mad. You know how it goes . . . a mother would rather be dead than stay and take care of her kid and all that stuff. But then Garrett confessed to Wyatt on his deathbed that he'd killed his wife to keep her quiet after she found out about the abuse. Ellie is sad because for all those years she was mad at her momma."

"That is very valuable information, Cin, and thank you for telling me."

Cin glared at Wyatt. "You guys are all messed up because of secrets. If you want Ellie to get better, start talking."

Aaron stifled a smile. He liked Cin. She was loud and proud. He turned to Wyatt. "Do you remember the first time Garrett molested you?"

"No. It was just what he did . . . how we lived . . . we didn't know any different for years."

Aaron remembered the early videos Garrett had made of Ellie. She couldn't have been more than two. "Where was your mother when all that was happening?"

"Praying. Momma always prayed. She would go to bed and pray a lot back then."

"Then who took care of you?"

"Daddy. She gave us to Daddy, went to bed with God, and look what happened."

Chapter Twenty-One

One week later:

The patients at Mind and Body ate their meals in their rooms, but when it was free time—time to watch television, or play a game of chess or checkers, or just sit near a window in the sunshine, all the patients who were able came to the common room—a huge, wide-open space with windows that circled the room on three walls. There were dozens of large round tables with folding chairs, a bookshelf along the far wall with a few books, a stack of newspapers and some magazines.

Ellie had looked at them briefly, noted the newest newspaper was more than a month old and the magazines were from last year. The first book she opened was missing the first three pages. So much for entertainment.

But knowing this led to her realization of what the mind-set of the patients must be like. Either no one read, or if they did, they didn't notice or care that what they were reading wasn't current, or that they might have read it before.

Her first day in the common room she'd pulled a chair into the corner of the room and sat without moving, trying to assess what was and wasn't done in here.

It was like when Sophie had first come to live with them and how hard Ellie had worked to learn the rules of polite society. Something told her that in here, knowing which fork to use and saying *please* and *thank you* wasn't going to be as pertinent. Even more troubling to her, Sophie would be of no help in here.

Wyatt had taken one look at the group, said it was like living in a zoo and rarely came back. But Sophie went often and when she did, she liked to sit in the sun and read. Cinnamon was a regular and tuned in to her favorite soap opera when she could control the remote.

After the first two tries, Ellie wouldn't go back. Some of the patients scared her as much, if not more, than Daddy. They'd get loud and shriek, or stand in a corner and pull strands of hair from their heads and put them in their pockets.

A young man, who she learned was schizophrenic, seemed fascinated with her hair and kept trying to brush or braid it. Ellie didn't like to be touched any more than she liked the skinny woman with brown hair and gray roots who kept calling her Charlotte. Being among people like that made her think she was like them, and she wasn't. She still didn't know why the court had put all of them in here. This wasn't a real jail and Wyatt was the one who shot Daddy.

Cinnamon was right in the middle of watching a scene in her favorite soap when someone tapped her on the shoulder. "What?" she asked, without turning around.

She got another tap on her shoulder.

Aggravation added to the tone of her voice. "What?"

And one more tap.

Cinnamon lost it. She got up and turned around, ready to berate whoever it was who was making her miss her show, and then forgot what she'd been going to say.

The man standing behind her chair was probably the tallest man she'd ever seen. Just guessing, she would have put him near seven feet. His hair was long and white with a beard to match but his face appeared ageless. His eyes were such a pale blue they appeared transparent, and with the white pants and shirt he was wearing, she didn't know whether he was an employee or a patient.

"Uh . . ."

"I have come to speak with Ellie."

Cinnamon blinked. "You want to talk to Ellie?"

He nodded.

"She doesn't come in here. She doesn't like it."

"She needs to talk to me."

Cinnamon threw her hands up in the air. "Look, no offense, mister, but if you're one of the loonies then you're not hearing my words. Ellie doesn't come here. You people make her nervous."

"Tell Ellie I'll be waiting here again tomorrow."

"Fine. I'll pass along the message, but don't blame me if she doesn't show."

"Tell her that I'm listening. She will come."

"Okay. What's your name?"

He walked away without an answer.

Cinnamon sat back down and then looked at the television and groaned. The show was over and she'd missed the big reveal of the day.

"Dang it." She relinquished the remote and was on her way out when one of the doctors came hurrying toward her.

"Ellie, my name is Doctor Moira Ferris. I need to ask you a quick question."

Cinnamon stopped. She'd seen her in the hall with Doctor Tyler before but didn't remember her name. "I'm not Ellie, I'm Cinnamon."

"Oh. Sorry. I wanted to ask you something about that man you were talking to."

"You mean that old tall guy?"

"Yes. What did he say to you?"

"He wanted to talk to Ellie. I told him she doesn't like coming here, but he kept pushing the issue, so I said I'd tell her. Between you and me, I don't think she'll come."

"Did he say why he wanted to talk to her?"

"Nope. Just said for me to tell her he had been listening, whatever the heck that means, and that he'd be back in here tomorrow."

"Thank you," Moira said, and then hurried away.

Cinnamon thought nothing of the moment and by the time she got to their room, had forgotten it.

Ellie was lying on the bed with her eyes closed, but Cinnamon knew she wasn't asleep. She could see her eyelashes fluttering. "Hey Ellie, stop pretending you're asleep and sit up."

Ellie frowned, but pushed herself up to a sitting position. "What?"

"There was a man in the common room who asked you to come see him tomorrow."

"What kind of a man?"

"A really tall man."

"Was he a doctor?"

"No—maybe—I don't know. He was dressed all in white, but didn't have a name tag on his shirt."

"Well, I don't want to talk to him."

"That's not fair. He wasn't acting all weird or anything. I wouldn't have said anything if I thought he would hurt you. He was just really big and quiet."

Ellie frowned. "You know I don't like to go to that room. What did you tell him?"

"I said I'd give you the message, that's all."

"What's his name?"

"I don't know. Are you going?"

"Why would I go?" Ellie asked.

Cin shrugged. "You're not doing anything else. Why not?"

Ellie sighed. It was difficult to argue with her logic.

Cin added. "Oh, one other thing. He said to tell you he's been listening."

"Listening . . . listening to what? What does that mean?"

"You'll have to ask him yourself."

Ellie's stomach rolled. She was tired of making decisions.

"I'll think about it. Where's Wyatt? He has an appointment with Dr. Tyler in ten minutes."

Cin sat down beside Ellie. "Why don't you go, too? Dr. Tyler is nice enough. He doesn't get mad or ask stupid questions. He's just trying to help all of us."

Ellie frowned. "The only help I need is for God to let me die, but I'm not talking to Him anymore."

Cin's eyes filled with tears. "You make me so sad."

"Why?"

"I know how to be happy. If I was out of here tomorrow I'd know what to do. I would be ecstatic just being alive."

Ellie started to shake. "That's not fair. You don't know what you're talking about. You want my life? I wish I could give it to you."

"You still don't get it," Cin said. "One of these days I'm going to disappear. The doctor will integrate us and that will be that."

Ellie frowned. "What do you mean, disappear and integrate what?"

"Ellie, Ellie, you know the answer. You just don't want to face it."

There was a knot in Ellie's stomach as she rolled off the bed and started pacing back and forth in front of the window. "Stop talking in riddles. I don't know what you're talking about."

Cinnamon wanted to shake her. Ellie's refusal was typical. If it was scary, pretend it didn't exist.

"You would know what I was talking about if you'd show up for your therapy sessions instead of hiding in the corner like a coward and making one of us go in your place. We're not real, Ellie. We're people you made up in your mind to compensate for a lack of stability in your real life."

Bile rose in the back of Ellie's throat as she backed into a corner. "You lie," she whispered.

"No, honey, I don't. Remember when I told you that I knew I

wouldn't live long . . . that I wouldn't grow old? That's because I knew one day you'd have to let us go. Doctor Tyler calls it *integrating.* He means we all go back into you, but we'll take each of our strengths with us, and when we're all together you'll be strong enough to face the world on your own."

Ellie started to sob. "You lie, you lie. Sophie is real. And Wyatt is my twin. We've been together forever. He's the other half of my soul. I can't live in the world without Wyatt."

"Then you better start liking this place, because as long as you keep talking to people who aren't real, they'll never let you leave."

"Get out!" Ellie screamed. "Get out! Get out! Get out!" She threw herself back down on the bed and pulled the pillow over her head.

Cinnamon left, but what she'd said stayed behind. Ellie was horrified and saddened and scared—so scared. How could any of that be true? As little children, she and Wyatt had slept together—played together—shared meals and gone to school together. She refused to consider anything Cinnamon had said as true. She was just jealous because she wasn't real family.

Her anxiety increased as she glanced at the clock. The aide would be here any minute to take Wyatt to therapy and he was nowhere to be seen. If he didn't show up, Dr. Tyler would be unhappy and the repercussions would probably roll over onto all of them.

Irked that he was putting her into such a spot, she got up from the bed and washed her face and combed her hair. She'd have to go and hopefully explain Wyatt's absence away. This was all such a waste of time.

Aaron Tyler's pulse kicked into gear as he glanced at the clock. *Almost time for another session with Ellie Wayne*, then he amended the thought. In the three weeks she'd been here, he hadn't talked to Ellie more than a couple of times. He'd broached the subject with Wyatt, who came occasionally and remained noncommittal each time. He would talk about his experiences, but never gave anything about Ellie away. It was apparent that Wyatt was the guardian and would not be talking Ellie into anything she didn't want to do.

Sophie came to therapy on a regular basis. She liked having a therapist and talked incessantly, but rarely about anything that was helpful to him. It was apparent that Ellie had created Sophie based on her perceptions of her mother. Fern hadn't known what was going on with her husband and Ellie, and neither had Sophie.

Cinnamon was interesting. She obviously represented everything Ellie wanted to be. She didn't take crap from people and spoke up for herself and for Ellie. She'd told him that if Ellie ever showed up, to offer her a Hershey bar. He had a handful in the drawer, but had yet to unwrap one.

But Ellie was still the enigma. As he was making last-minute notes, there was a knock at his door and then it opened.

One of the aides escorted Ellie into the office. "Ellie is here for her session." He gave Ellie's shoulder a quick pat. "I'll take you back to your room when you're done."

When Aaron saw Ellie pull away from the contact, his heart skipped a beat. Cinnamon liked the aide. Sophie often held his hand. Wyatt talked to the aide more than he talked to Aaron, but Ellie didn't like to be touched.

Hot damn.

"Come in," Aaron said.

Ellie walked in, but didn't sit. She eyed the doctor, noting his very kind brown eyes and long, slender face. "I'm very sorry. Wyatt wouldn't come. I don't know where he is."

"That's alright, Ellie. I appreciate you coming to let me know."

Relieved that Wyatt wasn't in trouble, she began to relax.

"Have a seat," Aaron said. He took a Hershey bar from the drawer and laid it on the desk in front of her. "Do you like chocolate?"

Ellie's mouth watered. She hadn't had a Hershey bar in such a long time.

"Yes, thank you," she said, tore into the paper and broke off the first square.

Aaron stifled a smile. *Thank you, Cin.* "You're welcome." He sat down and took one for himself then mirrored her actions, breaking off a square and putting it on his tongue.

"Umm," Ellie said, and then frowned and absently rubbed at the frown between her eyebrows.

"Headache?" Aaron asked.

Ellie nodded. "It's that baby." She broke off another piece of chocolate and placed it on her tongue as precisely as a priest with a communion wafer. "It just never hushes. I don't know anything about kids, but I don't think they cry all the time. Do you have children?"

"No, I'm not married, but I have nieces and nephews. You're right. They aren't supposed to cry all the time."

Ellie nodded. "That's what I figured." She licked chocolate off the end of her finger then laid the candy bar in her lap so she wouldn't eat it too fast. She wanted to make it last.

"When did you begin hearing the baby cry?" Aaron asked.

"A day or so after the abortion. It's the ghost of the baby I killed."

Aaron kept watching her expressions and keying in on the tone of her voice as she talked. She didn't seem the least bit remorseful about the abortion.

"You're sure?"

She shrugged. "What else could it be? I had an abortion and then start hearing a baby cry. It's just God reminding me that I sinned. I'm gonna be haunted until I die."

She looked down in her lap and broke off another square.

Aaron's eyes widened. She was religious? This was something he hadn't known about Ellie Wayne. "Do you belong to a church?"

"Yes. Preacher Ray was a good preacher."

"Did you go often?"

"Daddy took me every Sunday. I liked it the most when the choir sang. Music in church soaks into your skin. We always sat in the same pew so I could sit in the colors."

Aaron was excited about what she was saying. He made a quick note and then took another bite of chocolate, as well.

"You sat in the colors? How do you do that?"

"It was where the sunlight came through the Jesus window. If I sat in the right place, all the colors spilled onto my chest and in my lap."

"Why did you like to sit in the colors?"

"They were from the Jesus window. You know that part of the Bible where Jesus says, *suffer the little children to come unto Me?* That window had Jesus sitting in a garden with little kids all around Him. There was even one sitting in His lap. I liked to sit in the colors because I thought He could hear me praying better."

Ellie's head was buzzing, but she put another piece of chocolate in her mouth and it almost stopped.

"What did you pray about?" Aaron asked.

"I prayed for Daddy to leave me alone but it never happened. Not even after I got my period. I don't pray to God anymore."

"Why not?"

Ellie's hands began to shake. She took two squares at once and put them in her mouth.

"He wouldn't listen. I got tired of praying for things that never happened. The last time was when I prayed I wouldn't be pregnant, but I was. I told God then we were done. I haven't talked to Him since."

She wrapped up the last half of the chocolate bar.

"May I take this with me?"

Aaron felt her pulling away. There was so much more he wanted to ask her, but he didn't want to pressure her to stay.

"Sure," Aaron said. "When you come back, I'll be sure to have another one for you."

All of a sudden Ellie looked up at Aaron. A big smile broke across her face and then she crossed her legs and laughed. Just like that, Ellie was gone.

"I told you Hershey bars would work."

Aaron smiled. "And I thank you, Cin."

"Anything for our girl," she said. "Why don't you give Charlie a call. Tell him we're ready to go back to our room, okay?"

He made the call then leaned back to talk to Cinnamon while they waited.

"So what's been going on with you?"

"Not much. Watching TV, hanging out with Ellie and the loonies in the common room."

Aaron frowned. "I hope you don't call them that to their faces."

"I don't, but between us, they are nuts. This afternoon there was even this great big guy who interrupted me right in the middle of my favorite soap and made me miss the best part."

"What did he want?"

She laughed. "Like everyone else, he wanted to talk to Ellie."

Aaron frowned. "Ellie? Not you or Wyatt or Sophie?"

"No. He specifically said he needed to talk to Ellie."

"What was his name?"

"He didn't say. But he was for sure the tallest guy I've ever seen, with this really long white hair and beard and dressed all in white. Kind of freaky if you ask me."

Aaron abruptly leaned forward.

"He talked to you? As in opened his mouth and spoke?"

Cin made a face at him and then laughed. "How else can you talk without opening your mouth?"

"What exactly did he say?"

"I don't know 'exactly'. I don't have a photographic memory, you know."

"Take a guess."

Cin looked up at the ceiling, gathering her thoughts then started counting them off on her fingers.

"He just kept saying, 'tell Ellie to come see me,' that he needed to talk to her, and to tell her that he had been listening."

"Shit."

Cinnamon laughed. "I knew there was a reason I liked you."

Aaron actually blushed. "I'm so sorry. That slipped out."

There was a knock on the door.

"That will be Charlie. When you see Ellie again, tell her how much I enjoyed our talk."

"Okay. See you later," Cin said.

The minute the door closed behind her, Aaron grabbed the phone and dialed an extension.

"Moira. I need to talk to you."

Chapter Twenty-Two

Moira Ferris liked her job as a psychiatrist at Mind and Body, and for the most part felt she was making a difference in her patients' lives—except for Luther Dunn.

At nearly seven feet tall, Luther was quite a sight among the other patients. Even though his hair and beard were extremely long, he was neat to the point of obsession. When he'd first come here, he'd sat in his room naked, refusing to wear clothing until they'd brought in a pair of white scrubs long enough to fit his near seven-foot height. The loose-fitting outfit, along with his white hair and bare feet had earned him the nickname "Hippy" from the aides.

Luther had been here for more than five years now, and in all that time had never talked. Not to aides, or doctors or other patients—not while he was eating—not during sessions—not even after shock therapy. He never willingly left his room and only then when someone came after him.

Then for some reason, today everything changed. When it came time to go to the common room, Luther went unaided.

As soon as Luther walked in, he began circling, eyeing faces, pausing to listen to conversations while staring intently at the patients' faces. Then for no obvious reason, he suddenly stopped behind the sofa where Ellie Wayne was seated and touched her shoulder.

That was the second bombshell.

By the time Dr. Ferris got the news that Luther was out of his room and talking, over an hour has passed. She hurried down in an attempt to intercept him, but was too late and grabbed the nearest aide instead.

"Charlie. Where is Luther?"

"He was just here . . . I guess he left already."

"Who was he talking to?"

Charlie pointed. "That girl with the long hair who's watching television. Her name is Ellie Wayne, but you might not get much out of her."

Charlie's warning had proved to be right. When Moira caught up with Ellie, she got someone named Cinnamon, who had no idea who Luther Dunn was, or why he would want to talk to Ellie Wayne.

At that point, she headed for Luther's room, trying not to break into an out-and-out lope. As always, she found him sitting by the window with his eyes closed and his face to the sun.

"Luther. It's me, Dr. Ferris."

Luther didn't react.

"I heard you made a friend today. What was her name?"

Luther was mute and motionless.

Moira felt like she was talking to a wall. If she hadn't seen his eyelids fluttering, she might have thought he was dead.

"Maybe another time," she said. "I'm glad you've found a friend though. That's a positive move. So, we'll talk again at your next session."

She started to leave, then leaned over and moved her hand in front of his face just to make sure he was breathing.

Luther opened his eyes.

Startled, Moira straightened abruptly and walked out. "That was embarrassing."

So Luther was back on shutdown mode. She just had to find another place to start. She headed for her office to find out all she could about Ellie Wayne, but after an hour of reading through both Luther and Ellie's files, she couldn't find one connection that made sense. Not only were they not from the same part of the country, and of different sexes, there was also a forty-year difference in their ages.

She was still struggling to make sense of it all when her phone rang. "Dr. Ferris."

"Moira, it's me, Aaron. I need to talk to you."

She knew from reading Ellie's file that Aaron was her doctor. "And I you. My office or yours?"

"I'll come to yours. Be there in five."

He made it in four.

Moira had the door ajar for his arrival. "That was quick."

Aaron got straight to the point. "Have you heard?"

"You mean about Luther Dunn wanting to talk to your patient, Ellie Wayne? Yes. I venture to say most of the hospital knows it by now."

Aaron dropped onto the sofa, chose a piece of hard candy from the candy dish and popped it into his mouth. "*Eww*, butterscotch."

Moira rolled her eyes. "You're worse than my patients. Choose another. They always do."

Aaron tossed the candy and dug through the dish again. "What do you make of it? Have you talked to him?"

Moira shrugged. "I don't know what to think, and yes I spoke to him, but got nowhere. He was in his usual spot, sitting in front of the window with his eyes closed and the sun on his face. I spoke to Ellie but got one of her alters instead."

Aaron nodded. "Was it Cinnamon?"

Moira nodded.

"I thought so. She already told me about Luther talking to her. She's the one who's Ellie's age. Pretty outrageous but I like her. She's got a good head on her shoulders. I'm not sure Ellie will show up though. It's impossible to predict what she might do."

"So what exactly did this Cinnamon tell you?"

"That Luther wants to talk to Ellie. How the hell he knew there was more than one personality to choose from is a mystery, and why he chose Ellie is an even bigger one. But there is an interesting aspect to this that you don't know."

"Like what?"

"I think at one point in her life, Ellie Wayne was very religious. She may still consider herself religious, but in her words, 'right now she's mad at God'."

"I might be mad at God, too, if I'd had to endure what that child has gone through."

"I know, and you haven't seen the videos."

"Oh my God, there are videos?"

"About sixteen years' worth."

"Wait. That would have made her—"

"Two years old when he started to film them together."

Moira shuddered. "Jesus. No wonder she came undone."

"Anyway . . . here's the point I was trying to make. Ellie said she used to go to church every Sunday with her father and pray to God for help, but it never came. She said God never listened to her."

Moira frowned. "I don't get it."

"Cinnamon also told me that when Luther was talking to her, the last thing he said was to tell Ellie he was listening."

It took a few moments for Moira to grasp what he was saying, and then she gasped.

"No way!"

"Way. So explain to me, how your patient, who has refused to talk for the past five years, and who believes that he is God, suddenly goes looking for Ellie Wayne to make sure she knew he was listening?"

Ellie sat in the middle of her bed with the last half of the candy bar unwrapped in her lap. She put a small square on her tongue and then closed her eyes so she could garner every aspect of the chocolate experience without being distracted.

The baby was still wailing, but Ellie had been thinking about it for weeks and was beginning to wonder if it might not have something to do with the fact that the baby kept crying because no one answered—no one came to pick it up.

She knew what that was like. She'd talked to God for years without being heard. Maybe that baby just wanted to be heard as well. She was toying with the theory that if the baby knew it had been heard, maybe then it would stop. But that would mean talking to God again to intercede on the baby's behalf. Obviously the baby couldn't hear Ellie. But if it was a ghost, then God certainly could. Spirits and ghosts and angels were part of God's realm, not hers.

She broke off another piece of chocolate and was about to put it in her mouth when Sophie popped in.

"Oh. Chocolate."

Ellie knew Sophie liked her sweets. "Dr. Tyler gave it to me during session. Would you like a piece?"

"Yes, please." She ate it quickly, savoring the taste and licking her fingers as she scooted down onto the bed beside Ellie. "He gives out candy? I had no idea. He's never offered me any."

"I'll share."

Sophie leaned in to get closer. "What? What did you say?"

Ellie raised her voice. "I said, 'I'll share.'"

Sophie patted her on the arm. "Yes, you are a dear."

"No, I said 'I'll share,' not 'I'm a dear.'"

"Ah . . . I knew that didn't make much sense. You realize I'm getting very hard of hearing."

Ellie nodded. "It's okay, Sophie. We'll all talk louder."

Sophie took Ellie's hand, something she always did when she wanted to make a point. "You know one of these days my hearing will be completely gone. When that happens, you won't be able to talk to me anymore."

Ellie felt all the blood drain from her face, and for a few seconds she had to grab hold of the bed to stop it from spinning. "What do you mean?"

"Just what I said, darling. I'm losing my hearing because you don't really need me anymore. I'm still here, only because you're clinging to the past."

Ellie felt sick. "No. That's not true. I love you, Sophie. I'll always need you."

"I love you, too, but I'm not your mother. I can't ever take her place. When I'm gone, it will be alright. You'll see. I'll still be with you, but we just won't talk anymore. You'll feel my love and strength and remember what we've shared, but that will be all. That's how memories are supposed to be."

Ellie handed Sophie another piece of chocolate in a subconscious need to appease the horror of what she was saying.

"No, Sophie. Your ears are fine. You'll see. I'm full of this chocolate now. Would you like to have the rest?"

Sophie sighed. "I can't eat your food for you, Ellie. It's your candy. It's your life. Take charge. It's time."

Ellie shoved the rest of the Hershey into her mouth at one time in a desperate attempt to assuage Sophie's demands. "I'm eating it. See. I took charge. You don't need to leave. You don't need to go anywhere."

Sophie patted Ellie's cheek. "Don't worry, Ellie. I'm still here . . . at least for a while."

Cinnamon bounced onto the bed and then leaned against the wall. "What's going on? I heard a lot of angry voices."

Chocolate was dribbling from the corner of Ellie's mouth as she began to cry. "Sophie's leaving us. She said she won't come back."

"There's chocolate on your chin," Cin said, then got a tissue and wiped Ellie's face.

"I don't care about the chocolate on my face. I care about Sophie. Talk to her. Make her stay. You have to make her stay!"

Cin tossed the tissue in the trash and then folded her arms across her chest. "I'm not the one in charge of us, Ellie. That's you."

Ellie screamed. "Stop saying that. I don't believe you. I'm not in charge of anything."

Wyatt slid into the conversation so smoothly Ellie didn't even know he'd come in. "It's obvious you're not in charge of anything or we wouldn't be who we are."

Ellie flinched as if she'd been slapped. Wyatt never criticized her. "I can't believe you said that. Stop being mean."

Wyatt put his arms around her, holding her so tight against him that she could feel their hearts beating as one. "I'm not mean. I'm honest. When you learn to be in charge of your life, you won't need us anymore."

Ellie erupted, spewing huge, hiccupping sobs that felt like knives being poked into her chest. "If I don't have any of you, I'll have no one. I don't want to be alone. I'm afraid of being alone."

Wyatt sighed. "But Daddy's gone now, Ellie. I killed him so he could never hurt you again. There's nothing to be afraid of anymore."

Ellie rolled over onto the bed and turned her face to the wall. All three of them began talking to her at once, but she didn't want to listen. She pulled the pillow over her head and shut her eyes. Just when she thought life couldn't get any worse, it handed her a mutiny. "I hate you, God. I hate you."

At the other end of the building, Luther Dunn suddenly reeled as if he'd been shot and fell out of his chair onto the floor.

Aaron tossed a new stash of Hershey bars in his desk drawer for when Ellie Wayne's therapy time rolled around. After his first success with the candy, he didn't want to be caught short. It was just in time as Charlie knocked and then let Ellie in.

Aaron knew within seconds it wasn't Ellie, and from Wyatt's attitude, Aaron figured Ellie probably wasn't going to show. Still, he thought he'd try speaking to her in the hope that she'd hear him and come forward.

"Good morning, Ellie. I hope you slept well last night."

Wyatt strode into the office and slid into the seat like a typical teenage boy, his legs sprawled, his shoulders slumped.

"I'm Wyatt. No, Ellie didn't sleep well. She's pretty mad at all of us."

"Really? What happened?"

"She's still struggling with the fact that we're not real. She sees us just like you see her and is afraid to be alone."

Aaron was fascinated by how adeptly Ellie's brain had found a way to cope with unbearable trauma. Knowing there were other personalities was one thing, but he hadn't been aware that Ellie physically saw them. "So who told her you weren't real?"

Wyatt shrugged. "I think it was Cinnamon who told her first, but it was what's happening to Sophie that freaked Ellie out."

"What's happening to Sophie?"

"She's losing her hearing, right?"

"Yes, I've noticed, but—"

"Sophie claims she's losing her hearing because Ellie doesn't really need her anymore." Wyatt shoved his hand through his hair and then doubled up his fists. "She got so mad. She freaked. She's never been that mad at us before. It was hard to see."

"I'm so sorry, especially for you. You two have been together almost from the start."

Tears welled, but Wyatt blinked them away. "We know you're doing your best to integrate all of us, but I have to tell you there's nothing you can say that will make it happen. Either we talk her into accepting it, or she's lost."

Aaron didn't know how to respond to a statement like that. It felt weird, having an alter talk treatment with him as if they were peers. He scrambled to remember some of the things Ellie had said to him that might sway Wyatt. He needed for all of them to trust him, not just Ellie, but Sophie decided to put her two cents in as well.

"Dr. Tyler, it's me, Sophie. Wyatt's right, you know. He's always right about Ellie, whether we like it or not. Maybe when the first of us leaves, it will convince her we're right, that she can exist without us."

Aaron found this fascinating—an alter being willing to cease existence. Everything he'd read about this indicated the opposite—that they often took on a personality they didn't want to give up. There were even a few documented cases where the original person completely disappeared and the alter took over and lived out the rest of the life.

So why was this case different? What made all three of these alters willing to "die" to make Ellie well? Was it something innate within Ellie that had caused her to create alters with empathetic personalities, or was there another reason—something he didn't understand?

"What's the scoop on this guy who wants to talk to Ellie?"

Aaron blinked. "Uh . . . Cinnamon, is that you?"

"One and the same. I told Ellie about the guy but she didn't seem interested. What's he in here for?"

"I can't comment upon that. Doctor-patient privilege, you know."

"Then I'm going to tell Ellie to stay away," Wyatt said. "For all we know, he could be some crazy killer. She doesn't need any more grief."

Aaron was torn. He was curious as to how Ellie would react if she knew the basis for Luther's delusion, but he couldn't recommend them meeting on the chance it might do her some good. He wasn't in the business of playing with people's lives just to see what might happen.

"I can tell you he wasn't admitted for any crimes, but other than that—" He shrugged.

"Did Ellie tell you about the ghost baby?" Sophie asked.

He nodded.

Sophie started to cry. "We don't know how to help her with that, and it's the one thing I fear might push her over the edge. She's been hearing it cry for weeks now. I don't want her to go so far away that she can never come back. We've all worked so hard to try and help, but we don't understand the baby or where it came from."

Aaron was surprised. "You don't think it had anything to do with the abortion?"

"No," Wyatt said. "And if you'd known how bad Ellie hated Daddy, you wouldn't even ask that. That pregnancy was like a plague to her. If she hadn't been able to get the abortion, she would have killed herself before she would let it grow."

Cinnamon interrupted. "If you all remember, she *did* try to kill herself, and it was only by the grace of God that I was with her when she bought the sleeping pills and still with her when she tried to take them. I flushed them all down the toilet. And that was *after* the abortion. She was freaking out because she thought the baby was haunting her and she couldn't take it."

Wyatt nodded. "That's when Sophie and I found out about the abortion. I'd thought about killing Daddy a lot of times but never did it. That was the last straw."

"Do any of you have an idea as to why she might be hearing a baby cry? Is there anything in her past that it might be connected to?"

Cinnamon threw out an observation that startled Aaron and almost made sense. "What if Ellie isn't 'hearing' the cries, but is remembering them instead? What if the baby she hears crying is her?"

Chapter Twenty-Three

The therapy session ended later with the arrival of Cinnamon's favorite aide, Charlie. Dr. Tyler sent her off with a Hershey bar for Ellie.

"So how did it go today?" Charlie asked, as he walked Ellie back to her room.

"Ellie wouldn't come," Cinnamon said. "She's mad at all of us right now."

Charlie was used to the oddities of the patients, but this one was fascinating to him. "Sorry to hear that but I'm sure she'll get over it."

"Hey Charlie, what's the deal with that great big guy who was talking to me in the common room today?"

"You mean Luther?"

"I didn't know his name."

"Luther Dunn. He's been here for several years."

"Why is he here?"

"I don't know the medical term for what's wrong with him, but he's delusional and don't tell anyone I said so. We're not supposed to discuss patients with other patients, but Luther is different. Everyone in here knows about Luther."

"Except me. So what's his deal?"

Charlie grinned. "He thinks he's God."

Cinnamon stumbled. If Charlie hadn't been holding onto her arm, she would have fallen flat on her face.

"Easy there," Charlie said, and stopped at her room. "We're here. They'll probably be serving lunch within the hour. Beef and noodles and I think chocolate cake, one of their better menu choices."

"Okay, thanks," Cin said, and darted into the room and shut the door. "Guys. Come here quick. I have something to tell you."

"What is it? Is it about Ellie?" Wyatt asked.

"Just a minute," Cin yelled. "Sophie."

"My goodness, were you calling me?"

"Yes."

"Sorry, I had no idea. What's happening?"

Cin moved closer then lowered her voice. "You two need to hear this. This Luther Dunn, the man who wants to talk to Ellie—"

"What about him?" Wyatt asked.

"He thinks he's God."

"What the hell?"

Sophie frowned. "Wyatt. I won't have cursing."

"Sorry, but I don't get it. So he thinks he's God. What about it?"

Cin rolled her eyes. "You pay absolutely no attention to anything I tell you, do you, Wyatt?"

Wyatt glared. "I'm listening now."

"Then hear this. You know Ellie says she won't pray to God anymore because he never listened to her prayers, right?"

Sophie and Wyatt nodded.

"So guess what the last thing this Luther guy told me to tell Ellie?"

Wyatt threw up his hands. "I give up."

"Remember, he never told me his name, or who he thought he was. He just said for me to tell Ellie that he was listening."

Sophie gasped.

Wyatt looked stunned. "Are you serious?"

Cin nodded. "So my question to you guys is this—do we tell Ellie? Would this help or do you think she would believe him and make everything worse?"

"I don't know. I need to think about this," Wyatt said.

"Don't take too long because Ellie may decide to see him for herself this afternoon purely out of curiosity."

"See who?" Ellie asked.

"Oh. Hi. There you are." Cin handed Ellie the Hershey bar. "Dr. Tyler sent this to you. Said for you to come back and see him next visit."

"Thank you," Ellie said, and started to open it when Sophie stopped her. "You'll ruin your lunch. Save it for after."

"Oh. Right." Ellie looked at it wistfully, laid it on her table then moved to the window.

"It looks so pretty outside. I hate being locked up like this. Remember when we used to walk to the pharmacy whenever we wanted? It's so weird not being able to go where you want to."

Wyatt slipped up beside her. "We're stuck in here because of what I did, remember? Are you mad at me?"

"No, Wyatt. Never. You saved us. I'd rather be in here for the rest of my life than living free under the same roof with Daddy." Ellie's focus shifted instantly from wanting out of the hospital to grabbing her hair by the handfuls and pulling it in frustration. "My head hurts. I don't feel so sorry for that ghost baby anymore. I just wish it would shut the hell up."

Cin laughed. "Way to go, Ellie. I like to see some fire back in your soul."

"But without the cursing, of course," Sophie said.

Cin rolled her eyes and sat down on the bed. "Whatever. I am so bored. No wonder people are crazy in this place. There's nothing to do. I suppose they want us to get well, but sticking us off in these stupid lizard-green rooms with no televisions or books and leading us around like we're in kindergarten seems counterproductive to me."

"If you paid more attention to where we are you'd know some of the patients in here aren't capable of putting food in their own mouths. These safeguards are here for everyone's protection."

Cin glared at Wyatt. "Thank you, Dr. Wyatt, for the health lesson."

Before any more barbs could be slung, the door to Ellie's room opened and an aide came in with her lunch. "Enjoy, Ellie. I'll be back later to pick up the tray."

Wyatt headed for the table. "Finally. Lunchtime."

"Save some for Ellie," Sophie said. "You eat far more than your share and you know it."

Cin laughed. "You're guys are nuts. It all goes to the same place no matter who's chewing."

Ellie stared at the food tray. She could still hear Cinnamon's laugh and Wyatt arguing with Sophie, but there was a moment of clarity that shook her to the core. She could hear them, but they were no longer visible. On the verge of panic, she suddenly heard Wyatt whisper.

"Breathe, Ellie. Everything is as it should be."

The heat of the sun coming through the window was warm on her back as she sat down, picked up her fork and began to eat.

Luther Dunn ate food to fuel his body, unaware of taste or texture. If there was something left on his tray when he was finished, it had nothing to do with like or dislike. It was more likely from having been distracted. The voices he lived with were so loud and insistent that he didn't bother to set them aside for any length of time.

Today when they brought his lunch tray was no different from any other until he sat down to eat. As he did, he felt a moment of quiet so startling he looked up at the aide and smiled.

She was rattled enough by the interaction that she stumbled, then hurried off to tell what he'd done.

Unusual things were happening with Luther Dunn and no one could put their finger on what had triggered it, only that it had begun after Ellie Wayne's admission.

Dr. Ferris was notified that Luther had made eye contact with an aide and actually smiled at her. At that point she abandoned her own lunch in the hopes that he'd still be open to communication. When she got to his room, she knocked a couple of times before entering.

"Hello Luther, I see I'm barging in on your meal. I just had a quick question for you."

Luther didn't respond as he picked up a piece of bread and took a bite.

Sensing he wasn't thrilled by her presence, Moira stayed in the doorway instead of walking into the room. "You never make special requests of any kind and it occurred to me that you might be in need of something and just hesitant to ask. Is there anything I can do for you?"

Luther reached for the glass of iced tea on his tray and took a drink. Just when Moira thought she'd made another wasted trip, he stood up.

"I need colored markers that will mark on glass."

Moira stifled the urge to squeal. "Markers that will mark on glass? Right. I'll go check on that right now. I'll be back. Soon. Okay?"

Luther walked over to the window and sat down in the sun, but Moira was already gone.

When free time in the common room came around, Luther was one of the first to arrive. He headed straight to the wall of windows on the west side of the room where the sun came through onto the floor. Each window consisted of sixteen small panes of glass set into an iron framework, not unlike quilt squares set into a quilt, and extended from the windowsills up, all the way to the ceiling. The frames were made so that no matter how many glass panes were broken, no one would have been able to escape. Decorative iron bars, but iron bars, just the same.

Luther laid his sack of markers on the windowsill, took out a roll of toilet paper and began to clean the glass.

"What's he doing?" Moira asked.

The nurse standing next to her shrugged. "Looks like Luther does windows. All these years we've been missing out."

Aaron Tyler walked up. "Hey, Moira, I got your call. What's up?"

Moira pointed.

"Ah. The elusive Luther is in the room. Washing windows?"

"I don't think so," Moira said. "Earlier he asked for colored markers that would mark on glass."

"Interesting, I guess we'll—" Aaron jerked as if he'd been slapped. "Colors on glass?"

"What are you talking about?" Moira asked.

Once again, Aaron's reality was being altered in a way he didn't understand. "It can't be."

Moira grabbed Aaron's arm. "Can't be what? For God's sake, Aaron. Stop being so mysterious."

"Give me a couple of minutes to check something out. I'll be right back."

He hurried back to his office and began searching for his notes from his last session with Ellie, then sat down to read, scanning through the text to where she'd talked about church.

". . . sitting where the sun comes through the Jesus window . . . spills colors onto my chest and into my lap . . . closer to God."

"Damn."

He looked up, his gaze falling on his three framed degrees hanging on the wall, then to an award he'd won a few years back for a paper he'd had published on the study of paranoia in children under the age of eighteen. There wasn't one single thing in all of the education and experience he had that would explain what was happening here. And yet it was happening.

He headed back to the common room, curious to know if Ellie would show up.

Charlie opened Ellie's door. "Who's up for some television time?"

"Me," Cin said, and swung her legs off the bed and finger-combed her hair.

"Me too," Wyatt said. He intended to check out this man who thought he was God.

Charlie grinned. "The more the merrier. What about Ellie?"

Wyatt paused to listen then shrugged. "Nope. Don't think she's coming."

"I hope that old woman who calls me Charlotte doesn't come today," Cin said. "She makes me sad."

"She's easily distracted. Just walk away from her," Charlie said.

"Yeah, okay."

They turned a corner and came face to face with Aaron. "Hey Dr. Tyler, how's it going?"

Ah, Cinnamon's in the house today. Damn.

"Just fine, Cinnamon. Ellie not coming today?"

"I guess not, but Wyatt's here."

"So here we are," Charlie said, and opened the door. Cinnamon walked in with Dr. Tyler as if they were on a date, her hand through the crook of his arm and a smile on her face.

Moira saw them come in and thought Aaron had gone to get her. She started to speak when Aaron shook his head and then looked away. Confused, she watched him walk with her to the television, talk to her briefly, then leave her there on her own.

"What's going on?" Moira asked. "Why did you bring her here?"

Aaron shook his head. "I didn't. I went to my office to check something. I just ran into her in the hall."

Moira pointed. "Look at Luther. What do you suppose he's doing?"

Aaron sighed then shoved his hands in his pockets. "If I was to make a guess, I'd say he is making a stained-glass window."

Moira's eyes narrowed as she looked again. Luther had just begun using the markers and was making short jerky strokes at the corner of one glass.

"I don't see it."

But as she continued to watch, it began to appear that Aaron was right. Luther was methodical in his intent, filling in bright primary colors in geometric shapes and then outlining them with a black marker to tie them together. It was then she began to see his intent. None of the other patients showed any interest in what he was doing, not even Ellie Wayne. She was still at a loss.

"So Ellie is here and Luther isn't even paying any attention to her."

"No. That's not Ellie, that's Cinnamon and Wyatt. Wyatt is checking Luther out and Cinnamon is checking out the soaps."

"Oh. I keep forgetting about that. Still, Luther would have no way of knowing."

"He knew the other time," Aaron reminded her. "As for the stained-glass window he's making, in one of Ellie's sessions with me she told me that when she went to church, she always sat in the pew where the sun came through the Jesus window, which by the way was a stained-glass window depicting the Bible verse "suffer the little children to come unto me." She sat there so that the sunlight made it appear that the colors were spilling into her lap. She thought God could hear her better there."

Moira grabbed Aaron by the arm and dragged him out into the hall so they wouldn't be overheard. She wanted to shake him.

"That doesn't make sense. I know what you're thinking and you know how crazy it sounds. We're doctors, and you're starting to think like a patient. I'm not going to buy into Luther being God any more than thinking he's in any way connected to God, and I'm not about to believe he 'knows' Ellie Wayne because he's been listening to her prayers."

"There's more. Ellie doesn't talk to God anymore. She's mad at Him."

Moira backed Aaron against the wall, jabbing her finger into his chest to punctuate every word. "I know damn good and well you do not believe Luther Dunn is God."

"Of course not."

"Then where are you going with all this?"

Aaron pushed her hand away. "That maybe God moves in mysterious ways?"

He went back inside, leaving Moira to stew in her own interpretations. He wasn't about to admit how staggered he was by what was unfolding. He didn't understand it, but he couldn't ignore what he was witnessing either.

He moved to where Ellie was sitting, but could tell by the way she was glued to the television program that it was Cinnamon who was present, so he went to the windows where Luther was working, pulled up a chair and sat down to watch.

The ends of Luther's fingers were stained in a mishmash of colors. The intensity with which he was working was almost manic—coloring windowpane after windowpane in perfect detail, aligning colors that didn't clash within random geometric shapes. Then all of a sudden he stopped. It took Aaron a few moments to figure out that the markers had all run dry.

Luther gathered them up, dropped them into the sack and then turned around.

Moira was standing at the back of the room. When she took a step forward, her movement caught Luther's eye. He went straight to her and handed her the sack.

"That's very beautiful. Are you through?" she asked.

"No. I need more."

"Oh . . . I didn't—" Then she took a deep breath and started over. "I'll have them here tomorrow."

"A lot of them?"

Moira smiled. "Yes, Luther, a lot of them."

"Tomorrow."

"Yes, tomorrow."

He started to walk past her when she reached out and stopped him. "Wait. I thought you wanted to speak to Ellie today."

The moment the question left her mouth, she knew it had been a mistake. The look in his eyes was somewhere between pained and unflinchingly patient, as a parent would have been with a recalcitrant child.

"She isn't here," he said softly, and walked away.

Moira's fingers curled into fists of frustration as she strode across the room to where Ellie Wayne was sitting. "Hi, Ellie, I'm Dr. Ferris."

Cinnamon answered without taking her eyes from the screen.

"Ellie's not here."

"But you—"

Cinnamon turned. "There's no one here today but me and Wyatt. Do you want me to give Ellie a message?"

Moira was too rattled to think. "No, no message." She saw Aaron watching her. It made her angry all over again.

It took three days, another twenty-five packs of markers, and a very tall ladder for Luther to finish the window, but when it was finished even the most disturbed patients had taken notice.

Twelve feet high from windowsill to ceiling, and more than eight feet wide with a perfect cross left uncolored in the center. It was, in a sense, an artistic masterpiece. But for Luther, it was merely a means to an end.

Aaron had scheduled therapy sessions around this time to watch the drama unfolding. Moira kept popping in and out without speaking to Aaron, but when she found out it was finished, she was curious as to what came next. Like Aaron, she'd come to the common room on the last day to watch.

Luther came down off the ladder, sacked up the markers, and then cleared everything away from the window. Outside, the day was brutally hot, although it was comfortable inside.

Luther turned around to face the window.

Aaron moved a few steps to the right, trying to get a glimpse of Luther's face. "What's he doing now?"

Moira frowned. "The usual. Standing at the window with his eyes closed."

"His eyes are closed? He spends four days painting and then steps back to look at it and closes his eyes?"

She shrugged. "It's what he does."

A minute passed, and then another and another and Moira was about to go back to her office when all of a sudden the sun's rays scored a direct hit on the window and turned it into something holy.

The clear glass panes of the cross lit up as if someone had struck a match to them. The surrounding colors brightened as they bled onto the floor. Luther lifted his arms toward the stunning beauty of what he'd made. He looked like he was glowing.

"Holy Mother of God," Aaron whispered.

Moira's vision suddenly blurred with unshed tears.

There was an audible gasp from attendants and patients alike. An old woman started weeping. A man who played checkers with himself every day put his head down on the table and hid his face.

Cinnamon was sitting in front of the television when it happened. She looked up. Her eyes widened, her lips parted with a silent "aahh" then she turned off the television and stood up.

"Ellie."

Ellie had already made it plainly clear that she wasn't going to the common room to see some stranger just because he wanted her to. "I'm busy."

The timbre of Cinnamon's voice rose perceptibly. "Ellie. Please. You've got to see this."

"No."

Cinnamon doubled up her fists. "Ellie."

Ellie jumped then slapped her hand over Cinnamon's mouth. "Stop screaming. People are staring."

"Let them look," Cinnamon whispered, then made her turn around. "Look honey. Look at that."

Ellie saw the window first, then the cross, then the giant man with long white hair glowing beneath it. He was a magnet and her feet were already moving before she realized she'd taken a step.

Excited that Ellie had surfaced to witness this, Aaron grabbed Moira's arm.

Still pissed at him, Moira started to pull away. Instead of stepping backward, she moved closer, but not of her own volition. What the hell had Luther done, reversed the field of negativity? She didn't want to be standing under Aaron's armpit, but she was.

A trio of nurses had come out of the office to stand spellbound at the sight and Charlie walked up behind Aaron with tears on his face. "Dr. Tyler, what's happening?"

"I don't know."

No one knew what would happen next, least of all Ellie. She just kept moving toward the man and the colors coming through the window. "Who—"

Still silhouetted against the light, Luther slowly turned to face her. His immense size and the glow around him made her forget what she was going to say. Startled, she quickly covered her face as if she'd looked upon something she shouldn't have seen.

"Hello, Ellie. I've been waiting for you."

The voice knocked at her soul. She had no other option but to let it in.

"Do you like the window? I made it just for you."

Hearing the voice elicited the same kind of fear she used to have knowing the monster was coming, only this time it wasn't fear for herself. It was a fear of discovery she wasn't ready to face. She moaned beneath her breath.

"Look at it, Ellie. Open your eyes. Face your fears."

She wanted to—tried to—meant to—yet couldn't bring herself to move—never heard him leave.

It was the sudden sense of being alone that made her look up. She was standing in the light, bathed in a kaleidoscope of colors with her fists clasped against her belly. She lifted her face to the light. "God, was that You?"

No one answered. It was disappointing, although she didn't really expect it. He didn't answer her prayers, so it stood to reason He wouldn't be answering her questions either.

"The window is beautiful. Thank you for making it for me, but just so you know, I'm still really mad at you. I guess you know Wyatt killed Daddy. I'm sure you also know I'm not sorry he's dead."

Ellie looked up at the window again, unaware there were tears on her face. "I'm not going to pray. Thank you again for the window."

When Ellie turned, she realized everyone was staring. She heard Wyatt whisper in her ear. "Keep your chin up and start walking."

"Did you see him?" Ellie asked.

"Yes."

"Who do you think it was?"

"I don't know, Ellie, just walk."

So she did, all the way to where Charlie was standing.

"Ellie, is that you?"

Ellie nodded. "Yes, Charlie. It's me. I'm ready to go back to my room."

Chapter Twenty-Four

Charlie didn't say a word to her all the way back, for which Ellie was grateful. When she got to her room, she closed the door behind her then collapsed on the bed, too stunned to talk. It didn't stop everyone else from talking to her at once.

Cinnamon was bugging her. "What did he say to you? Did he tell you who he was?"

Wyatt slipped into protective mode. "Leave her alone. Can't you see she needs to be left alone."

Sophie sat down on the bed beside Ellie. "Atone? Who needs to atone?"

And beneath the conversation, the baby kept crying in a plaintive and weak little wail.

"Stop talking. All of you, stop talking." Ellie pulled the pillow over her head and rolled over onto her side.

Sophie muttered an apology and politely popped off.

Cin lay down beside her. "Poor Ellie. We're sorry. We only want what's best for you."

Ellie threw the pillow across the room and sat up, her face flushed with anger. "Best for me? Exactly what would that be?"

Cin got back in Ellie's face, unwilling to let her pout herself back into a funk. "You know exactly what that is and don't pretend you don't."

Ellie slapped the mattress. "Oh. Right. Pretend none of you exist."

"No! Stop pretending we do."

"Shut up," Ellie muttered, then rolled off the bed and strode to the window, desperate to change the subject. "Look Wyatt, it's clouding up. It will probably rain before morning."

"Yes, I see. Remember when we were little how we used to sneak out of the house during a summer rain and run down to the creek to play? How did that rhyme go that we made up?"

Ellie leaned her head against the window and closed her eyes. "Water on my feet. Water on my head. Water, water everywhere except in Wyatt's bed."

Wyatt smiled. "Yeah, that was it. When you get out of here, do me a favor, will you?"

"Yes, always."

"Remember to laugh."

As soon as Ellie Wayne left the common room, everyone went back to their usual tasks. By the time their shifts were over, most of them had come up with a logical explanation for what they'd witnessed. They'd already seen too many weird things working in a psych hospital. Colored glass and a trick of the light were surely nothing remarkable.

Aaron wanted to talk to Ellie, but when he got to her room, he found her lying on the bed with her back to the door. Deciding he would bring up the subject tomorrow in therapy, he left her to her nap.

Ellie heard him come in, but she no more wanted to talk to him than she'd wanted to talk to anyone else. She couldn't get the man's voice out of her head or the message that had come with it.

Open your eyes. Face your fears.

Moira was determined to talk to Luther but felt intimidated by what she'd seen. She found a male nurse and then went to Luther's room.

But he wasn't sitting in his usual seat at the window. Instead, he was lying in bed, laid out with his hands folded across his chest and his eyes closed. It was so like a viewing at a funeral home that it gave her a start. She went straight to his bedside to see if he was ill.

"Luther, it's Dr. Ferris. Are you alright? Do you hurt anywhere?"

Luther opened his eyes. "Why must you always talk?"

A bit taken aback, it took Moira a few moments to respond. "I guess because that's my job. I ask questions that will help my patients."

"Sometimes you need to be still and listen."

"Is that what you're doing . . . listening?"

He closed his eyes. "Yes."

"What are you listening to?"

"Prayers. I'm listening to prayers."

"Because you're God?"

"Because I hear them."

Moira opened her mouth.

Luther opened his eyes. His lips weren't moving, but she heard his rebuke.

She blinked and walked out of the room.

Late that night, after she'd gone home, done a load of laundry and watched a couple of shows she'd recorded on her DVR, she finally crawled into bed. The day had been hot and the cool sheets were a welcome relief. She fluffed up her pillow, stretched out and finally closed her eyes.

Within seconds, she heard a voice.

Be still and know that I am God.

Aaron spent the evening reviewing the earliest videos from Ellie's case and found one he'd missed earlier. He was surprised to see that it had nothing to do with the molestations. It was a simple home movie of Ellie and her mother, taken at different times when Ellie was just a baby in her mother's arms. Since all of her trauma revolved around her father and what she'd first believed was abandonment from her mother, it occurred to Aaron that it might be helpful for her to see her mother in a different light. He put the tape in his briefcase, intending to use it during their next therapy session, ordered Chinese takeout for dinner, and drank a half bottle of wine while waiting for it to be delivered.

Hours later, he lay in his bed wide-eyed and unable to sleep. He'd seen it, but still didn't understand how a mentally ill patient, colored markers, and a setting sun had turned a wall of windows into a church. Even more disturbing was why it felt like he had witnessed a miracle.

It began to rain just after midnight, peppering Ellie's window with the wind-driven drops. When a particularly bright bolt of lightning struck close to the hospital, it lit up her room.

She woke abruptly. "Wyatt?"

"I'm right here," he said. "Go back to sleep."

Ellie closed her eyes. "Thank you, Wyatt."

"For what?"

"For always taking care of me."

"You're welcome."

"I love you, Wyatt."

"I love you, too, Ellie, but one of these days you're going to have to figure out how to take care of yourself."

"Not tonight."

"No, Ellie, not tonight."

It was still raining when Ellie woke. She had barely finished dressing when a message from Dr. Tyler arrived with her breakfast tray.

Cin snitched a piece of bacon from the plate and then picked up a folded piece of paper and opened it.

"Hey Ellie, the shrink sent you a message."

Ellie was opening a salt packet to sprinkle on her eggs and eyeing the last piece of bacon, hoping she got it eaten before Wyatt showed up. Back home Doris had always fixed plenty of food and set separate places at the table, but in here they all had to share. Sometimes it left Ellie hungry.

"*Shrink* is such a rude word," Sophie said. "I'd prefer you chose another."

Cin took a big bite of the bacon and licked her fingers. "I'll keep that in mind."

"Read it to me," Ellie said.

"Ellie, I have a special treat for you during therapy this morning. Be sure to come. I don't want you to miss it."

The excitement of a treat had her in a good mood as she finished her food. When Charlie came to get her, she was ready and waiting.

"Looking good, Miss Ellie," Charlie said.

"Cin did my hair."

Charlie grinned. He got along great with all of her alters except Wyatt. Wyatt didn't much like anybody, but Charlie didn't take it personally. He knew Wyatt was the one who'd offed the father and felt a measure of admiration and understanding. A couple of minutes later, they reached Aaron's office.

"So here you go. Have a good session and I'll be back to get you when you call."

"Thank you," she said.

Charlie knocked then opened the door for her to go in.

Aaron was waiting. When Ellie entered, he smiled. "Good morning, Ellie. That thunderstorm we had last night was a noisy one, wasn't it? I hope it didn't disturb your rest."

"Not much."

"Did you get my message about a treat?"

Ellie nodded. "Is it chocolate?"

He grinned. "I have some and you're welcome to it, but that's not the surprise. I was going through some of your information last night and found something I bet you haven't seen in a long time. Why don't you have a seat on the sofa while I start the VCR."

Ellie moved past the chair she usually sat in and chose a cushion next to the arm. Dr. Tyler dropped a Hershey bar in her lap and then sat at the other end and picked up the remote.

"Ready?"

Ellie unwrapped the candy, broke off a square and put it in her mouth, then nodded.

Aaron hit *Play*. Within seconds, the images appeared on the screen.

Ellie gasped. "That's Momma. Look Dr. Tyler. It's Momma."

"Yes and that tiny baby in her arms is you."

Ellie felt like she was dreaming. Momma was young and smiling, and she'd never seen her look that happy. "I've never seen this."

"Then I'm glad I thought to show it to you."

Unconsciously, Ellie scooted to the edge of the seat.

On the screen, Fern waved at the camera and tilted the swaddled baby in her arms so that her face could be seen peeking out from the blanket. She jiggled the baby up and down a couple of times and then leaned down and kissed her little cheek.

"Momma," Ellie whispered, unaware that she'd spoken aloud.

The next image showed Fern pushing Ellie in a baby buggy. The camera panned down into the buggy for a bird's-eye view.

"Look at you smile," Aaron said.

"I look happy. I didn't know I was ever happy there."

Becoming emotionally involved in a patient's life was a no-no in Aaron's world, but it was hard to keep a clinical distance from a patient like Ellie who'd suffered so many years of tragedy and abuse. "I'm very sorry, Ellie."

She sat through the rest of the video without a comment, but when it was suddenly over, she groaned out loud. "Oh no . . . is that all of it?"

"Sorry, yes. So tell me, what did you like best?"

"That Daddy wasn't in any of it."

"Having seen it, how do you feel about your mother now?"

"She looked happy. I don't remember her ever looking like that. And she seemed really proud of me."

"How do you remember her?"

"Nervous. On the defensive. Always praying."

"Praying?"

"Yes. Momma prayed about everything. If there was a problem,

Momma prayed to God to fix it. If she got sick, she prayed to God to make her well."

"And how did that make you feel?"

Ellie frowned. She'd never thought about her Mother's predilection for prayer like that before.

"I'm not sure, but maybe that she never took the initiative and tried to solve her own problems. She just prayed and expected God to do it for her."

Aaron nodded. "So, do you think you're like your mother?"

"I have her blonde hair and blue eyes, but I don't look like her. I don't really look much like either of them."

"I don't mean physically, I mean emotionally. When bad things happen to you, how do you deal with them?"

Ellie's eyes narrowed suspiciously. This was beginning to feel uncomfortable, but she didn't know why. "What do you mean?"

"Okay, let me ask this another way. Do you remember the first time you knew what your father was doing to you wasn't right?"

Her fingers curled into fists. "Maybe after I started school. I'm not sure."

"I'm not talking about an exact date. I mean was there ever a time when you thought about telling someone, like maybe a teacher, or a friend?"

"I never had a friend. I had Wyatt."

"You never had someone come home with you after school?"

"No. Daddy said no."

"What about you going to someone else's home to play?"

"No. I never did that, either."

"Was there ever a teacher you were close to that—"

"No."

The fact that Ellie didn't let him finish the question was telling, as was the tone of her voice. She was getting uncomfortable with the questions. "But you eventually told your mother?"

"By accident."

"I see. And how did she react?"

Ellie folded her arms across her chest. "She threw herself onto the floor and prayed. Then she went to the hardware store and got a lock and put it on the inside of my door so I could lock it to keep Daddy out."

"But she didn't tell anyone else either?"

Ellie began to rock back and forth. "No, she didn't tell."

"How did that make you feel?"

"Dirty. Bad. Had to keep it a secret."

"Did the lock work?"

"Only until after Momma died."

"Until after your father killed her?"

"I didn't know about that until the day Wyatt killed Daddy."

"Were you mad at your mother?"

Ellie started to cry.

Cin slid into the conversation so quickly Aaron didn't even know it was her until Ellie opened her mouth. "Ellie's through talking today. She wants to go back to her room."

"Oh. Well, could you just ask—"

Cin stood up. "Sorry, Doc. I could, but I'm not gonna. Would you call Charlie for me?"

Aaron sighed. He knew when he'd been bested. "Of course."

She sat back down on the arm of the sofa, idly swinging her foot as she finished off the chocolate Ellie hadn't eaten. "Hey Doc . . ."

"Yes?"

"Just so you know, Ellie got the message."

"What message is that?"

"That's she's reacting to problems like Fern did. Fern prayed to make them go away. Ellie thought us up to deal with her stuff instead of dealing with it herself."

"That's what she said to you?"

Cinnamon laughed out loud. "You almost forgot I'm Ellie, didn't you? Here's the deal. Wyatt exists because he's the one who always went with Garrett when he came to get her in the night. He would tell Ellie to stay in bed, or to hide her face, and so she did. Sophie came after her mother died. Ellie needed a mother and didn't have one, so she created a nanny. A nanny with a conscience who had no idea what was going on. She was Ellie's backup plan. If her father touched her again, she would tell Sophie and Sophie would tell everyone. Garrett would get arrested. End of story. Only Ellie was just a kid and once again she was outsmarted by the Devil. He knew how attached she was to Wyatt, so he showed her the movies he'd made of them together. Ellie was horrified. In her mind, if everyone found out about what Wyatt had been doing, he would be humiliated. To protect Wyatt, she went back to being Daddy Dearest's little love slave."

"Oh. God."

"And since you brought Him up, what's the deal with Luther Dunn? Does he really think he's God?"

Aaron was surprised. He didn't know she knew about that. "Does Ellie know this?"

"Not yet. Wyatt and Sophie and I haven't decided whether to tell her or not."

"I'd like to ask you not to tell. Falling into yet another illusory belief would be extremely harmful to her well-being."

Cinnamon licked chocolate from the ends of her fingers as she thought about what he'd said. "I'll tell the others, but I'm not promising anything."

"Why not?"

"Because we know her better than you do."

There was a knock at the door.

"That'll be my ride," Cinnamon said, and let herself out of the office with a wave and a wink, leaving one very surprised doctor behind.

Aaron took the old video out of the VCR and filed it with the others. "If I ever get all three of those alters back into Ellie Wayne, she's going to be one heck of a woman."

He thought nothing of the fact he was talking to himself just like most of his patients as he turned off his video equipment.

It wasn't until much later that he realized Cinnamon hadn't explained how she came into Ellie's life. He made a mental note to ask her some time, although he wasn't so sure he'd ever get an answer. When Cinnamon was on stage, she was definitely the one in charge.

That afternoon, Ellie didn't argue about going to the common room when free time rolled around. She didn't care who came with her and who stayed behind. All she knew was that she wanted to go see that window again.

The weather was still cloudy, which didn't bode well for a sunset revelation at Luther's window, but it didn't daunt her. Drawn by the colors and the cross, she pulled up a chair and sat down in front of it anyway, just as she used to do in the pew at church.

Luther was conspicuously absent. The old woman who called Ellie "Charlotte" was watching television and picking at a sore on her knee. The man who played checkers alone bounced from one side of the table to the other and accused himself of cheating. Nurses were calming crying jags. The young man who'd always wanted to play with Ellie's hair wasn't around, and Cinnamon told Ellie he'd been dismissed.

Aides came and went with patients.

Dr. Ferris sat in her office on a conference call with a colleague in New York City, and Dr. Tyler had slipped into the room to watch Ellie from a distance.

As for her, she was talking to God.

> *Just so You know, God, this isn't a prayer. I thought You should know where I am. It's a hospital for crazy people. My doctor is always asking me, 'how does that make you feel,' so now I'm asking You: How does that make You feel? I have prayed all my life and not one time did You answer. Do you see what happened? Do You feel sad for me? Do You feel bad that You didn't intervene?*

Ellie closed her eyes and took a slow, deep breath, making herself calm the rage within. She lived with so much hate on so many levels that sometimes it was hard to just breathe without screaming.

Outside, the wind was rising. She could hear the faint rumble of distant thunder. It was going to rain again, which meant no sunshine, but there was nothing she could do about it.

She thought about the video of her and Momma that she'd seen in Dr. Tyler's office. Knowing there had been a time in her life when all had been safe and normal gave her a new sense of herself. All along she'd imagined God had just given her to the Devil to do with as he pleased, but that no longer seemed the case. Once upon a time Momma had loved her and taken care of her just like any mother would do. Somewhere along the way Momma had fallen sway to the Devil, just like Ellie. It was a new thing to ponder—that Momma had been a victim, too.

The first raindrops splattered against the windowpanes like water on a hot griddle, hissing and popping as they danced along the surface before exploding in tiny bursts of steam.

Ellie opened her eyes. Rain ran down the outside of the window. Ellie thought about what she'd said to God—asking Him if He was sorry. It occurred to her that it had begun to rain right after she'd asked the question. She stared at the rain as hope began to rise within her. Was this truly her answer? Had God finally given her a sign?

The rain began to come down harder now, blurring vision to the outside world until Ellie felt as if she was looking through a veil of tears. She closed her eyes and began to rock back and forth with excitement. This was her answer. For the first time in her life, she believed this was a sign from God.

He was crying and the raindrops blasting against the windows were His tears.

Ellie clasped her hands against her belly as she continued to rock. The pores were opening in her skin, just like in church when the music of the choir used to fill her soul. She could hear God's sob in the rumble of the thunder, and when the wind would rise and wail, she heard it as despair. Ellie sat in witness, taking comfort in the knowledge that she was worth the storm of God's grief. In time, a measure of her anger began to subside. Her shoulders slumped. Her head nodded forward.

Then Wyatt whispered her name. "Ellie."

She jumped then straightened up in the chair. "What?"

"Momma loved you."

"I know. I saw it on the movie."

"We love you."

"I know that too. I've always known that."

"God loves you."

Ellie's voice was just above a whisper. "He's crying for me, Wyatt. Can you see? He's crying for me."

"It's time for you to love yourself."

A shudder rolled through her in such a wave that it made her shake. "I don't know if I can."

"Are you saying you know more than God?"

She was horrified that he would think that. "No. Never."

"If He cries for you, then you are allowed to cry for yourself."

Ellie let the notion settle. She would have to think about all she'd been given today. For now, it was enough to know that God had heard her.

Chapter Twenty-Five

Memphis—October

Autumn was coming to Memphis. There was a nip in the air and an internal rush to get summer projects finished and crops laid by. Animals had begun to grow their winter coats and the leaves were just starting to turn. The world was going on without Ellie, whether she liked it or not.

Her therapy sessions with Dr. Tyler were going nowhere. Every time he thought they'd taken a step forward, Ellie put herself two steps back. She was so unwilling to turn loose and trust herself that he was at his wit's end.

Cinnamon kept telling him the time was coming, and Wyatt subtly threatened him to stop pressuring her. Sophie's appearances were becoming less and less frequent. He didn't know if that meant she was getting ready to integrate with Ellie, or just tired of his prattle. He had never bonded with a patient as he had with Ellie Wayne. It wasn't healthy. It wasn't even wise. But it was too late for recriminations.

Meanwhile, Moira Ferris was back to square one with Luther Dunn. If it hadn't been for the constant presence of what was now referred to as Luther's window, she would have convinced herself that their brief moments of conversation had never happened. As for the times she thought she'd heard his voice in her head, she had chalked that up to the emotion of the moment and completely rejected it.

He had never come back to ask to see Ellie, and Ellie had not asked to talk to Luther, although she spent every moment of her free time sitting in the sunlight with a lapful of colors.

Excitement was at an all-time low at Mind and Body until the morning Ellie woke up and realized Sophie was missing.

It was just after seven-fifteen in the morning. Charlie and Walt were helping a nurse with a bedfast patient who had soiled his sheets during the night.

A visiting psychiatrist was doing rounds for another doctor who was having dental surgery, and one of the janitors was mopping up a stream of urine left behind from a patient who'd been walking the halls. There was nothing remarkable about the morning that would lead them to believe the turmoil that was to come. In fact, it was an uneventful day until a wail of complete despair suddenly sliced through the silence, followed by a long, ear-piercing shriek. It brought everyone within hearing distance out into the hallway trying to find the room and the source.

Then Ellie solved the problem by running out into the hall, screaming. "Sooophie! Sooophie!"

Charlie was the first to reach her, grabbing her by the shoulders. "What's wrong, Ellie?"

She slid to a stop and dug her fingers into his forearms in frantic desperation. "Sophie's gone. You've got to help me find her."

A pair of male nurses grabbed her by the arms and began physically restraining her, which only led to even more distress.

"Let me go. You don't understand. Sophie's lost. I've got to find her."

The nurses had heard it all before and weren't going to cater to a patient's hallucinations. "Grab her arm," one of them said.

At that point, Wyatt stepped in. "Turn her loose, damn it."

The men were taken unawares by the strength of her alter's reaction. Wyatt doubled up his fist as he pulled away, punched one nurse in the face, the other in the groin and took off running down the hall.

Aaron Tyler was just getting off the elevator and was on his way up to his office when he heard a woman screaming for Sophie. That had to be Ellie. He took off running in the direction of the screams.

Wyatt had gained some distance from his pursuers, and when he turned a corner that put him momentarily out of their sight, he darted into a janitor closet, then into the far corner and hid behind some mops and brooms.

Cinnamon arrived just as Wyatt was trying to catch his breath. "Well, that was smart. Now they're going to shoot Ellie full of drugs to keep her quiet."

Wyatt dropped his head. "Shit. I didn't think."

"You rarely do," she reminded him. "Don't worry. I'll get us out of this, but next time, talk to me first before you decide to take someone out by the balls."

Wyatt nodded. "Sorry, but what are we going to do about Sophie? She's gone."

"And we both know why," Cin said, as she stood up. "The issue comes in convincing Ellie. I'm going out now. Keep your mouth shut and let me do the talking."

"Right."

They'd come a long way from Wyatt's resentment of her arrival and Cinnamon was confident of her ability to keep everyone inside. She smoothed down the front of her shirt and pants, finger-combed her hair, and sauntered out of the janitor's closet as calmly as if she was taking a walk. At that moment, Charlie came around the corner.

Cinnamon waved. "Hey Charlie. No worries. I have everything under control. Help me find Dr. Tyler, okay?"

"Is it really you?" Charlie said, as he grabbed her by the arm.

She grinned and winked. "All five feet seven inches of me and my gorgeous red hair."

The two male nurses were right behind him, carrying restraints.

"It's cool," Charlie said. "Cinnamon's here. It's over."

"Like hell," one nurse muttered. "She hit me."

The other one was still holding his crotch.

Charlie grinned. "You're six foot two. Do you really want it to get around the hospital that a little female took you out?"

"Whatever, I'm putting her in restraints."

Cinnamon waggled a finger. "Let's don't. I promise I've got them all under control. We need to find Dr. Tyler. All of this happened because Sophie is gone."

Charlie immediately understood what that meant. "Aw heck, no wonder she freaked. Look guys, the restraints aren't necessary. I've got this," Charlie said, and took off down the hall holding Cinnamon's arm.

Aaron was out of breath and down to a walk as he, too, finally caught up.

"Hey Doc, we've been looking for you," Cin said. "Ellie has a problem. Do you have time to talk?"

Aaron was relieved to see Ellie had disappeared and the alter with the level head was now in charge.

"Of course. Bring her to my office, Charlie."

Cinnamon went along quietly, saving her bombshell for when they were behind closed doors.

Ellie's scream had been Luther's wake-up call. He sat up in bed, his heart hammering and the sound of her despair locked in his head. He got up and walked straight to the window. Sunrise had come and gone and the light of a new morning was softer than it would be later in the day. He pictured her face, and when he could feel her heartbeat, he closed his eyes.

Aaron didn't want to ruin the moment by setting up a video camera, so he turned on a tape recorder and settled in by throwing out his first question to Cinnamon. "What happened to Ellie this morning?"

"Sophie's gone."

Aaron blinked. "As in missing, or permanently gone?"

"As in not coming back ever," she said. "Sophie warned Ellie it would happen, but typical Ellie, she chose to ignore something she didn't want to face."

"Why do you think Sophie left?"

Cin crossed her legs and leaned back in the chair. "I know why she left. Ellie doesn't need her anymore now that Garrett's dead. The less Sophie was needed, the worse her hearing became. After your God guy painted that window, Ellie has pretty much abandoned all of us except when she's in her room. Then she wants to talk because she's so afraid of being alone."

"What do you think that window means to her?"

Cinnamon shrugged. "I don't know and I don't think Ellie does either. All she does when she sits down in front of it is talk to God, and I already told her she could talk to God anywhere. She didn't need a Jesus window to make it happen."

"So what's going to happen once Ellie comes back?"

"She's going to pitch a fit and then go into a state of depression for sure. You see, for Ellie, Sophie just died."

"Lord."

Cinnamon grinned. "Might be a good idea to clue Him in, too. Oh. Wait a sec . . . uh, wow . . . see you later, Doc."

Ellie sat up. "Sophie is gone."

Aaron blinked. What just happened? "Ellie?"

"Yes, it's me." Then she leaned forward and whispered. "Sophie is gone." Tears rolled down her face. "She left and never even said good-bye. Why would she do that?"

Aaron was impressed. Ellie had never moved Cinnamon aside and taken the forefront before. It was either a sign of how distraught she was, or that she was finally learning to take control of her own anger.

"Cinnamon said Sophie told you this would happen."

Ellie moaned and covered her face with her hands. "She's gone and I don't know how to get her back."

"But Ellie, do you really think you still need a nanny?"

Ellie kept sobbing, her shoulders shaking so hard her whole body was trembling. "No."

"Then why are you so distraught? This just means you're becoming an adult. One day you'll be on your own and you have to learn how to do that before you can leave here."

"I don't want to live alone. I'm afraid to be alone."

"Why?"

"I don't know how to be that way. I don't want to be that way."

"So one day you'll meet someone and get married."

Ellie shuddered then looked up. "That's not going to happen. I will never get married."

Aaron stifled a sigh. He didn't want to get into this, but they were here just the same. "With therapy you can—"

She leaned forward, pounding her fist on his desk—her eyes burning with hate. "You listen to me. I would never trust a man. I don't trust you. I don't trust Charlie, and you're both good to me. I will never have a child for someone else to destroy. I will die first. You don't talk to me about this ever again. Do you understand?"

Aaron felt chastised and ashamed in the way only his grandmother had ever made him feel. "Yes."

"Sophie is dead and I'm sad. And I'm mad. I don't need therapy today. I need to cry. Tell Charlie to come get me or I'm going on my own."

Aaron picked up the phone and quickly paged Charlie's number. "He's on his way."

Ellie covered her face. "The least she could have done was say good-bye."

"Ellie."

"What?"

"Lots of people die without getting to say good-bye to their loved ones."

She swiped the tears from her cheeks and looked up.

He had her attention. Now he needed to drive the point home. "Think about it. When people die in accidents, they don't know they're going to die, so there's no way for them to tell their loved ones good-bye. When people die on the operating table, they don't get that chance. When people drop dead of heart attacks or strokes, they don't get that chance. You're not the only person who's ever lost a loved one. You can grieve and get mad and blame God and whoever else you choose, but it doesn't change the fact that bad things happen and lives end."

All of a sudden Ellie stood up.

He thought she was about to run again, and then he realized she was listening to something. He assumed it was one of the alters. "Is Cinnamon talking to you?"

Ellie's eyes widened as she slowly shook her head.

"Then who do you hear?"

"I think it's God."

Oh great. Sophie's gone, so now she's pulling out the God voice.

"Why do you think it's God?"

"Because of what He said."

"So tell me, Ellie. What did you hear the voice say?"

"Come to My window."

Aaron stifled the urge to roll his eyes.

Ellie started toward the door. "I need to go to the common room now."

"It's morning. Free time isn't until this afternoon."

"I need to go now. He said, 'Come to My window.'"

"There's a window. You can use that one."

Ellie looked at Aaron as if he'd lost his mind. "He said, 'My window.' Not 'A window.' I have to go now. You have to take me or I'll take myself."

Aaron could see another screaming fit coming and didn't know whether to medicate her or let her have her way. Then Charlie knocked.

"Charlie will take me," she said, and bolted.

Aaron followed. "We'll both take you," he said, well aware he couldn't handle her by himself if she became hysterical again.

"I need to go to the common room," Ellie told Charlie.

"I'll come with you," Aaron said.

Charlie looked a little startled. "Yeah, sure, whatever you need," but Ellie was already on the move. They had no option but to follow or get left behind.

Aaron didn't know what to expect, but when they got to the common room, it certainly wasn't finding Luther Dunn standing beneath the window.

"How did this happen?" Aaron muttered.

Charlie frowned. "He's not supposed to be here. Do you want me to take him back?"

"No. We're here because Ellie said God told her to come here. I just wasn't expecting this," Aaron said.

Charlie paled. "He's not God . . . is he?"

"Of course not."

"Then how come he's here waiting for Ellie?"

"We don't know that's why he's here," Aaron muttered.

"Yes, we do."

Aaron glared. "And how do we know that?"

"Because I just saw him say it to Ellie."

"You saw it?"

Charlie nodded. "I read lips. He just said, 'Welcome, Ellie. I've been waiting for you.'"

Ellie walked straight up to Luther without hesitation. "I'm here."

"Welcome, Ellie. I've been waiting for you."

Ellie shivered slightly, but stood her ground. "Are you God?"

"Who I am is not important. I felt your pain."

Her chin quivered. "Sophie's gone. I think she died."

Luther laid a hand on Ellie's shoulder, and as he did, the hair on her arms suddenly stood on end. "Sophie isn't dead. She's in you."

Ellie's eyes welled. "She can't be *in* me. That would mean she wasn't—"

"Real? She was real to you, and at the time, that was all that mattered. But you know different now, don't you, Ellie?"

Ellie covered her face and shook her head, rejecting his words.

"Look at me."

Ellie tried not to, but there was strength in more than his voice. She did as he asked and burned in the fire of his gaze.

"Hear my words, Ellie Wayne. You will be well. You will be happy. You will be loved."

But Ellie needed it now. "Do you love me?"

Luther smiled. "It doesn't matter who loves you, Ellie. What matters is that you love yourself."

Ellie didn't want to hear the hard stuff. She just wanted proof the easy way, like maybe a miracle before her eyes. "If you're God, then tell me why the ghost baby cries all the time. Why won't it leave me alone?"

Luther laid a hand on the top of her head and briefly closed his eyes. "There is no ghost with you."

"But I hear it crying. It cries all the time in my head and won't leave me alone."

"Have you cried, Ellie?"

"Sometimes."

"Why do you cry?"

"When I'm sad. Sometimes when I'm mad. Sometimes when I'm afraid."

"But do you cry for yourself?"

She didn't answer.

"Do you? Do you weep for what you have endured?"

"Not anymore."

Luther moved his hand from her head to the side of her face. "What you hear is not a ghost, but yourself . . . your inner child, crying for you when you do not cry for yourself."

Ellie shivered from the touch of his hand against her cheek. It filled her, and at the same time made her feel lacking in his presence. He said pretty words, but she wanted proof.

"If you're God, then make it go away."

Luther's sigh was that of a parent whose child has just disappointed him. It enveloped her. "You are the only one who can make it go away."

"How?"

"You give away your pain for others to feel, but the pain is yours. Claim it. When you can cry for yourself, you will be well with God."

"You don't hate me?"

Luther opened his arms.

She walked into them. Peace enveloped her and with it came an unbearably beautiful light. She closed her eyes against the glow as it filled her—cherished her—cleansed her.

Luther touched the top of her head once more. "You are heard. You are loved." Then he walked away, passing by the two men at the door without making eye contact.

Aaron was still struggling with the shock of watching Ellie accept Luther's touch and walk into his open arms.

"Make sure he gets back where he belongs," Aaron said. "I'll take Ellie to her room."

"Yes sir," Charlie said, and followed Luther.

Aaron waited for Ellie, but when she didn't move, he went after her. "Ellie, it's time to go."

When she turned, her expression was one of shock and disbelief. "God loves me, Doctor Tyler."

Aaron frowned. "Is that what Luther said, that he loved you?"

"I have to claim my pain. I have to face my fears. I have to cry. That will be the hardest."

"He said that?"

She sighed. "I'm hungry. Can I go back to my room?"

"Yes, of course."

"If I'm not there, will they still leave breakfast?"

"I'm sure they will, but if they don't, I'll bring you some myself."

"Thank you," Ellie said, as she followed Aaron out of the room.

They had walked in silence for only a short distance when he heard a sob and realized she was crying.

"See, you're already crying and you said that would be the hardest."

Ellie frowned as she shook her head at him and again, he realized he had failed her in some way. "I'm crying because Sophie is dead. I still hear the crying baby, and we need to hurry or Cinnamon will eat all my bacon."

"I don't understand. What other kind of crying is there?"

"I never cry for me. He said I had to quit giving everyone else my pain and cry for myself. When I do that, the baby will go away."

Aaron felt like Alice who'd fallen down the rabbit hole. Up was down and down was up and he was forever late in trying to keep up with Ellie Wayne's brain. "Why will that make the baby disappear?"

Ellie sighed. "Because the baby is me. He said it was my inner child, and that it cries for me because I won't cry for myself."

The logic was so brilliant that it stopped Aaron cold. "Luther said that?"

"Yes. Tell everyone I'm very sorry for causing such a scene. I saw Momma when she was dead and I didn't cry. But I need to go cry for Sophie, even if I can't see her again."

She walked in her room, checked the table for her food and pointed. There were still tears on her cheeks. "My breakfast tray is here and so is the bacon."

"Okay. So I'll see you later this afternoon in the common room."

Ellie didn't answer.

He quietly closed the door and walked away, refusing to dwell on what he'd seen or that the advice Luther just gave Ellie was as good, even better than what he might have said.

It was somewhat daunting to know there was a delusional patient dispensing very good advice. He didn't know whether to worry that he kept missing the connection with Ellie, or be grateful that someone had finally gotten through to her.

At the other end of the long corridor, Charlie saw Luther to his room.

"So Luther, is there anything you need before I go?"

Luther paused then turned around. "Your tire is going flat."

"What? My tire is—?" Charlie took a deep breath, then turned around and left the room.

Luther sat down at the table, removed the cover from his plate of food and began to eat.

Out in the parking lot, Charlie had already taken the spare from the trunk of his car. He didn't want to think about how Luther had known this. He was just glad he knew it now instead of at quitting time.

Ellie ate the bacon, but couldn't down anything more. Her heart was broken and her world was out of control. She knew what she was supposed to do, but knowing and doing were two entirely different projects.

She tried one last time to call Sophie to her, but it was to no avail, and that baby's wails, while faint, were constant. She crawled back into bed, pulled the covers up over her head and cried herself to sleep.

Cinnamon sat on one side of the bed and Wyatt on the other, keeping watch over Ellie. They knew, like Sophie, that their time was growing shorter. And unlike other alters who had no desire to leave, they both loved Ellie too much to demand their existence continue beyond her need.

"I wonder what it will feel like?" Cinnamon asked.

Wyatt frowned. "It? *It* what?"

"Dying."

He shrugged.

"Are you scared?"

"I'm scared for Ellie," Wyatt said.

"We just won't leave until we're sure she can handle life on her own."

"Right."

"In the meantime, what can we do to help her grieve for Sophie?"

"According to Luther, we need to quit helping her, right? She has to learn how to grieve and heal on her own."

"Wyatt. That's brilliant."

"I have my moments."

"That you do, my brother . . . that you do."

"I'm not your brother."

Cin laughed. “In a manner of speaking, yes you are. We’re all a part of Ellie, so that makes us kin.”

“Shit. Just when I thought things couldn’t get worse.”

Had anyone been passing in the hall outside Ellie’s room, they might have thought it strange to hear laughter coming from a place that, only an hour earlier, had been a place of despair.

Chapter Twenty-Six

December—Christmas Week

There was an eight-foot Christmas tree in the common room and garlands of green plastic ivy and pine boughs that had been draped around doorways and up and down halls. Every six feet or so, a staff member had fastened a red bow into the garlands, giving the corridor leading to and from the room a very festive appearance.

A group of women from the local ladies auxiliary had made little red stockings for the patients so that every door had a stocking with the patient's first name, painted in glitter, hanging on the doorknob.

The staff seemed to have taken on a bit of their patients' mania in an effort to keep the holiday intact for the people within. A craft table had been set up, and during their free time every day there was an inordinate amount of coloring and gluing. If something needed cutting, a local crafter who'd volunteered to help with the project was there with a pair of scissors she carried in her pocket for such instances.

Ellie wasn't much into glitter and glue, and she understood the need to curb sharp objects, but it was kindergarten all over again. Then, the teacher hadn't trusted them with scissors, and here she was now, a brand-new high-school graduate, and back to the "no scissors" rule. If her situation had not been so frustrating, she might have laughed. She spent a good portion of her free time sitting in front of Luther's window, talking to God. She had yet to offer up another prayer, but Ellie was evolving.

Now the common room was in an uproar. A squabble had just erupted between two women at the craft table over a bottle of gold glitter glue. One wanted it for her craft project. The other one wanted it to paint her fingernails.

Wanda Buford was a thirty-seven-year-old bottle-blonde divorcée with two teenage kids at home who drove her crazy. She looked a little like Meryl Streep with a Chelsea Handler personality. She'd volunteered to organize the crafts at Mind and Body, thinking she would be getting a break from the ongoing drama at home, but after fifty-five minutes with twenty patients, she was wishing she'd stayed home and baked sugar cookies.

Working with people who were short on reality and long on mania was harder than she'd expected. She had a piece of green felt taped to her butt where a pocket should be, and a red felt bow glued to her bleached blonde hair because one of the patients wanted it there, and she'd been too afraid to tell her no. She kept watching the clock, praying for her last hour to soon be over.

Across the room, Ellie was at the window chasing sunlight. She scooted her chair a little to the south to catch a better angle on the rays coming through the window, and when she was satisfied with where she was sitting, made herself ignore the crying baby and settled in to discuss her latest concern.

> *I hope you're not busy, God, because I have something I want to talk to you about. Every time I look in the mirror, and I do this quite often to brush my hair or my teeth, all I see is Ellie Wayne, the victim.*
>
> *Dr. Tyler says I'm progressing, but I'm not so sure. Back home, I wore my hair a certain way because Daddy liked it that way. I didn't wear any makeup for the longest time because of the same reason. Sometimes I wear lipstick now, but it's almost gone and I can't go to the pharmacy to buy more, and my hair just keeps getting longer and longer. I feel like I'm stuck in a time warp. If I changed my appearance, would it change me inside as well?*

She closed her eyes and waited.

Moments later, she heard a voice, but it wasn't from God. It was Wanda, the craft volunteer. "Ellie? That's your name, right? Wouldn't you like to come to the craft table and make something?"

Ellie answered without opening her eyes. "No thank you, Wanda, I would not."

"Why not, sugar? It's lots of fun."

"I don't have any friends or family, therefore I have no need to make a gift. Now if you don't mind, I need to be quiet. I'm waiting for a message from God."

Wanda stared for a moment, wondering what had happened to such a pretty young girl to make her so dad-blamed nutty. But since she didn't know how to rebut a statement like that, she took herself back to the glitter glue and pieces of felt.

Ellie sighed. *"Sorry about that, God. It was Wanda, but she's gone. About my appearance—?"*

Change is growth.

Ellie smiled. *"Thank you, God. That's how I felt. I'll let you know how it goes."* She got up and headed for the craft table.

An older man named Dewey, who had a tendency to walk around with his fly unzipped because he claimed it all needed airing it out, had discovered the red felt bows. He decided one of them would make a good zipper pull and was trying to glue it onto the zipper in the fly of his pants. Wanda had already called for an aide and was on the verge of tears.

Ellie could see she was in something of a state, so instead of bothering her by asking for the scissors, she just took them out of Wanda's apron pocket and walked out of the room.

Wanda missed the scissors within a couple of minutes and let out a shriek that brought both nurses and aides running. "My scissors. They're gone," she screamed.

Her panic sent the room into an uproar as the search for scissors began.

In the meantime, Ellie had gone back to her room, then into the bathroom. She left the scissors on the counter while she went to look for something to put up her ponytail. After she found a ponytail band, she brushed all her hair into a topknot at the crown of her head and fastened it off.

At that point, Cin came in. "Hey. New hairdo? You look kinda like the I-Dream-of-Jeannie girl on Nickelodeon."

Ellie turned sideways, then faced front again.

"Kind of . . . at least the hair does . . . What are you going to do?" Cin asked.

Ellie picked up the scissors. "Make a change."

Cin shrieked, but it was too late.

Ellie was already making a cut through her hair about three inches above the band. The scissors weren't meant for hairstyling and Ellie's hair was thick, but she didn't give up. Eventually, long lengths of it began to fall at her heels and when she was done, there was more hair on the floor than she had left on her head.

Cin groaned. "You have ruined your hair. Now they'll for sure think you're crazy."

Ellie undid the rubber band and then finger-combed her hair back into place. It fell around her face in a wispy, pixie look that made her smile.

Cin's despair turned to glee. "Holy crap, Elizabeth Ann, that's actually cute."

Ellie smirked.

"How did you know to do that?" Cin asked.

"One of those makeover shows on TV."

"Now you need some makeup."

"All I have is lipstick."

"I have some mascara and eye shadow."

Ellie frowned. "Have you been holding out on me?"

"No. I didn't know you wanted makeup."

"I have to make a change," Ellie said.

"Who said?"

"God said change is growth. I need to grow to get better to get out of here."

Cin said nothing in return, which for her, was unusual.

"What?" Ellie asked.

"Nothing. Are you looking forward to leaving here?"

"Yes. Aren't you?"

Cin laughed, but it was a very happy sound. "Honey, it's not up to me. You're the one with too many people living in your head. The sooner we're gone, the sooner you're out of here."

Ellie froze. "But—"

"No *buts*. The bottom line is you have to let go of us to get out."

Ellie's eyes filled with tears. "Why do I have to give up the only things that were ever good in my life to be free?"

"Oh, sugar . . . do you hear what you just said? Do you know how sad that is to hear?"

"Yes, I heard myself, but I don't know what you mean."

"If Wyatt and I are the only things you consider good about your life, and we're not real, then what does that say about you?"

Ellie suddenly shivered. "That there's nothing good in my life?"

"Pretty much, but there can be good things you have yet to discover only you can't find them in here."

"I don't want to lose you and Wyatt."

"You can't lose what's inside you."

Ellie sat down on the toilet seat and thought about what Cinnamon had said. It was frightening, but at the same time she wanted out. She didn't belong in here with old crazy people. She needed to go to college and figure out what she wanted out of life for herself—not have doctors who knew nothing about her telling her what to do.

"I have to take the scissors back," Ellie said.

Cin poked a toe in the hair. "Tell someone to send housekeeping back to clean up this floor, too."

"I will."

Ellie gave herself a last careful look, then picked up the scissors and went to find Wanda.

When Ellie got back to the common room, Wanda was bawling and the nurses were frisking every patient personally before they were allowed to leave.

She walked past the line of patients waiting at the door, then over to where Wanda sat and laid the scissors down at her elbow. Wanda registered the haircut before she saw the scissors, and broke out into an even louder wail.

Ellie frowned. "I only borrowed them, and I brought them back the minute I was through with them."

Wanda's mascara was running as she grabbed the scissors, stuffed them in her purse and headed for the door, pausing only long enough to deliver the news. "I have my scissors back. I hope all of you have a Merry Christmas, but I won't be able to return to finish our little projects."

The staff began talking at once. "Who . . . where did you—"

Wanda pointed at Ellie, then clutched her purse against her chest and headed for the nearest exit. She was actually looking forward to getting home to her kids. They were looking better to her by the minute and they no longer ate glue, which was more than she could say for some of the residents here.

However, Ellie's troubles had just begun.

The head nurse, a twelve-year veteran of the hospital who went by Nurse Jolly, which Ellie privately thought was a misnomer, grabbed Ellie's arm and yanked. "Did you take Miss Wanda's scissors?"

"You're hurting me," Ellie said. "Daddy hurt me and Wyatt killed him."

Nurse Jolly got the message and released her, but didn't back down. "About the scissors you stole."

"That's not true. They were borrowed, not stolen," Ellie said and pointed to her own head. "How do you like my new look?"

The nurse wasn't having it. "You are in trouble, Ellie Wayne."

Ellie's delight quickly shifted to anger. "Why?"

"You stole something that didn't belong to you."

Ellie looked at Nurse Jolly as if she'd just lost her mind, then looked around at the others for a familiar face. It turned out to be Charlie. "Charlie, can you come here a minute? I need your help."

"Nice hairdo," he said. "What's up?"

"Nurse Jolly is hard of hearing like Sophie was. I've told her twice now that I didn't steal Wanda's scissors, but she can't hear me. I borrowed them to make my new look. I'm supposed to be changing. Dr. Tyler said so, and God told me growth was change and change is good. So I was only doing what God and Dr. Tyler told me. Can you explain that to Nurse Jolly and tell her I'm sorry she can't hear good anymore. Tell her she needs to get a hearing aid, or she'll just disappear like Sophie did."

Charlie grinned. "Yeah, sure kid, I'll tell her."

Ellie beamed. "Thank you." She waved at Nurse Jolly and then yelled, "Charlie will explain. Have a nice day."

Ellie could hear people laughing as she walked out. Momma always said the holidays were good for making even the cranky people glad. Momma was right about that.

She dawdled on the way back to her room, wanting to be somewhere and let people see that she was different. Maybe if they recognized the change, it would make her feel it stronger.

She thought about showing Dr. Tyler, but she wasn't his only patient and he might be busy. She wasn't allowed to go to his office alone anyway, so that idea was discarded.

Then Luther popped into her head. She stopped in the hall and closed her eyes. She wasn't sure this would work without the window, but she thought she'd give it a try.

Want to see how I'm changing?

She stood there for a good three minutes without moving, and then opened her eyes to see Luther coming toward her. Without thinking, she stood a little straighter and smiled at him. Luther saw the smile and the haircut and rejoiced in the change he was seeing in her.

"You heard me, didn't you?" Ellie asked.

Luther smiled.

Ellie was almost dancing from one foot to the other. "What do you think?

He knew she meant her hair, but it was the light in her eyes that gave him joy. "You are glowing."

Ellie did a three-sixty turn so he could see it all. "I did it myself. Scared Cinnamon, too. She thought I'd ruined it."

"You scared her? Now that truly is a change."

Ellie laughed out loud. "You're right about that."

She kept talking, unaware she was turning into the lively chatterbox that Cinnamon had been, or that when the transformation was complete, Cinnamon would be gone.

"Ellie."

"Yes?"

"Have you forgiven yourself yet?"

Her smile slid sideways as she looked away. "I don't think about it."

"That's not change. That's hiding. You can't change if you don't come out of hiding."

All of a sudden, her lack of hair had taken a backseat to another truth and it seemed she hadn't done all that much growing after all.

"Don't be sad, Ellie. Don't hide what hurt you. Take it out into the light and beat it into so many pieces that it will never be a whole pain again."

"Into the light?"

"Yes, and until you do that, your father is still controlling you."

Ellie frowned. "But Daddy's dead."

Luther laid a hand on her head. "Not in here, he's not." He pointed to her heart. "And not in there, he's not. You're holding onto everything that had to do with him."

All of a sudden, Ellie got it. Her eyes welled and her chin began to quiver. "You're not just talking about the memories of what Daddy did, are you? You're talking about Wyatt and Cinnamon, because they are a huge part of that life. You're telling me I have to let them go, too."

"Do you see? Already you understand that without me saying the words. Do the work, Ellie. I can't do it for you."

He cupped her cheek lightly then ran his forefinger down the side of her hair. "The change is good. What's next?"

Ellie watched him walk away. He was all the way down at the far end of the hall before it dawned on her that she hadn't said good-bye. And no sooner had she thought it, than she heard him.

No need for good-byes.

Her heart thumped. She watched him walk into his room and then he was gone.

Ellie's steps were slower as she returned to her own room. There was a note on the door from Dr. Tyler, but she didn't bother to read it. Dr. Tyler talked around her problems and wanted her to guess what he was getting at and figure them out for herself. Luther didn't waste time with all that. He just laid them out and told her to fix them.

It was action versus reaction.

She liked action best.

Wyatt showed up right after lunch. When he saw Ellie, he freaked. "Cinnamon, what the hell did you do to Ellie's hair?"

Ellie frowned. "Don't yell at her. I did this."

Wyatt couldn't believe it. "Are you kidding?"

"No, I'm not. What's so shocking about it? I got tired of looking in the mirror and seeing Daddy's victim."

Understanding quickly surfaced. "Oh."

Cin gave Ellie a hug. "She's growing, Wyatt . . . by leaps and bounds."

"I see that." He ruffled his fingers through the short length and grinned. "Good job."

She sighed. She and Wyatt had been through so much together. It mattered that he approve. "I'm going to free time. You guys coming?"

They looked at each other then shrugged. "We might show up later."

"Okay. See ya.'"

As soon as she was gone, Wyatt's expression went from smiles to shock. "What the hell?"

"She's getting well, Wyatt." Cin had already experienced the revelation a day or so earlier. "It's what we want for her, right?"

He shoved his hands through his hair then dropped onto the bed. "We don't have much time left, do we?"

"No, and in the words of our inimitable Dr. Tyler, 'how does that make you feel'?"

Wyatt shuddered. "Scared."

"Me too."

"I never really thought about this before."

Cin sat down beside him. "I can only imagine. You've been with her for so long. I'm the new kid on the blockhead, and by the way, that was meant to be funny."

"Ah, God, I can't laugh right now."

"Me either, but we're still staying true to the plan, right? We let her call the shots. We do not control the situation or jump in and bail her out if she gets into trouble."

"I remember," he said.

"You're not going to change your mind?"

"No. I've seen her sad too long to take this away from her now. Besides . . . it only seems fair that I bite the dust since I'm the one who committed murder."

"No, Wyatt. That wasn't murder. That was a rescue, and you'll always be my hero."

The memory of Garrett's brains splattering against the headboard of his bed slid through Wyatt's mind and then out again. He couldn't look at Cin and remember that.

"So what do you want to do?" she asked.

The change of subject was welcome. Wyatt slapped his legs. "Hell. Let's go hang out with Ellie while we've still got the chance."

"That's what I'm talking about."

Ellie was careful to sidestep Nurse Jolly when she got to the common room. She didn't quite understand why Jolly had been so set on accusing her of theft, but was thankful Charlie had run interference. In fact, he'd assured her all was well when he'd come to get her, but she wasn't taking any chances. She waited until the woman's back was turned, then slipped past the Christmas tree on her way to Luther's window. She got a chair from a nearby table and dragged it along behind her until she found the sun, then sat down in it.

Outside, the sky was spitting snow at Memphis with a disdainful attitude, tossing the feeble flakes to and fro with a weak but bitter wind. Knowing how cold it was outside, sitting with the sun on her face made Ellie most grateful. At least for today, it was better to be crazy than homeless.

> *Hi, God, it's me, Ellie. I just cut my hair today, so I thought I should give You a heads-up in case You didn't recognize me.*
>
> *Lots of things have been happening. They're all positive, but they're also getting harder. This isn't a prayer, but if You have any advice, I would definitely take it. And there's something else I need to say, but I don't want You to take it the wrong way. It has been pointed out*

to me that every time Momma was faced with something difficult, she dumped it in Your lap. She ran away from solving her own problems and I've been doing that, too. It's why Sophie and Wyatt and Cinnamon came to live with me. Instead of facing my problems, I made them do it. I tell You this so that, in the future, if I don't talk to You as much as usual, You don't take it the wrong way.

She took a breath and paused to think if there was anything else she wanted to say when she felt a tap on her shoulder.

"Ellie, it's me, Dr. Tyler. Do you mind if I sit with you a minute? I promise I won't stay long or intrude on your meditation."

"Okay, but I don't meditate."

Aaron pulled up a chair and sat. It took him a few seconds to adjust to the light, but then he began to understand the appeal of this place, of the colored light. It felt peaceful.

Then he focused on what Ellie had said. "If you don't meditate, what do you call it?"

"Talking to God. Not praying, just talking."

"I can see how this would feel like a good place to do that. Does He ever answer you?"

She nodded.

"Really? You said He never answered you when you prayed back home."

Ellie held up a finger to correct him. "I don't pray here, remember? I talk. God talks back. I don't think I know how to pray, that's all."

"Ah. Makes sense. Say, I like your new look."

"Thank you, so do I."

Aaron already knew she'd made off with the scissors without asking, but was curious to know which alter did the deed. "Who cut it for you?"

"I did."

The surprise showed on his face.

Ellie rolled her eyes. "You're just like Wyatt. He nearly had a fit when he saw it. He blamed Cinnamon."

"Yeah, my money would have been on her, too. Poor girl. She gets all the blame, doesn't she?"

"That's my fault. I've been letting everyone take the blame for my deeds. It has to stop."

Aaron couldn't help but stare. The words coming out of Ellie's mouth were diametrically opposed to how she'd been when she'd first arrived. He was thrilled that she was getting better, but wondered just how much of her healing he could legally claim. He leaned forward, resting his elbows on his knees as he watched the colors from the window flickering on her face.

"How did you get so smart?" he asked.

"God and Luther. Although sometimes, I think they're one and the same."

Considering she'd pretty much left him out of the equation, Aaron figured he'd gotten his answer.

Chapter Twenty-Seven

A few days before Christmas

Aaron had been watching Ellie's reactions throughout their session, trying to make sure he was still talking to Ellie. "What do you want for Christmas, Ellie?"

"Out of here."

Aaron was a little surprised by her vehemence, but tried not to show it. "I see. You do know you have a ways to go yet?"

Ellie's shoulders slumped. "I know exactly what you're not saying. You want Wyatt and Cinnamon gone, just like Sophie."

This surprised him again. "Well, yes, there's that." She was unconsciously picking at a hangnail, something only Ellie did, which reinforced his earlier identification.

"I'm not saying it will be easy, but I can't stay here much longer."

"Why not?"

"Why not? You say you want me to get better, but the only people in here are really crazy. That's like putting a sick person in a room with a whole bunch of people who are sicker than she is and asking her to get well without catching what they have."

It was interesting to Aaron that she viewed herself as sane, even though she had, at one time, conceived three extra personalities and murdered her father. He leaned back in the chair, watching the changing expressions on Ellie's face. "I understand your logic, but if you remember, there were some very serious reasons why you came here."

Ellie sighed. "Yes, Wyatt killed Daddy."

"Not if you're ready to claim your own mistakes."

Ellie flinched. The urge to go somewhere else was strong. Where was Wyatt when she needed him? "You know what I mean," Ellie muttered.

"Yes, and you know what *I* mean. When you know better, you do better."

Ellie stared. "Did you get that off the Oprah show?"

Aaron laughed out loud. "Sorry, but I'm having a few ego issues here. First God, then Luther, now Oprah. I fear I have been seriously failing you."

"Oh no, that's not true," Ellie said. "I'm sorry. You've been wonderful."

He grinned. "It's okay, Ellie. I have a tough hide, even if it doesn't show."

Silence stretched out between them. Ellie waited for him to say something else, and when he didn't, she closed her eyes.

The truth will set you free.

Ellie's eyes popped open. She grabbed Aaron's hand so fiercely he flinched.

"I shot Daddy. I don't really remember how many times, but probably not enough to make him pay for what he did to me before he died."

Tears burned the back of Aaron's throat, but he swallowed past them. "What made you say that?"

"Before you sat down, I asked God if He had any advice for me. And just now when I closed my eyes, I heard Him say that the truth would set me free. I want out, so I told the truth."

"Lord, Lord, Lord," Aaron whispered, and looked up through the cross in the window to the blowing snow outside. He didn't know what was going on inside her head, but he would have given an entire year of his life to be able to hear it.

"Good for you, Ellie."

"For shooting Daddy?"

He would have laughed, but the tragedy of her life was far bigger than the irony. "Not that so much. I meant . . . good for you for not only recognizing the truth, but for admitting it. That couldn't have been easy."

"Oh."

"We'll be working on some more of your truths in the coming days, but in the meantime, keep your ears and heart open, okay?"

"Okay."

Aaron got up and started to leave, then stopped. "Merry Christmas, Ellie. I hope this time next year you will be in your own home celebrating it as a free woman."

"Me, too, and thank you."

Aaron nodded, but he felt like he should be the one saying thank you as he walked away. She'd given him the best present he could have asked for.

Wyatt sat down in the chair beside Ellie. "Hey you."

Ellie smiled. "You came."

"So did I," Cin said.

"What do you think about when you're here at this window?" Ellie asked.

Wyatt eyed the window. It made him feel a little guilty, like the Jesus window did back at Preacher Ray's church, but he wasn't going to tell Ellie that. "It's a good place, honey."

"I think so, too. What do you think, Cin?"

"I think someone must have loved you very much to have done all this just for you."

Breath caught in the back of Ellie's throat. She'd never thought of it like that before.

"So what did the Doc want?" Wyatt asked.

Ellie frowned. "I'm not sure. He talked about my haircut and asked me what I wanted for Christmas."

Cin giggled. "What did you tell him? Makeup?"

"No. I said I wanted out of here."

A look passed between Wyatt and Cinnamon, but they didn't comment. For them, there was nothing left to say.

Ellie was still picking at the hangnail on her thumb as she leaned back and closed her eyes.

Wyatt knew she was hiding something. "Ellie."

"What?"

"What else did you say?"

She didn't answer.

"Ellie, open your eyes and answer me."

"I confessed."

"To what, sugar?" Cin asked.

"To killing Daddy. I told him that even though I let Wyatt take the blame, I was the one who did it."

Wyatt felt like he'd just been kicked in the gut.

Cin reached for his hand, but he pulled it away.

The shock of the moment was broken by one of the aides who'd come to get Ellie for the Christmas party. "Hey Ellie. The party is starting, and they have a special treat for you up at the snack table. Christmas cookies. Come on. I'll walk you over there myself."

"Go on," Wyatt said. "I'm not hungry."

"I'm staying with Wyatt," Cin said. "Eat one for me."

"Okay," Ellie said, and walked off, leaving her best friends behind.

For Wyatt and Cinnamon, it was yet another nail in their coffins. Ellie didn't know it yet, but she was learning how to be strong and was moving on without them.

Her next session with Dr. Tyler was a few days after Christmas. When she came into his office, he sat at the computer, and to the right of his elbow there was a present wrapped in pink paper with a big pink bow.

"Have a seat, Ellie. Let me save these notes and then we'll begin."

Aaron entered the last bits of data and then saved it to his laptop, but he could see she was already curious about the present. Wyatt had mentioned in a previous session that Ellie's favorite color was pink, so Aaron's choice of wrapping paper had been on purpose.

"Sorry about that," he said, as he faced her.

"It's alright."

"I have something for you."

Ellie's eyes lit up. "Is that for me?"

"Yes, it is," Aaron said, and handed it to her. "Open it and then we'll talk about it."

The smile on Ellie's face was enchanting. In many ways, her emotional growth was far below her actual age. She tore through the bow and the paper, giggling when tape from the bow got stuck to her elbow before she finally opened the box. She dug through the tissue paper to the pink leather-bound book inside.

"It's a journal, Ellie. There's a pink pen in there as well."

"Like a diary. Oh thank you. I always wanted a diary, but I would have been afraid to write in it. Daddy went through my things all the time."

Aaron smiled. "Yes, like a diary. This will be part of your therapy, but I won't read it. No one will read it but you, unless you choose to share it, okay?"

"Okay."

"I want you to write something in it every day. It doesn't matter what. Maybe it's what you had for lunch, or what you saw that was funny, or that you might be sad and missing someone."

"I will. I promise."

"Just getting things out of your head and on paper is healing in itself. The more you give away, the less of a burden you have to carry."

Ellie's eyes widened. "I love that. That's going to be the first line in my journal. Wait. I want to write that down right now. May I?"

"Sure, go ahead." He then watched the reverence with which she opened the book and the intensity of her expression as she wrote on the first page.

He was glad he'd followed his instincts on this. Six months ago he would never have hazarded a guess as to when, if ever, he would be able to integrate Ellie's alters. The only reason she was at the place she was now was because they were the ones pushing her healing.

Ellie finished writing, closed the journal then held it against her chest. "Is this journal for Wyatt and Ellie, too, or just me?"

"What do you want it to be?"

"Is it selfish to say me?"

"Of course not."

"Do you want them to keep a journal separate from mine?"

"I don't think so, do you?"

She was silent for a moment then her eyes began brimming with unshed tears.

"I'm losing them, aren't I?"

"Yes, if you want to be well."

"I wish I could lose that crying baby instead of them." Tears rolled down her cheeks as she looked away. "There's something else I need to do to get well, and I'm going to need your help."

"That's what I'm here for. What can I do?"

"Ask the family lawyer to either call me or come see me."

"I can do that, but can you tell me why?"

"I'm going to change my last name to Momma's maiden name. I don't ever want to write the name Ellie Wayne again. I want to be Ellie Strobel."

Aaron was impressed. "That's actually a very good idea. I can certainly get that information from your file and contact him on your behalf. After that, the rest will be up to you." Then he added. "Can I ask you something?"

Ellie grinned. "Don't you always?"

"Touché. I'm curious. Have you thought about what you want to do when you leave?"

"Oh yes. I already had plans before Daddy got me pregnant. I still want to follow through."

"Follow through on what?"

"College. I don't know for sure what I want to do, but I think something with computers. You don't have to talk to so many people to do that well. I will figure it out after I'm there."

"Did you have a school picked out?"

"Yes, but I hadn't enrolled. Daddy was controlling all that until I turned eighteen. I do know I will never live in that house again. It has nothing but bad memories. I'll sell it and get a place of my own."

"I think you can do anything you set your mind to. Anyone who is as focused as you are can do anything they want."

"Are we through yet?"

He smiled. "We can be. Why?"

"I want to go write in my journal."

"Then we're done. I'll call Charlie."

"Thank you, Dr. Tyler. Thank you so much for the gift."

"You're welcome, Ellie. Happy writing."

Memphis—Late March

Spring had come early to Memphis. The tulip beds on the grounds around the hospital were starting to bloom. Ellie had watched the show from her window, from the first shoots of green leaves cutting through the earth to the thick fat buds. Now they were opening, coloring the bleak landscape in colors of bright reds and yellows. It made her miss seeing Momma's flower beds come to life after a winter's sleep. Back home there would be tulips and forsythia and even lilac already blooming around the house. It was strange to be homesick for part of her past and so ready to let go of the rest.

She'd already taken a big step in putting the past behind her. Legally, she was now Ellie Strobel. She'd written it on every page of her pink journal just for the pleasure of seeing it there.

Wyatt had reminded her only this morning that when she got to her new place, she could plant all the flowers she wanted, but Ellie wasn't so sure. Flowers were a permanent thing, and she still didn't know where life was going to take her.

But she hadn't been feeling well and was in no mood to debate with Wyatt. She'd managed to eat breakfast, but a couple of hours later it had come back up. After that, stomach pains were added to the nausea. She'd spent most of the day in bed, even canceling her meeting with Dr. Tyler and opting to miss spending time at Luther's window.

When they brought her lunch tray, she drank her iced tea and shoved food around on the plate, but was still unable to eat. She'd napped off and on throughout the afternoon while the pain in her stomach got worse.

By late evening, she was sitting up in bed and reading when they brought her dinner tray. "I don't feel like eating," she said.

The aide frowned. "You're never sick," she said. "As soon as I get these trays delivered, I'll come back and check your temperature."

But a small emergency a few minutes later derailed her intent and she went off duty later without remembering to check back in.

Night fell, bringing more pain with it. Ellie was in so much misery now that she could hardly think.

Cinnamon came in and sat down beside her. "Honey, are you still feeling bad?"

Ellie nodded and pulled the covers up over her shoulders.

"Want me to go get someone to come see about you?"

"No. Surely I'll feel better soon."

Cinnamon patted Ellie's leg. "Is there anything I can do?"

"I'm just going to sleep."

"Okay, but I'm here if you need me."

Wyatt came in behind her. "What's wrong with Ellie?"

"She said she doesn't feel good and wants to sleep, which means we need to make ourselves scarce."

Except for the faint wails of the crying baby, the room got quiet. Within a few minutes Ellie drifted into a fitful sleep filled with crazy dreams and old memories—memories that kept waking her in a state of panic, then dropping her off into limbo again.

Hours passed.

The pain in Ellie's side had become so severe she was shaking, and the fever in her body so hot she'd thrown off the covers. The room was cold, but her pain and fever were rising. That's when the hallucinations began.

The monster was coming. She could hear the shuffling sound of his steps against her carpet. The sounds morphed into voices out in the hall. There were sirens in her yard—loud ones—screaming, screaming, like the voices inside her head.

Momma face down on the bed. She's not dead. See everyone, she's not dead. Then Momma rolled over. Her face was purple and even though her eyes were slightly open, Ellie could see that she was no longer there.

All the tires were flat on her car and she was running, trying to get home before

Daddy found out, but when she got home there was blood everywhere.

A light appeared above her head, but it wasn't from the Jesus window. Someone was running a vacuum cleaner. Tell them to stop. She didn't want to hear the noise.

Blood everywhere. Daddy moaning. Gunshots. The smell of gunpowder up my nose. Sirens in the yard again.

The look of horror on Doris's face. Poor Doris.

Poor Ellie, the keeper of secrets.

Luther Dunn had been asleep for nearly an hour when he suddenly opened his eyes. His skin was burning, his belly on fire.

Ellie!

He threw back the covers and left his room, unconcerned that he was naked.

A nurse on the night shift saw him running up the hall and called for help in a panic, certain he was having a psychotic episode. "Luther! Stop! You're not wearing any clothes and you're not supposed to be out of bed. What's going on?"

"Ellie is sick. She needs a doctor or she's going to die."

"What?"

"Run, woman," Luther cried, and took off down the hall to Ellie's room, dragging her with him.

Once they reached Ellie's room, the nurse was shocked by Ellie's condition. When the nurse turned on the light, Ellie rolled over on the side of the bed and vomited. She was feverish and incoherent.

The flurry of activity on the floor increased tenfold as an ambulance was called and nurses came running. Someone wrapped Luther up in a bedsheet, then an aide took him back to his room. He went willingly, knowing he'd done what needed to be done.

By the time the paramedics arrived, Ellie had slipped into a state of unconsciousness. She never knew when they wheeled her out of her room on a gurney, or the frantic 2:00 a.m. ride to All Saints Hospital in Memphis. They wheeled her into ER in an unresponsive condition with a fever of 105. Shortly thereafter she was diagnosed with appendicitis and on her way to surgery.

The diagnosis took a deadly turn after they opened her up to find the appendix had already ruptured. After that, it was a race against time. A half hour into the surgery her blood pressure suddenly dropped, adding another measure of intensity to an already dire situation.

An anesthesiologist suddenly shouted. "We're losing her."

The doctor looked up at the dropping pressure just as she flatlined. In that moment, Ellie Wayne was dead.

"I need a crash cart."

Ellie felt light and empty *of every negative thing she'd ever endured. The field of daisies in which she stood was filled with butterflies and hummingbirds vying for the nectar, while the sun lit a path toward a large stand of trees, just like the ones above the creek behind her house.*

Ellie pointed, laughing at a pair of hummingbirds that were dive-bombing each other for the rights to a single bloom. "Look, Wyatt. That's you and me fighting over the last pancake."

Wyatt moved up beside her and put an arm around her shoulder. "I love you, Ellie."

She looked up, smiling. "I love you, too, Wyatt."

Cinnamon came up behind her and handed her a handful of daisies. "From me to you with love," she said.

"Thank you, but why so solemn? Look at this place! It's beautiful. How can you not be happy here?"

"You're not supposed to be here," Wyatt said.

"What do you mean? You and Cinnamon are here. Why can't I be here, too?"

"You're dying, Ellie. They're trying to bring you back to life but it's not happening."

All of a sudden the sun was gone and the sky was black. The wind began to whirl, tugging at their hair and clothing and pulling the petals from all the daisies until they spun in the air like snowflakes in a storm.

"Go back, Ellie. Go back," Cinnamon said.

Ellie screamed at them, desperate to be heard against the rising wind. "We'll all go back!"

Wyatt pushed her away. "We can't. You're not strong enough to take us back with you. If you don't go now, we all die. You have to go back, Ellie. You have to live."

The storm was within her now in a new and frightening way, ripping at what she'd been, but she wouldn't give way.

"I don't want to live without you. I can't. I won't."

Wyatt and Cinnamon began to disappear. But even after she could no longer see them, she could still hear Wyatt's voice, shouting at her, begging her to understand.

"Yes you can. Yes you will. Go back, Ellie. Go back, or Daddy will have won."

A nurse looked up. "I've got a pulse."

Someone muttered, "Thank God."

The surgeon shifted back into gear. "Let's get this finished, people."

Aaron Tyler got to work to find a note on his desk stating that Ellie Strobel wouldn't be in for her session because she'd been taken to the hospital in the night.

Frowning, he picked up the phone and called the nurse's desk. "This is Dr. Tyler. What happened to Ellie Strobel?"

"I just came on duty. Let me check, Dr. Tyler."

Aaron waited a few moments, and then the nurse was back.

"She was taken by ambulance to All Saints around 2:00 a.m. It says here she was unconscious, with nausea and high fever. Oh. And one other notation here . . . something about being alerted to her condition by Luther Dunn, although I'm not sure what that means."

Aaron's stomach knotted. "I think I do. Thank you."

He hung up, then glanced at his calendar. Ellie had been his only session this morning. There was plenty of time for him to go check on her. Even though this did not fall under the auspices of his duty to a patient, he knew if he didn't go, there would be no one but strangers seeing to her welfare. But before he went, he wanted to talk to Luther—if, of course, Luther was willing to talk to him.

He left his office and ran into Charlie on the way down the corridor. "Charlie, do you have a minute?"

"Yeah, sure Doc. What do you need?"

"Walk with me to Luther Dunn's room. I need to ask him a couple of questions, but he doesn't really know me, so I'd prefer you went along as a familiar face."

"No problem. Is he in trouble?"

"No."

"Good. I like the old Hippy. He doesn't make waves, which is more than I can say for most of the patients in here."

"Yes, I suppose that's so."

A couple of minutes later they were at his door.

Charlie knocked then poked his head in the door. Luther was sitting in a chair in front of the window with his back to the door.

"Hey Luther, it's me. You have a visitor."

There was no indication that he'd heard.

"Wait here for me," Aaron said and went in. He walked around the chair where Luther was sitting to face him. "Luther, I'm Ellie's doctor. I wanted to thank you for calling attention to her condition last night."

"You're in my light."

Aaron jumped, then moved off to one side. "Sorry. I didn't realize."

Luther turned his head and looked straight into Aaron's eyes. "They all died last night."

Just like that, the air went out of the room. Aaron reached for the wall to steady himself as a wave of despair rolled through him. "No . . . God, no."

"Only Ellie came back."

And just as quickly, oxygen returned. "What do you mean?"

"You'll see."

"I'm on my way there now."

"She won't talk to you, but that's okay. Later she will remember you cared enough to come."

Aaron walked out of the room with Charlie at his heels. "Is that true, Doc?"

"I'm about to find out."

Chapter Twenty-Eight

Ellie never knew how many times Aaron visited her in intensive care. When she finally woke up enough to realize where she was, all she remembered was seeing the tulips from her window.

She wouldn't think about being dead, although she remembered it had happened. Knowing Wyatt and Cinnamon had willingly sacrificed themselves to save her was breaking her heart. She wasn't worthy of such a sacrifice. Whatever pain and discomfort she was feeling she considered just punishment for surviving when they had not.

The day they moved her from intensive care to a regular room, she was still weighed down by guilt and unable to accept what she'd lost. And then she heard the voice.

You can't get past it without going through it.

Ellie heard it—got it—and finally lost it.

It started with an ache in the back of her throat. Then her vision blurred. She reached for a tissue and knocked the water off her table. When it hit the floor with a splat, sending ice and water all over the floor, she groaned and reached for the call button.

A few moments later, a nurse answered. "What do you need?"

"I spilled my water," she said, quietly swallowing a sob.

"We'll be right there."

The connection was gone, but her pain was not. She kept hearing Wyatt's voice . . . *Yes you can. Yes you will.* And the tears began to roll.

A janitor came in to clean up the water. "Hey, no need to cry about that. I'll have it cleaned up in no time."

But Ellie couldn't stop. Pain grew within her faster than she could let it out. Tears fell harder, choking her, ripping her up from the inside out.

The janitor called for a nurse.

By the time the nurse arrived Ellie was sitting up in bed, sobbing.

"Ellie. Are you in pain? What's wrong? You have to tell me before I can help you."

"They're dead. They're all dead," she cried, then threw herself backward and began to scream.

The first thing Ellie heard when she came to was the silence. She didn't know how long she'd been out, only that she'd been drugged. She recognized the feeling and the taste in her mouth from meds she'd been given at Mind and Body.

She lay without moving—trying to figure out what had happened—what was different. It took her a few moments to realize the crying baby was gone.

She put her hands over her ears, then took them off, then put them over her ears again, testing to see if the quiet was real. And it was.

She couldn't believe it.

It had taken nearly a year for it to happen, but the crying had finally stopped. So her inner child wasn't sad anymore, but she wished she could say the same for herself. Without Wyatt and Cinnamon, she was horribly alone. The true state of her life was like a knife to the heart. How did one live without joy? How could *she* find the courage to move forward?

I rejoice in your peace.

And just like that, the panic that threatened her receded, leaving a message in its wake. As long as she kept God in her life, she would never be completely alone.

God is forever.

She took a deep breath and then let it out while holding on to the wash of solace.

"I won't forget that again."

Memphis—July

Ellie had been packed since before breakfast, although the car that would be taking her home wasn't due to arrive for another hour. She was, in the words of Nurse Jolly, who had never quite forgiven her for taking the scissors, a success story in spite of herself.

Dr. Moira Ferris had given up trying to understand the link between Luther and Ellie—mostly because Luther refused to cooperate and Ellie couldn't explain it.

Dr. Tyler felt somewhat like a parent watching a child leaving home for the first time. He didn't know if she was completely ready, but it was time to let her fly.

He glanced at the clock, then shut down his laptop and headed for her room to wish her well and tell her good-bye. He was almost out the door when he remembered something and ran back to get it.

Ellie hadn't worn a dress in more than a year, but she was grateful to Doris for having the foresight to send it to her. It was the little dress with the cap sleeves and the tulip skirt that she'd worn the night she graduated high school. It felt right, since leaving here was, in a way, another graduation. And it was pink, which was for Ellie the color of joy, and this was a joyous occasion.

She eyed herself in the bathroom mirror, feathering her funky new haircut and then used up the last of her lipstick.

"Just in time," she said, and tossed the empty tube in the trash.

It was exciting to know she would, once again, be making her own decisions, buying her own food, stocking her own home with the necessities of life, although it was daunting to be doing it alone. Just as she was stepping into her white sandals, there was a knock at her door. She walked out of the bathroom as Dr. Tyler peeked in the door.

Aaron stopped in the doorway, stunned by the sight of her, then he smiled. "Ellie. You look beautiful."

"Thank you. I'm excited."

"I can imagine. Are you nervous about anything?'

"No. I spoke to Doris a couple of days ago. She was our housekeeper and a really nice lady. She packed my clothes at the house, and saw to getting my car serviced. I needed a new battery and an oil change . . . stuff like that. She also found the keepsakes I'd asked for and boxed them up. The rest will be sold with Daddy's car and the house, but the lawyer is dealing with all that. All I have to do is load my things in the car and wave good-bye to Memphis from the rearview mirror. I think Doris is a little glad I'm leaving so she won't have to actually quit. I doubt she could have taken much more of me. Truthfully, I am stunned by how loyal she stayed to the family, putting up with Momma's prayers and Daddy and me, although to be fair, she didn't know about Daddy."

Ellie paused, the corner of her mouth turning up just enough to prove she was happy. "She once said that living with me was like working in a boarding house. There were too many people. Daddy upped her pay and she stayed on."

Aaron listened to her rattle, just like Cinnamon used to do, but he knew it was Ellie. He couldn't help watching for signs of panic, or the telltale picking of hangnails that was a sure sign she was keeping something back, but he saw none of it. "Do you have your finances in order?"

She nodded. "I don't suppose you knew it, but I inherited everything when Momma died. Daddy still had a job at Strobel Investments, but the business, house and property were mine. The irony was he didn't know Momma had changed her will until he'd killed her. She'd done it after she found out about what he'd done to me. There is an executor until I turn twenty-one. I'll be fine."

"Good." One more worry checked off his list of concerns. "Do you know where you're going?"

"Waco, Texas."

He didn't bother to hide his surprise. "Waco? What's in Waco?"

"Baylor University. It's a private Christian-based university. I think it will suit me."

"Ah . . . and I think you're right. But I wouldn't feel like I'd done my duty without warning you it's going to be hard and sometimes dangerous for a young girl like you, living on your own."

The minute he said it, he got one of those, I-can't-believe-you-just-said-that looks for which she was famous. Then when she laughed, he knew he'd somehow put his foot in it again.

"I'm sorry for laughing, Dr. Tyler, but that has to be one of the dumbest things you've ever said to me. My past was not sheltered. I spent thirteen years in school without a single friend and managed to graduate with a 4.0. I went home to a mother who talked to God more than she talked to me, and a father who made my life a living hell. I killed a person to save myself. After all that, living alone will be a breeze. Ellie Wayne was naïve, but Ellie Strobel is not. Stop worrying."

"You're right, but you're still going to need therapy. I will find a good doctor for you in Waco. Will you promise to go see him?"

"I guess, although I don't feel like I need any more help."

Aaron knew that wasn't the case. There would be days when the world crashed around her, and days when she felt too alone. She was going to have to learn how to make friends. She'd never had a real friend in her entire life. This was a skill children learned in kindergarten, although by that time, Ellie hadn't needed a friend, she'd needed a savior. And when He hadn't come, she hadn't bothered to look elsewhere.

"What if Wyatt comes back, or Cin? You'll need someone to talk to. Trust me on this, will you?"

She looked at him as if he'd lost his mind. "What do you mean, if Wyatt comes back? They're dead. I think you've been with these crazy people too long. Sometimes the things you say make me think *you're* the one who needs a shrink."

And once again, Aaron was left with no way to answer. Just like she'd believed them real, she now knew they were dead. In a way, he could see the wisdom in leaving well enough alone, but as a doctor, he didn't dare.

"I still want you to promise me you'll maintain a regular relationship with your doctor. Even if it's no more than once a week, or once a month, or whatever makes the both of you happy."

She shrugged. "I can live with that."

He started to shake her hand, then remembered she didn't like to be touched. To his surprise, Ellie extended her hand instead. He took it.

"Thank you for everything you did for me."

"You're very welcome. Don't forget to write in your journal. When it's filled up, begin another one and remember, the more you give away . . ."

Ellie finished it. ". . . the less of a burden you have to carry. I won't forget."

"Best of luck then, and if you need me, you know how to get in touch. Oh. I almost forgot." He took a video tape from the inner pocket of his jacket. "I thought you might like this. It's the one of you and your mother when you were a tiny baby."

Ellie beamed. "Thank you. Thank you so much. Yes, I definitely want it."

He waved and then left her at the door. Ellie popped the video into her suitcase as she glanced at the clock. Still forty minutes before the car came to get her. She had one more person she needed to see, and she wanted to do it without company. She closed her eyes and sent out one last message.

I'm leaving. Please come to the window. I want to say good-bye.

The common room would be empty at this time of morning. She hurried down the hall and then slipped inside. Her footsteps sounded doubly loud in the empty space, but she kept on walking toward the window. It was the perfect time and place for one last visit here with God, as well.

> *Hi God, it's me, Ellie. As You can see, I'm leaving today. The next time I talk to You I will probably be in Texas. I'm going to college there. I wanted You to know that I don't have any hard feelings toward You anymore. One of these days I'll say another prayer, but not until I figure out how to do it better. I guess that's all for now. Talk to You later.*

There was a touch on her shoulder but she was already smiling before she turned around. "You came."

Luther's eyes smiled first, but his lips soon followed. "I could not miss my good-bye."

A quick burn of tears blurred Ellie's vision, but she blinked them away.

"You saved my life."

Luther touched the wispy bangs on her forehead then suddenly dropped his hand as if he'd transgressed. "You saved yourself, Ellie."

"Cinnamon said once that someone must have loved me a lot to paint something as beautiful as this window. I've never said thank you for that, but I am now."

Do unto others as you would have them do unto you.

Ellie heard it, even though his lips never moved. When she looked up, he was so tall she had to squint her eyes against the sunlight to see his expression. "I know your secret."

His eyebrows arched, but he didn't respond.

"I know you're not God."

Luther waited.

"You're psychic, aren't you, Luther?"

His eyes suddenly twinkled.

"I won't tell," she whispered.

Luther opened his arms and one more time, Ellie walked into his embrace. It wasn't a hug so much as a union of one soul to another, and then it was over. He turned loose as she stepped back.

"One last thing, Luther . . . I just want you to know that if you ever tune in and want to send me a message, I will be listening."

"And I will be listening for you."

She glanced up at the window as he walked away, memorizing every color and hue, then followed him out and hurried back to her room to get her things, suddenly afraid someone would change their mind and make her stay.

It was surreal to be riding through the streets of Memphis along with thousands of others on their way to somewhere else. But when the driver pulled up to her house to let her out, Ellie physically shuddered. Even though she knew it would be empty, it was still too full of ghosts and bad memories for her to want to linger. The only plus was that her car was sitting in the driveway, just as Doris had promised.

The driver looked up in the rearview mirror and spoke. "We're here, Miss. I was told to wait and help you load some things into your car."

"Oh. I didn't know. Just a moment and I'll go unlock the house."

She got out and hurried around to the back, got the key from under the mat and let herself in. She found the car key on the kitchen table along with a large envelope and her purse, but she would look at those later. She grabbed the car key and hurried through the kitchen to the front door. The driver was waiting outside on the porch and the bags and boxes she was taking with her were inside by the front door.

"Very handy and thank you, Doris," Ellie muttered.

She let the driver in, then aimed the remote and unlocked the car, thankful the SUV had plenty of space. "Just put these anywhere they'll fit."

"Yes, Miss."

She waited until he'd carried them all out and told her good-bye, then relocked the front door and turned to face the empty house.

She'd wondered how she would feel coming back to this place and was surprised to realize she felt nothing. Maybe knowing the Devil was dead had something to do with it.

She walked down the hall to her old bedroom and then pushed the door inward. The room seemed large compared to where she'd been for the past year, but the energy that had been in it—the same energy that came with fear wasn't there—the room felt just as dead as Daddy.

She closed the door, then moved across the hall to her mother's room. For a fraction of a second she flashed on the sight of Fern's dead body sprawled face down on the bed, and then it was gone. Her gaze moved from the bed to the wall and the array of crosses and icons that had grounded Fern Wayne's world. Ellie wanted one. It would be like taking a little bit of Momma with her.

She looked them over, then finally chose a simple iron cross and took it down from the wall. She walked out, then paused a moment to gather her thoughts. Daddy's room was at the end of the hall, but she had no intention of wasting her time looking. She'd spent the best years of her life being tortured in there. She had no desire to take the memory with her. Instead, she headed for the kitchen, the one place where she had known peace.

She opened the large envelope by her purse. It was from her executor.

Miss Strobel,

I have taken the liberty of transferring your bank account into your new legal name. There are new checks and a new ATM card as well, and Mrs. Bailey, your housekeeper, has packed the rest of your checks into your luggage. You will also note I have secured your high-school transcript, along with the paperwork regarding your name change which you will need to secure college entry. Since you are leaving the state, I recommend you get the name changed on your driver's license after you get settled there. Remember to take the paperwork with you to the tag agency for proof.

It has been my pleasure to serve you over these years and I will continue to do so until you have reached the age of twenty-one, at which time the entire proceeds and property of your mother, Fern Strobel Wayne, will be turned over to you.

You have my contact information. I am at your service.

Regards, Milton Crossley, Esq.

Ellie put the new checks and ATM card in her purse and checked to see if her old driver's license was there as well. Doris had packed her Momma's china and silverware and they, along with the other stuff she was taking, were in Ellie's car. But there was one more thing she wanted that she hadn't thought to tell Doris about, and that was Momma's rolling pin.

She took it out of the drawer, then got a sack from the pantry and put the cross, the envelope with her papers, and the rolling pin inside. She was getting ready to leave when she noticed a note taped to the refrigerator. It was from Doris.

Ellie,

I say prayers for you every day, and I want you to know I think of you as family. When you get settled into your new place, I would be honored if you wanted to stay in touch. You know my address. If you need anything else done at the house before it sells, all you have to do is call.

Love, Doris,

PS, I left you a treat in the refrigerator.

Ellie appreciated the invitation, but she already knew she was cutting ties with everything and everyone connected to this part of her life. Still, she opened the door to see what Doris had left and found a box of homemade oatmeal-raisin cookies and a cold bottle of Pepsi, just like when she and Wyatt were kids. As the memory slid through her mind, she realized it was the first time she'd thought of Wyatt without a huge sense of loss. That had to be a good sign.

She took the cookies and the pop, locked the door as she left and put the key back under the mat. By the time she got off the porch, she was running for her car. Only one more stop and then she was out of Memphis and never coming back.

Stanton Brothers Funeral Home wasn't far from Franklin's Ice Cream Parlor, where she used to work, so she had no trouble finding the place. She pulled into the driveway and got out, brushing cookie crumbs from the front of her dress as she headed for the entrance.

A bell dinged as she entered, which brought a forty something man in a light-blue summer suit up from behind a desk. He folded his hands against his waist and walked toward her.

Ellie guessed it would be hard to figure out what kind of an expression to use when you worked in a place like this. You couldn't frown because people were already sad or they wouldn't be here, and you couldn't smile in welcome, because they were here because someone was dead. She wondered if he'd practiced that zombie look or if it was his natural appearance and thought the bald head he was sporting didn't help.

"Hello. My name is George. May I help you?"

"I've come to pick up my father's ashes."

His expression instantly shifted to one of deep concern. "We call them cremains. Please have a seat at my desk so I can pull the file."

Ellie sat.

George moved to a set of file drawers. "What was the name of the deceased?"

"Garrett Wayne."

She watched George reach for the lowest file drawer, which figured, since *W* was near the end of the alphabet, then pull out a file and open it. She braced herself, waiting for the moment when it dawned on him she was the girl who'd killed her father.

"Oh. My. I, uh . . ."

Ellie sighed. "If you don't mind, I'm kind of in a hurry."

"Yes, of course. I just wanted to—"

"I've already spoken to my executor. Everything has been paid for and you were to keep what's left of him until I got out of the hospital. So as you can see, I'm out."

George tried to smile, then wasn't sure it was the proper thing to do, then wondered if it was safe to turn his back on her as he headed for their storage area to retrieve the deceased.

He was close to running when he came back with a square black box about the size of a box of tissues. He set it on the desk and then discreetly removed his handkerchief and wiped the sweat from his head. Ellie noticed it made his head shine even more than it already did, which then set her to wondering if bald people had shine spray like people with hair had hair spray, then made herself focus on the box.

It was smaller than she'd imagined it would be and very nondescript. There was satisfaction in knowing that much evil had been reduced to such a small pile of waste.

"Uh, Miss Wayne, it's customary to choose an urn for the cremains, if you would like to follow me into the viewing room I have some on display."

"No need," Ellie said. "He isn't going to be in there long."

"Ah. I see. You have a special place where you intend to scatter the ashes, which is often another favorite family choice."

"Yes. I have a place in mind. Is that all?"

He took a couple of papers from the file and spread them out before her. "If you would just sign here, and then here, as well, you'll be on your way."

Ellie signed the name, Ellie Strobel.

He saw it and frowned. "I'm sorry. I thought you were—"

"I am. I had a horrible father and no desire to carry his last name any longer than I had to. I had it legally changed to my mother's maiden name. I'm sure you know of Strobel Investments here in Memphis?"

"Why yes, I do, but I had no idea—"

Ellie suddenly laughed. He'd just said, "I had no idea"—what had been Sophie's favorite phrase.

And George had no idea why she'd suddenly laughed with her father's remains only inches away from her nose, nor was he going to ask.

"Alright then. This is your copy, and here is your—the, ah . . . cremains."

Ellie folded up the paper, ignoring George's horror; she pulled a plastic Walmart bag from her purse and dropped it and the box inside. She walked out of the office, swinging the bag in one hand and her car keys in the other.

"Lord have mercy," George muttered, and wiped his bald head a second time as Ellie drove away.

Chapter Twenty-Nine

It was just after 1:00 p.m. when Ellie pulled up to a big truck stop just off Interstate 40 in Forrest City, Arkansas. She was hungry and this was as good a place as any to grab a bite to eat. She filled up with gas first, paid at the pump, then drove up to the station and went inside carrying her purse and the Walmart sack with Daddy's ashes.

The deli case next to the register was full of greasy offerings of corn dogs, potato wedges and hunks of fried chicken, or if she wanted to go ethnic, she had a choice of *taquitos* or nachos with thick canned cheese sauce that tasted more like yellow paste than cheese.

Ellie bypassed the fried stuff for the Subway sandwich area and ordered a ham and cheese sub on flatbread, and a Pepsi. It was so different from what she'd been eating for the past year that her mouth was actually watering when she took her first bite.

She ate without thought, thankful for the freedom to be sitting here and choosing her own food. When she was finished, she dumped the remains in the trash, picked up her purse and her Walmart sack and headed for the ladies' room.

There were six stalls, including the one for the handicapped, and they were all empty except for one, which she quickly bypassed. She could get to it later.

Ellie used the bathroom, flushed the stool then took the box with her father's ashes out of the sack.

"Right where you belong," she muttered, as she dumped some in and flushed.

She waited until the smoky contents had more or less gone down the hatch before she moved to the next empty stall where she repeated the process, dumping ashes, then flushing, moving from toilet stall to toilet stall until she'd covered them all and there was nothing left to flush.

She dumped the box in the trash, then calmly moved to the sink where she soaped and rinsed her hands over and over until she was satisfied there wasn't an iota of the Devil on her person.

In the meantime, women had been coming and going, doing their business, then washing up and moving on. Ellie waited until she was once again alone in the room before she said her good-byes.

"So, Daddy . . . I feel you have earned your final resting place, which is in the sewer. It's where your mind always was. It seems only fair that your remains rest there as well. With, of course, the added benefit of having women shit on you with daily regularity. It saves me the trouble of telling you to go to hell, because you're already there."

When she walked out, there was a bounce in her step and a slight smile on her face. She stopped in the candy aisle and bought herself a Hershey bar, then left the station heading west.

Epilogue

It had taken Ellie a couple of days to find just the right house near the Baylor campus. It was a small, one bath/one bedroom with a great kitchen, a living room and a tiny dining nook. The draw had been the fenced-in backyard. Ellie was toying with the idea of getting a dog. She'd always wanted one, but had never been given the option. After another two days of unpacking, she was finished.

She stood in the middle of the living room, eyeing her new furniture and fluffing a pillow here and there, then finally stopped fussing and stepped back for a final look. The suncatcher Wyatt had given her for her eighteenth birthday was hanging in the front window. It gave her hope for the future.

You will be happy here.

Ellie's heart skipped a beat. "Wyatt?"

But when she turned to look, he was nowhere in sight. She swallowed past a sudden lump in her throat as reality hit. Then she took a deep breath and lifted her chin.

"You're right, honey. I *will* be happy here. I promise."

As promised, she called Dr. Tyler, who gave her the name and phone number of a psychiatrist there that he wanted her to see. The doctor's name was Butterfield. She liked that. It made her think of butterflies. Tyler told her that he had already filled the man in on her history, which was good. It saved her the trouble of rehashing it with a stranger.

It had taken some fancy paperwork, as well as letters of recommendation from Preacher Ray, her executor, and her banker, to get her into the fall semester at this late date, but when school at Baylor College began, Ellie Strobel was listed as a freshman.

She'd dressed for the day as carefully as a bride would have dressed for her wedding, choosing just the right clothes and shoes—even the right backpack, with just a touch of pink.

In honor of the free spirit within, she'd kept her funky haircut.

When she finally found a parking space on campus, she grabbed her backpack and got out. Armed with a schedule of her classes and a map of the campus, she started walking.

The day was hot and sunny without a cloud in the sky—the kind of day that made her wish for a creek bank and cold water to wade in, but that was before, and this was now.

Students were everywhere, some looking as lost as she felt, others with their heads down on the paths that led to the rest of their lives. She paused to check her map, and as she did, something zipped past her line of sight. She turned to look and saw a pair of tiny hummingbirds fighting for the same bloom on a crepe myrtle bush.

As she stopped to watch, she thought of the hummingbirds back home that spent their days on her Momma's flowers and in that moment, knew it was a sign from God to remind her she was never alone. The hair on the back of her neck stood up as her vision blurred, but she pulled her sunglasses out of her purse to hide the tears.

This was no time for sorrow.

She had places to go and people to meet.

About Sharon Sala

Sharon Sala is a long-time member of RWA, as well as a member of OKRWA. She has 85 plus books in print, published in four different genres – Romance, Young Adult, Western, and Women's Fiction. First published in 1991, she's a seven-time RITA finalist, winner of the Janet Dailey Award, four-time Career Achievement winner from RT Magazine, five time winner of the National Reader's Choice Award, and five time winner of the Colorado Romance Writer's Award of Excellence as well as winner of the Booksellers Best Award. In 2011 she was named RWA's recipient of the Nora Roberts Lifetime Achievement Award. Her books are New York Times , USA Today and Publisher's Weekly best-sellers. Writing changed her life, her world, and her fate.

CPSIA information can be obtained at www.ICGtesting.com
Printed in the USA
LVOW101444141112

307307LV00004B/48/P